FINAL PLAY

SHADOW OPS: CHARLIE

First Published in Great Britain 2020 by Mirador Publishing

First edition: 2020

Any reference to real names and places are purely fictional and are constructs of the author. Any offence the references produce is unintentional and in no way reflects the reality of any locations or people involved.

A copy of this work is available through the British Library.

ISBN: 978-1-913264-92-5

Mirador Publishing
10 Greenbrook Terrace
Taunton
Somerset
UK
TA1 1UT

Final Play

Shadow Ops: Charlie

Sarah Luddington

1

MY EAR PIECE GAVE ME Stanton's voice clear and even. "Echo 7, go right."

I turned my head, the NVG – night vision goggles – picking up the void to my right. Another tunnel entrance. The heat inside the tunnel made sweat run off me as if I were in the monsoon rains and the air smelt of dirt and soiled humans.

This place brought forth some disturbing imagery in my head. We moved through the dark and sticky interior of a monster's bowels, seeking answers to riddles our superior officers would untangle when we brought home our prizes of hard drives.

With my Heckler and Koch G36k carbine pressed close to my cheek and folding stock closed because of the tight confines of the tunnel, I tucked it once more into my shoulder as I peeled off from the other seven in the team, and went right keeping my back to the wall and walking with sure but quiet steps. My trigger finger checked the safety for the hundredth time, the selector turned to 'F'. A part of me knew I didn't have to check, and check again, but these days I couldn't help myself. Stanton had a nasty habit of sending me in first at every opportunity but being the 'only gay in the village' made me a target and it's *put up* or *fuck off* in the Regiment. I had long since begun to wonder why I *put up*.

The tunnel bent around to the right, the dirt walls held in place by bamboo mesh and a few tree trunks. You wouldn't think bamboo could carry the weight of the soil above our heads, but it did, at least until we started blowing things up.

"Echo 4, go left," I heard in my ear. "Echo 7, sit rep."

I spoke into my mic, the headset tight under my tactical helmet and night vision goggles. "Echo 1, all clear and quiet so far," a soft murmur of words at my call sign.

"Roger that, Echo 7. Rejoin the group."

"Received, Echo 1. Coming to you." I dropped the barrel of my weapon to turn back in the narrow tunnel when I picked up a noise. I stopped and held my breath for a moment, the incredulity of the sound making me pause.

"Echo 1, I'm picking up voices, or a single voice. Going to take a look."

"Do not engage unless necessary, Echo 7."

"Understood, Echo 1. Out."

I moved the barrel of my G36k back to my previous direction of travel and approached the corner, the sound growing louder. I hit the pressel in my chest opening a channel to my commanding officer. "Echo 1, I can hear someone singing the Star-Spangled Banner."

"Say again, Echo 7."

"I think there's an American down here," I whispered.

Then I heard, "Contact!" from several team members on the net and suppressed gunfire behind me, the *phut phut*, strange in its quiet deadness.

A movement of a ghost green human form rushed forwards, lifting the barrel of an assault rifle. My suppressed weapon spat twice, I didn't even think, the training so embedded it happened without my heartrate or breathing increasing. The form dropped after a spray of dark green fluid arced out of the target. I continued on until I reached a dead end. I turned to my right and saw bars over a deeper hole and in the dim light of my NVG I saw a figure hanging behind the bars. The song, badly out of tune, came from the person.

I checked my six before approaching the bars. "You alive in there?"

The singing continued. The first few lines on repeat like a stuck CD player.

"Echo 1, are you receiving?" I could no longer hear gunfire.

"Receiving, Echo 7."

"I have a prisoner here, American."

"Our orders were clear, Echo 7. This is a search and destroy not a rescue."

I growled inside my chest. That was my CO, all fucking heart. "We can't leave him here." Assuming the figure was male. In the light from the NVG I couldn't tell, they couldn't function without some kind of light from somewhere and this place was darker than the devil's colon.

"Echo 7, your orders are to rejoin. We have what we came for, we are returning to the RV point and moving onto the LZ."

"I just need five mikes, Echo 1."

"Be it on your own head, Wilde. You have 15 mikes to get to the LZ."

"Roger that, out," I muttered while kneeling in front of the bars. I forced the anger at my CO's dismissal out of my head. It wouldn't help my current thinking and if I let it leech into me, mistakes would happen.

A simple chain and padlock held the metal grill in place. They'd also used concrete to maintain the cell's integrity. They must really want to keep this prisoner because Myanmar didn't use concrete unless necessary, especially not the drug cartels.

I glanced around the tunnel in front of the cell and saw a chair with a small table tucked against a wall. "Damn me," I muttered. A set of three keys were on the table. It turned out the last key was the one to open the padlock, this did not surprise me.

I walked into the cell backwards, my nose pressed against the central mass of my weapon. I remained alone. When I reached the hanging figure, who turned out to be male after all, I dropped the G36k, allowing it to hang by the lanyard.

The singing continued.

Sunken eyes didn't focus on me. Glancing up I could see his large hands were chained together and hanging from a hook in the ceiling only a half a metre more than his reach. His legs didn't hold his weight and his hands looked swollen from the trapped blood.

"Hey? Can you hear me? You have a name?" I reached out and touched his face.

His entire body jack-knifed away. "No!"

I stepped back. "Steady, I'm a friendly. I need to get you down."

A vague noise came from the man.

"I'm going to unlock your hands, but I need to touch you. My name is Nick Wilde, I am with the British Special Air Service. Who are you?" I reached out and placed a hand on his hip. He was naked with no shoes. His body flinched but he held still. With care I wrapped my arm around his waist and lifted. Someone his height should weigh considerably more. I held his mass and reached up with the keys I still held. The first key slotted in and turned. The padlocks were mercifully free of rust and snicked open. I removed the lock from the chain, and it unravelled from the man's wrists. He collapsed into my body and air rushed out of him. The smell repelled me for a moment, but I didn't release him. A sense of unknown power rippled through the core of my being, like I'd been plugged into the universe, not a mere national power grid.

"Can you walk?" I asked.

A small whimper came back.

"Hey, buddy, I need you to walk out if you can because we are on a timetable." I heard in my ear piece the others had reached the rendezvous site. They'd be moving on to the landing zone soon for the helicopter due to return us to our forward operating base. We were here under sufferance from the Myanmar government, but they weren't happy about it and anything that went against the rules of engagement would give them the right to retaliate.

I shook the man I held just a little. He managed a weak, "I can walk."

"Can you hold a weapon?" I asked.

"Yep."

"Know how to use it?"

A small laugh. "Ranger."

I moved him back onto his feet and held him steady. "You're a US Army Ranger?"

"Was." He managed to lift his head. The NVG hid his colouring but I could see the sharp angles of a handsome face despite the patchy beard.

I removed my side arm and pressed it into his hand. I watched him try to chamber a round. His fingers were unable to perform the task on the Sig Sauer P226.

"I can help," I whispered.

"No."

Voices were coming towards us through the tunnels – or maybe they were moving past – to be honest the acoustics in the underground sweatbox were impossible to navigate. The prisoner needed help, he needed to trust me.

"Here, water." I thrust my canteen under his nose, partly to distract him.

He looked confused, frowning, trying to figure out how to hold the gun and remove the stopper of the flask simultaneously. His eyes were black pits in the NVG's green tint.

I pulled out the stopper. He glanced into my face for the first time, though how much he could see in the dark I wasn't certain. I couldn't work out the colour of his eyes, but they were large and surrounded by long lashes. Slim lips sipped at the flask and I found myself so transfixed I forgot we stood in a part of what had once been Burma and a death camp to many British soldiers during WWII. I gave myself a mental shake.

He handed the flask back with shaking hands. "Thank you." He wasn't just meaning the water.

"Let's get out of here."

He nodded just once and returned the gun to me so I could chamber the round. Then he curled his fingers around my webbing as I gave him my back. Together we moved out. I heard his breathing and my heartbeat. I kept the sights of my weapon on a constant pivot. Soft grunts of pain and broken shuffling steps behind me slowed us down, but I couldn't rush him. The rest of my team had hit the RV and were ordering an update from me.

"Echo 7 receiving, Echo 1," I murmured.

"Where the fuck are you, Wilde?" barked Stanton.

"Still in the tunnels, Echo 1." I held up my closed fist and sensed my passenger shrink back against the wall. Two armed figures rushed past the tunnel opening I'd come down.

"We can't wait."

"Understood." I didn't. They could have helped. They could have backed me up, come and saved the US soldier. The intel we were here to get and the damage we were seeding to the drug shipment due to hit Europe in a few weeks weren't our only priorities. Surely we had an obligation to save the lives right in front of us as well?

"Make your way to the border, Echo 7. Don't get caught."

Yeah, and fuck you as well, I thought. "When I get back to Credenhill you'll owe me a pint, sir."

"If you make it back," came the last retort before my comms unit went silent in my ear.

"Motherfucker," I muttered.

The man behind me pulled on my webbing. "We're alone?"

I didn't glance over my shoulder. The most important thing right now was getting out in one piece and that meant paying attention to my surroundings. "Looks like it."

"What happened to no man left behind?"

I snorted. "That's you guys, not us. We don't risk lives to save bodies or each other if it places the rest of the mission in danger. We do have to move though because the drug shipments here are tagged for a missile strike when the higher-ups deem it expedient."

"Shit."

"Yeah. So let's keep moving."

"Don't let them take you alive," was the last comment he made before following my lead.

We were now 10 metres from the entrance to the main tunnel and so far, no problems. After that we needed to cover at least 50 metres before reaching the exit. The jungle camp buzzed like a poked hornets' nest, they'd found the bodies of the sentries we'd neutralised. They wouldn't consider one idiot still lived and breathed in their camp. With any luck they'd all fuck off and race around the jungle trying to find the rest of my supposed comrades.

Once at the entrance to the tunnel I checked both directions, doing an east-west sweep with my rifle.

"Clear," I murmured. "Going right. Move."

"Moving right," came from behind me.

At least we spoke the same language.

Traversing this hostile territory with a naked man at my back felt surreal. I made quick work of covering 10 metres. I paused and listened for any changes. Nothing. The fetid air around us didn't stir. I moved on. Another 5 metres and the man behind me breathed more heavily and I heard him fighting the need to cough.

A change in the air of the tunnel alerted us. I turned even as my companion raised my Sig. *Phut, phut, phut.* I fired my suppressed weapon. The Ranger didn't fire at all, keeping noise to a minimum. The enemy dropped. I approached and fired once more into each head. Removing a small torch from one hand and an AK-47 that might date back to the Vietnam War for all I knew, I returned to the Ranger.

"I can't," he whispered when I tried to hand him the rifle.

"Why?"

"It's too heavy. I can't hold it and you and if I lose you, I'm fucked."

I tried to think of a way to make him carry the rifle. The range would be far better over a distance than the side arm but if he knew his limitations then I had to trust him.

"Okay. Let's move."

I gave him the torch and dropped the rifle. With dead bodies in the main tunnel they'd know I existed. Time for discretion had fled. I moved with more speed than before and knew the Ranger struggled to keep up. We reached the main tunnel entrance and I pushed us back against the wall.

My NVG's were now a hindrance. Daylight filtered in from outside and from the electric lights they must have repaired already.

Two men were stationed one either side of the tunnel entrance. I couldn't take out both without raising the alarm.

The Ranger tapped my arm and pointed to my knife. I carried a short double-edged blade with a narrow blood gutter through the middle. It wasn't showy but damn she'd proved herself more than once. I removed her from the thigh sheath with a sense of loss, but he was right. With a knife he could kill someone. I'd have to do it with my bare hands.

I hated close combat. Too many opportunities for things to go wrong. Shooting your enemy from a distance might not be heroic but it made your odds of survival better.

Either side of the tunnel entrance we crept the last 5 metres. The Ranger was a lean creature of smoke and shadow. A denizen of myth and legend. I must look like the Hulk in comparison.

Two metres and no one knew we were there, as one we shared glance, a nod and sprang forwards in the same moment. My arms wrapped around the smaller Asian man. Left arm around his face, right pinning his weapon to his chest so he couldn't fire it and warn others. A muffled shout came from my left. I had my hand around the back of the Asian's skull and even as he kicked and thrashed, I used my bulk and height to separate his skull from his spine, breaking the atlas. The thick bones in his neck cracked against my right ear and his body grew heavy in a single heartbeat.

I dragged him into the dark tunnel entrance and took the radio on his old-style webbing. He also had a knife and when the Ranger joined me, now smudged with another man's blood, I swapped the blade out and returned mine to my thigh.

The Ranger and I took in our surroundings for a handful of heartbeats. Thick jungle in the distance, maybe 100 metres. A single dirt road rutted and wet. Red dirt stained everything, the sky lightening enough to see the filth. Men with guns were mustering to our left. Trucks were being filled with more men, but I could see a dirt bike. The Ranger tugged at my clothing and pointed. A big man for someone in Myanmar, close to the Ranger's size, stood near the bike. He watched the muster but appeared to be busy trying to unlock a case that might contain anything from an RPG to more drugs for all I knew.

I lifted the muzzle of my assault rifle. Taking careful aim through the sights, then a gentle squeeze on the trigger and a soft *phut phut* came next. The man dropped.

"Fuck, you're good, English," said the Ranger. He shuffled off without another word and I maintained over-watch as he huffed and puffed to move the body out of the way of the muster. When I saw him safe, I rushed to cover the same ground and dropped to one knee beside him, keeping him at my back.

Under the cover of a tin shed, which smelt like the shithouse, he began stripping off the man's clothing. I helped him as much as possible. Shirt, trousers, boots. With daylight almost breaking through the thick monsoon clouds overhead, I could begin to see the damage done to the American soldier.

Scars littered his body. Most of them fresh and some still open and leaking. There were bruises over his back and large welts. What looked like burns over his backside, thighs and I thought I saw them over his genitals before he covered himself up. He had longer hair than an army man would normally sport and a beard from neglect covered his cheeks and jaw. I could count every rib and bone in his spine as he bent over. His hair was the colour of pitch and his hollow eyes were black. He looked more Hispanic than white American. We were roughly the same height but where his muscles were long and lean, I'd make a rugby lad look petite and truth to tell, prettier.

He'd taken two minutes to change and the muster at the gates of the terrorist come narcotics camp had decided to move out.

"Lose your kit," he whispered.

"What?"

"We need to look like them."

"No one is going to think I look like a native of Myanmar, fella." I tugged at the dark blond and thick beard I sported.

He took me in properly and cocked his head. "Shit, you're right."

"Just hang tight and they'll leave. A skeleton crew we can handle."

The panic in his dark eyes made it clear he didn't believe me. How would I feel about waiting in this place if I'd been held and tortured long enough to grow a beard?

2

THE MORE DAYLIGHT CREPT OVER the camp the more people were moving about, women in particular and what a sorry sight they were, petite, piteously thin and dressed in rags. I realised with a rising sickness in my gut they too would die if the call came in to destroy the drugs in the camp rather than on the container ship bound for the European drug market. Also, we'd soon be spotted if I didn't make some decisions.

"Can you manage the back of the bike?" I asked the Ranger.

He shook his head. "I doubt it. Listen, what you did for me – staying behind –"

"Don't," I said. "We go together, or we aren't going at all. I'm not leaving you here." I looked around. In the corner of the camp sat a Land Rover, probably older than me, possibly older than God. There were strange tokens of the British Empire all over Myanmar and not just its fucked up politics.

I looked the Ranger in the eyes. "Listen to me. Stay here with this," I removed my assault rifle from its lanyard, "I'll take the Sig. You see a problem shoot first. I'm going to get that vehicle and come pick you up. Can you cover the necessary distance if I drive here and cover our six as we make a run for the gate?"

He studied me a moment. "You won't leave me?" A tremor swept through his body and I saw how parched his lips were, the green wash of colour from the night vision hadn't done him justice. An old scar ran from the bridge of his nose of his right cheek and into the beard but other than that and the starvation he was beautiful.

"No, I won't leave you."

"Go."

I gripped his shoulder for a moment, checked my surroundings, and bolted for the Land Rover. The flat sprint covered just shy of 70 metres. I kept low, the crouched run slowing me just a little over the short distance. I reached the vehicle and checked all four tyres. They were old but were fully inflated. I tried the door handle. It opened. The dusty colour had been stained with the red of the earth in this part of the world and several of its panels had dents and scratches. I checked my back, still no sign of being spotted by someone, and slid into the truck. I rifled through the sun visor for a key. Nothing. Next the ashtrays. Nothing but the foul-smelling local cancer sticks. Pushing my fingers under the driver's seat I struck gold. The good fairy of keys seemed to be on my side for a change.

With a stupid grin I stuck the Land Rover key into the ignition and turned it. The engine coughed, barked a fart of black smoke out the rear end and rumbled to life. A sturdy diesel engine juddered under my hands. The steering wheel was made of Bakelite and I knew it would be a bitch to drive with no power steering, but we'd manage. Who needed a team of SAS brothers at your back to get out of enemy territory? Not me. Wait until I made my way to Thailand, I was going to make those bastards regret leaving their token gay in the jungle.

I crunched the gears but when I released the handbrake it lurched forwards and trundled, rather than raced, to the tin hut behind which the Ranger waited. So far, no screaming from the enemy that we'd been noticed.

Almost 10 metres from the Ranger and everything changed.

A shout rang out. A dozen men spilled from the tunnel and gunfire *cracked* through the humid air. A round hit the truck. The Ranger rose and began his shuffling run towards me. Another round caught the truck and more people swarmed towards us. I wished I'd spent a little time setting some simple explosive traps to distract and disable but I hadn't, we were just going to have to keep moving.

The Ranger fired my assault rifle, the suppressor keeping noise and flash to a minimum, as he ran and despite his fear, he maintained his training, keeping his bursts short and controlled to save ammo. I hit the brakes when he reached me and turned to open the rear doors.

The windscreen shattered and I bellowed as a round caught me on the forearm, shattering my GPS locator, and clipping my shoulder on my left side. The pain lashed at my senses, a hurricane tearing at a willow tree, and stole my breath, shutting down parts of my brain.

Acting on instinct, trained and honed by hours and hours and hours of relentless work, I dragged the Ranger into the back of the truck, gunned the engine and we lurched forwards. Pushing us into third gear enabled me to drive at speed and I just about forced my left hand to grip the wheel while I fired my side arm through the smashed window at a man 20 metres ahead and closing. He took his time, lining up his iron sights on his AK, aiming for my chest. I could almost feel the bullet ready to go, a hunting dog on a leash, baying for blood. My blood. I forced the wheel to turn but without power steering I didn't have the manoeuvrability I needed to get away from his laser focus.

Movement behind me and the Ranger rose from the backseat, the rear stock of my weapon close to his face, the suppressor gone. He fired right next to my ear. The sound was terrible, a wash of noise in my head that gathered together the pain of my arm and formed stars across my vision. The man with the AK managed to fire one shot before his head and body exploded in a fountain of gore and a heartbeat later the truck bounced over his corpse.

I managed to haul the truck around to face the gate and keep the pedal planted to the rusty floor. The engine roared and I changed up a gear to gather more momentum. Bullets screamed around us.

"RPG, left, left, left!" yelled the Ranger.

I yanked the wheel left and the rocket propelled grenade hit the ground exactly where we had been just a second ago. The entire truck rocked off two wheels from the impact. Dirt and stones rained down hitting my arms and face through the empty windscreen. We smacked into the ground and I aimed for the gate again. Now, there were two men trying to shoot into the front of the beast I drove. We made the gate. We also hit one of the men and the sickening crunch and scream as we lurched over his body to grind him into the red dirt of the jungle would live with me forever.

The Ranger sat in the back of the truck, kicked out the glass from the broken rear window and fired to cover our rear until the chamber emptied. I pulled out a new magazine and handed it back to him.

"How many?" I yelled after I heard the chamber click into place.

A pause. "None?"

"Are you asking or telling?" I said, trying to control the vehicle at speed on a bad road with an arm that didn't work. Pain clawed its way up my neck and over my scalp making my stomach twist.

"Oh, shit, you're bleeding." The Ranger reached through the gap between the front seats.

I managed a grunt. He began rummaging in my webbing and checking my body armour. Flashes of long fingers searching close to my skin made bits of me tingle; I gave myself an internal bollocking. He found my med-kit. Unable to stop the truck he couldn't do a good job, but he fought to get a dressing on it and wrapped it tight.

"How does it feel?" he asked.

"Horrible," I muttered.

He chuckled. "Try electrodes on your balls, then you can bitch about a scratch."

I glanced at him, but he didn't lift his eyes from the wound.

The old truck lurched and bounced sending the Ranger into the back with a grunt of pain.

"Sorry." I wrestled with the wheel and dragged the vehicle back under control. "Are we still clear?"

Silence from the back.

"Hey, are we being pursued?" I tried to look behind me and out of the window. I couldn't do both while wrestling the wheel to keep us on the road, so I opted to slow the truck. When the vehicle juddered to stillness, I turned in my seat.

The Ranger lay in the back, holding his ribs on the right side and gasping for air. His body trembled and his eyes were screwed shut. "Don't stop," he gasped. "It's just pain."

"I'm sorry."

"Not your fault. I just caught an old wound." The pallor of his skin and the whispered gasp weren't reassuring. I glanced down the road behind us and decided I needed to press on. I couldn't help him if we were caught and our proximity to the camp meant we were still in danger.

"Just hang on," I told him, and I forced the truck back into movement.

We trundled forwards and I tried to think through our predicament. My team were long gone. Even if I could make the LZ it would be impossible to recall the heli, my comms unit was out of range now and with the GPS locator gone I couldn't send a message using that either. Our orders were clear: go in, get the job done, get out. If you fuck it up, we cannot come to get you. Standard operations procedure for Special Forces the world over. Despite the SOP I realised it hurt being left behind by my team so easily. Not one member of our squad had asked Stanton to wait, to give us a chance to reach the landing zone.

I gritted my teeth and tried not to think about the implications of such an act. Stanton was a first class bastard, if you weren't white, straight and able to play football and rugby – not cricket, that wasn't a real sport – then you weren't worth his time. He'd made sergeant because ultimately, he was good at his job, if you were part of his team. If you stood out, he made your life hell until you moved on. SOP for him. I'd called him on his bullshit more than once but by doing so I'd driven a deeper wedge between us and forced men to start taking sides. Needless to say, no one wanted to stand in the gay kid's corner.

They'd effectively left me to die. I wondered when or even *if* any of them would be haunted by that thought over the coming days as I tried to figure out how to get back to the UK.

The Ranger's breath huffed out of him at every bump in the road and I glanced in the rear-view mirror which had somehow survived the gun fight. His eyes were closed, the hunger and dehydration had made his skin tight on his face and I could see the remains of a recent beating. I flipped through my belt packs and found some energy bars.

"Here." I held them over my shoulder. "You need to eat and drink some more water."

He peeled open those dark eyes and stared at me in the mirror. "Thank you, but we need to share them. We'll need your strength before we're done."

I wished he was wrong.

"The legal border crossings are maybe our best option. Blend with the tourists, then when we get caught, surrender to the Thai police."

"Not on the border. They are paid by the cartels and the minute they know I'm missing my face will be on all their computers and phones. We have to get to the right kind of police or army in Thailand to be safe."

"Do you know who the right people are?" I asked. "If we get to a phone, we can call them. My team might come back if we can get to a safe place for extraction. Though I'll need an exact location."

"Don't you have a cell phone on you?" he asked.

I held up my left arm. The GPS locator which acted as a low-grade mobile phone was fucked. It had probably saved my arm though through the deflection. "Smashed. The battery might be working though so they might still be able to locate me on GPS, though I can't communicate with them. They'll know I'll head to the FOB as soon as possible, as fast as possible." I didn't add that the chances of my team admitting to the higher-ups I was still alive when they left me was slim to none. They wouldn't be looking for me, they wouldn't come and find me. I knew it in my heart, and it made me feel very tired, alone, scared and really fucking angry.

"Where is your forward operating base?"

"The Bay of Bengal," I said. The doom-laden statement made him smile. It might as well be on the moon. I caught my breath at that smile; with some meat on his bones those handsome features would be devastating.

"How much fuel do we have?" he asked.

I glanced at the gauge, a fortunate distraction. "Just under a quarter of a tank. In this beast we probably only have another 20 clicks at most."

He leaned forwards and tangled his bloody fingers into the thick black curls on his head. "I can't go back."

I kept half an eye on the dirt track and placed a hand on his head. "Hey, it's alright, we'll figure this out. We just keep moving."

He surprised me by moving one of his hands to cover mine, pressing my fingers into his scalp. I let them form small circles, a comfort, a gentle acknowledgement that his fear was real, but I'd help. He wasn't alone in that cell any longer.

"What's your name?"

He looked up in surprise and my hand fell away. I returned it to the wheel and tried to ignore the tingles in my fingers.

"Gabriel. Gabriel Cabrera. Everyone calls me Gabe though."

"It's a pleasure to meet you, Gabriel."

The corners of his eyes crinkled as he smiled, and I realised he was probably older than me. "We need a plan," he said.

"Yes, we do, because for the moment we are on our own."

3

"WHERE ARE WE EXACTLY?" GABE asked after opening and nibbling at one of the energy bars from my kit. He drank water in small amounts as well.

"You don't know?"

He shook his head. "I was inserted into a trade delegation from Venezuela, that's where my father comes from though, I was raised in the US, so I could hold a legend better than most under those circumstances. Someone leaked I worked for the US, that I was CIA and they even knew I was a Ranger. They snatched me right off the street along with a Chinese national. They accused us both of being spies. They produced evidence and we were imprisoned." After a moment of silence, he started to climb into the front of the Land Rover, sweeping glass off the passenger seat.

"So how did you end up here?" I asked.

"I was sold."

"What?"

He sighed. "The government couldn't ransom me, obviously, but they could receive a kickback from a group like the one you raided. The Chinese woman taken with me wasn't as lucky. She screamed a lot while they lined up to take turns…"

Long fingers twisted in his lap and he started to shiver.

"Hey," I said, trying to draw him back. "You're safe, don't do this to yourself. It's not your fault."

He nodded, though the haunting memory remained in his eyes. "When they threw her back in the cell we shared she begged me to end her life." He stroked a series of scars on his arm, long and narrow. The scars wouldn't be the kind to stay for years so the wounds hadn't been deep.

"You did?"

He nodded. Still unable to look at me.

I put my hand over his restless fingers, and he surprised me again by holding on tight.

He continued his story. "After that they beat me, then moved me and kept moving me until I ended up in that cell. They couldn't understand why no one claimed me. I told them the CIA would deny I existed."

"Jesus, Gabe, how long have you been down there?" I asked.

"What's the date?"

"21st June."

"It's been three months," he said after a quick calculation. "Some of that time has been worse than others. This lot liked to chain me up for long periods, but they'd give me some food and water if I begged. The monsoon season has meant rain through the roof and walls of the cell. It's mostly clean. God, I'm tired." He leaned against the side of the truck and closed his eyes. I didn't have the heart to disturb him even though I could have done with someone watching our six.

He muttered a quiet, "They'll have road blocks once they radio about my escape." Then his body grew lax and I knew he'd drifted off.

I really needed a plan.

The legal borders were going to be complicated. We had no visas and little local currency. The money issue I could solve because I carried several hundred US dollars and some Sterling and Euros – good strong currency in this part of the world – but the visas couldn't be bought easily. Not without using groups such as the one Gabe had been sold to for ransom. If they caught me it would be torture for the hell of it and death. A British soldier out here would not be treated with any kind of compassion and the Geneva Convention had never bothered the government in this part of the world.

So, no visas equalled no legal border crossing. I already knew the borders with China and Laos were closed. We could get into Bangladesh but hostilities over the Rohingya people and the distance between here and there made it a bad option. The Thai border, long and mostly following the wriggling course of a single river with several names, had to be the best choice. It would be porous.

I snorted at the stupid pun and Gabe twitched. Even in sleep he didn't look relaxed. He shrank into himself as if trying not to be noticed. How much physical pain was he in? Rangers were tough men, but he looked almost delicate in the tatty old leather seat and stolen uniform.

Focus, doofus, I told my wandering concentration.

Trying to get through the jungle to the river, across the river and through the jungle on the other side to reach some kind of safe place in Thailand would be difficult if we were both fully fit and equipped. We had no communication device between us. Little food or clean water. No shelter and only the ammunition I carried. Gabe couldn't walk stupid distances and during the monsoon the weather could turn so fast and with such fury we'd be in danger of flash floods, mud slides and I couldn't begin to think about the animals out there wanting some human goodness in their diet.

The mosquitoes alone were dangerous; never mind the snakes, scorpions, spiders, and maybe the odd tiger – though this seemed unlikely. The snakes bothered me most because my kit might be good quality, but Gabe's was not, and his new trousers didn't meet the top of his boots.

I thought back to all those WWII films I'd watched with my grandfather while mum and dad had been busy with the farm. He hated Burma but then he'd been posted to Shanghai so his perspective was coloured by experience.

A river crossing seemed the most sensible but not in the monsoon season. We'd have to risk the land border. India or Thailand. I tried to visualise the map. To the north of Myanmar, we'd be running into the foothills of what would become the Himalayas covered in jungle. Also, we were a really long way from that side of the country. So, land crossing into Thailand by road if possible, rather than on foot through the jungle, avoiding all the places where people hated the British and Americans – that made the list really small – really, really, really small.

I knew we were in the mountain jungles to the south east of a small city called Mongpan on the maps we'd consulted before leaving the Royal Navy ship that brought us to the Bay of Bengal. The main 'road' for the area was number 45 and ran to a new border post called Kew Pa Wok. We could try for that but between here and there would be any number of small outposts both legal and illegal, some run by drug cartels, some by separatists, some might even be legal. Then there were the minefields…

I looked at the fuel gauge again. It didn't seem to go below the quarter full mark, and I realised we probably didn't know if we were anywhere near full or empty. Gauges weren't exactly reliable in old vehicles.

Once more I glanced at Gabriel. He twitched a little in his sleep and small animal sounds of pain were escaping his cracked lips. I wanted to make his pain go away so he'd sleep in peace.

A crack of thunder overhead made the vehicle shake and a deluge of rain to smash onto the road. With most of the glass missing from the windscreen I expected Gabriel to wake up, but he didn't. I had to further slow the truck just to be able to see in the darkness of a monsoon day on a jungle track. Within minutes we were soaked, and the road turned to slush but Gabe slept on. I didn't know if that was a good sign or a bad one.

The truck ambled through the thickening mud; a work horse vehicle designed for the most inhospitable places in the British Empire of old. We started to round another bend when the shadows in the rain became straight, man-made, lines right at the edge of my vision. I stopped the truck. We were surrounded by thick foliage, so I stuck us into reverse and backed the truck up with great care. I ran through my options at speed. I needed to see what the man-made objects were close to the road. Had I seen a guard point through the dismal light and thick rain?

I glanced at Gabriel – again – did I leave him asleep only to wake alone when I checked out the road? Or did I wake him and warn him I'd be leaving the Land Rover? The second option was the best one, he could run if something kicked off and have some kind of chance to get out. If I left him to sleep and something happened to me, they might find him, and I couldn't allow that to happen.

"Gabe?" I called several times with no reaction. Trying hard not to freak him out, I reached over and stroked his scarred forearm. He yelled, knocked my hand back, grabbed the knife at his belt and lunged for me.

Training kicked in and I deflected the knife strike to my throat, wrapped his arm, tucking his forearm into my body armour and mine against his triceps to force his elbow straight. The arm lock made him drop the knife. I pinned his head against the seat with my other hand, which tightened around his throat until he stilled. His strength surprised me considering his physical condition.

"Gabriel, it's Nick. Remember?" I asked with authority and calm. The awareness in his eyes took long moments to flood back but when he located me and himself in the present his body relaxed.

"Nick?"

"That's right," I said still holding his throat. "Tell me something you remember?"

"Special Air Service."

I smiled and relaxed, letting his arm return to his body and releasing his throat. Retrieving the knife from my foot well proved tricky in body armour but I gave it back, hilt first. "We okay?"

"Sorry." He looked properly sheepish, like a dog caught with his snout in the rubbish bin.

"It's alright. I know now. Nothing wakes you faster than physical contact. You've managed to sleep through everything else."

I handed him the water, but he pushed it back. "You need it."

"No, Gabe. You drink this, we'll collect more from the rain." I pointed to the water now gurgling in happy runnels through the smashed windscreen.

He nodded and drank. I also gave him another energy bar. "There's something on the road up ahead but I can't see what it is so I'm going to check it out. Stay here, take the driver's seat and wait out."

"No," he shook his head, "I should come with you."

I lifted my assault weapon from his side of the truck. "No. You remain here and keep the vehicle primed to move out if I return in a rush or you hear me engage."

He wanted to argue, I could see it, but he also knew he couldn't afford to let his ego get in the way of a simple recon. A small nod. It gave me the permission I needed to know I could trust him to follow instructions. I exited the vehicle. The mud immediately sucked at my feet and made walking hard work. The rain filled my vision, a curtain of it falling from the helmet I hadn't removed. Taking cover from the jungle on the side of the road, I walked around the corner, keeping my weapon live in my hands and my sights trained on the middle distance.

When I reached the point I'd stopped the Land Rover, I paused and knelt in the red mud and thick grass. I estimated only 30 metres separated me from the checkpoint, in the thick downpour and with sound being bamboozled by the rain on the leaves I couldn't hear anything ahead or from the truck behind me. I also couldn't see any human shapes moving around the shed, but I could see what looked like a pole across the road. Keeping my sights on the guardhouse I maintained a crouch to break up my shape and approached with smooth, small steps.

After covering another 10 metres I crouched and listened again. The water sluicing from the sky eased for a moment and my vision cleared a little. A guard post. My guess? Something to prevent anyone from reaching the cartel's camp without permission. They'd be able to radio the camp on short wave this close and they would know of our escape if anyone manned the barricade.

The rain eased further, and I heard voices for the first time, then made out the figures of four men and they all held weapons. These weren't old AK-47s either, these were black in colour. I couldn't quite make them out, but my best guess was MP5s, accurate and rapid fire.

I did not engage. Without removing my sights from the target, I pushed back into the jungle because if I could see them, they'd see me if I moved like a human. By slow increments I backed away from the target and only when the next thunder clap and deluge began did I stand, turn and run back to the truck.

Gabriel sat behind the wheel, my Sig in his hand. I walked forwards with my hands up and away from my weapon. His dark eyes were wild even at this distance. I didn't want to call out to him, so I stood still until the barrel of my personal weapon dropped.

I huffed out a breath I didn't know I'd caged in my chest. A quick jog returned me to the vehicle. "We can't go that way."

"Why?"

"Manned outpost for the camp, I think. Four tangos, heavily armed with MP5s. Thick jungle either side of the road."

"We can take out four men," Gabe said. I knew why he wanted to face those odds. We both knew why but I had to make him acknowledge it aloud.

"No, we can't." I stared at him and hated myself for the look of defeat that replaced his defiance.

"I'm too weak and we don't have a second rifle, we have limited ammunition and you're injured."

I nodded. "I'm loathed to backtrack in case they rallied enough men to come after us, but I think we'd be wise to move on foot right now."

Gabriel eyed the jungle in the same way I'd seen one of my few ex-boyfriends eye my dress sense, a mix of horror and resigned disbelief. "We'll get eaten by something."

"If we go along the road we'll get shot for certain. I'd rather risk the bugs and monkeys."

"I'd be more worried about the snakes."

"I'm trying not to think about the snakes." I made a brave attempt not to release my internal shudder at the thought.

"Denial is no defence against snakes," Gabriel told me while he eased out of the vehicle. He shivered as the rain began soaking his back. "They'll know exactly where we entered the forest if we go in from here."

"We'll backtrack a little and enter on an animal track," I said, wiping rain from my eyes.

Gabriel opened the back of the truck and began rifling through its contents. He pulled out a rain slicker in olive green and grinned at me before sliding it over his head. Next, he found water bottles and a couple of plastic shopping bags. I kept watch while he rummaged. A length of rope appeared and under it the real prize. An old and rusty but still sharp machete. He also found a crowbar and of all things an axe.

"Good scrounge."

He smiled. "Reminds me of what the Brits were like when you lot first came to Bagram. If you couldn't beg or borrow our kit, you'd nick it."

"At least we get better scran than you guys," I said. "And we're very good magpies, the British Army relies on our thieving skills to keep us in bullets." That wasn't too far from the truth on occasion. When the second war in Iraq began a friend of my father's from the other side of Somerset, who managed the Ministry of Defence's land, said they were cutting down the woodlands to sell the trees to pay for bullets. How true that was I didn't know; truth be told I didn't want to know as I'd just signed up for the Royal Marines.

"Come on, English. Let's go find some snakes." He touched my shoulder.

I took the crowbar off him and pushed it between my body and my armour. "You don't want to carry that unnecessarily." I also took the axe and hung it from my webbing.

The softness in his eyes as he looked at me made parts of me tingle and grow warm. "Come on, we've a long way to walk."

4

We trudged back up the road, with me on point and Gabriel checking our rear every few metres, his head on a permanent swivel. The rain continued to wash the world but for now we had no thunder from the glowering clouds overhead. After a quarter of a click I found what I wanted, an animal run for something large enough to leave tracks. Of course the downside meant a large animal used that track often enough to make it clear in the jungle. Large animals in the jungle came with teeth – lots of sharp teeth.

Before we left the road, I took a bearing on our direction of travel, looking for a high point to help keep us going in the right direction. I could see a ridgeline covered in thick jungle directly in front, which meant it ran perpendicular to the track we were on. The clouds lifted a little more and the sun, still marking time before midday, sat in the east which meant the ridgeline went south. Thailand was south. We needed to go south. I needed us to head towards the ridgeline and follow it south.

"I have our direction of travel," I said and explained my thinking. Gabriel nodded his agreement, though to be fair he'd probably follow me into hell if it meant escaping his captors for good.

"How much jungle training you had, English?" he asked.

"Some. Borneo mostly."

"Let me take the lead, I've done jungles in South America, South East Asia and bits of Africa." Gabe stepped off the path and we vanished into the thick jungle of Myanmar.

The heat hit me fast. The road we'd been on had at least permitted some air to travel in a breeze. The thick covering of dark leaves and wet soil under our feet meant we had no air stirring around us and as the monsoon passed over us, the sun started to work on the next set of clouds. The humidity meant I'd never dry out from the rainstorm and I needed water. Being big and holding most of the weight, made me vulnerable to dehydration. Also, we couldn't cut back the vegetation yet, we were still too close to the road, so pushing through became our only option.

We didn't speak, with the lack of noise from the rain, our voices would travel, and the monkeys weren't screeching yet. I had to admit, watching Gabriel pick our route with a practiced eye made me feel confident we might actually be able to get out of the forest and into Thailand. He moved with grace, despite his pain, and I watched him collect water into the empty bottles and my flask from the leaves of certain plants. If we found food near this trail we'd be set.

A part of me found some pleasure in our predicament. This is why I'd joined the SAS, to work with the best in the world, to survive against the odds and most importantly for me – to save people even if it meant killing others. Teamwork came easily to me, not one bone in my body sang to the tunes of a lone wolf hunter. I wanted to fit in, wanted to find a family in the Regiment. Men I could trust. Shame that feeling came from a man I'd known for an hour and happened to be an American Ranger.

After thirty minutes of travel we paused.

"I think we're safe, at least until someone finds the Land Rover." Gabriel handed me a water bottle which I guzzled.

After gasping my thanks, I said, "Agreed, but how far can you go?"

"Today? Without any more food? Not far but we can't make camp near any habitation, so we push on and look for food on the way. Snake is best if you spot something in a tree."

I pulled a face which made him laugh and we trudged on and on. After another hour the jungle thickened even more and Gabriel began using the machete to clear our path but his energy levels weren't high enough and I gave him my rifle and helmet while I hacked a path for us to take between the thick trees and vines. The tangle of leaves from unnamed – by me at least – plants at our feet made it hard to see the roots and stones, the potholes and patches of slick mud. If I thought I'd been sweating before, now I was soaked and the night's operation in the camp with the previous day's long tab from the landing zone drained even my strength. I now knew how a keg of beer felt being emptied by a tap draining all the liquid out.

Thinking about beer wasn't helping my thirst.

When the sun slipped past midday, we checked our position. I couldn't see the ridgeline above the thick and now raucous canopy of secondary jungle, but Gabriel pointed to the trees below the highest ones. "See how they have more leaves and branches on one side? That's south."

I didn't bother to point out I was a farmer's son and knew how to find south even before I joined the Marines. "Will the jungle thin out do you think?" I asked.

"Maybe. We're in stuff that's difficult right now, but if we keep going deeper, we'll reach a different part of the forest. This secondary jungle is the area the locals have been using for millennia, by cutting down the high canopy from larger older trees all this scrubby stuff can grow up and take over. The trees will be larger in the primary forest but so will the animals. I don't think we'll stumble into tigers though."

"Seems unlikely as there aren't any left," I muttered.

"It's one of the things I was doing here. Trying to dig into the illegal trade of animal parts, I was masquerading as the rich American."

"It's bad then?"

"Almost as much money is made by trading animals as trading drugs and slaves. This country is a mess of illegal activity," he said, and we began walking again, together this time. "Listen, I know you Brits don't believe risking the lives of your team to save one man but I'm really shocked they left you so easily and I'm even more surprised you didn't put up a fight for them to help you."

"It's complicated." I really didn't want to cover this ground with Gabriel. Our companionship wasn't old enough to take a hit of such magnitude and men in any armed force weren't overly accommodating to alternative lifestyles.

He pulled me to a stop and pointed. "Bubbi fruit. Good eating and we can use the bark to make a goo to spread on our wounds. Your arm must be hurting."

"It is," I agreed.

"Then we rest here for an hour before moving on." He wandered over to the tree and began pulling off giant sized grape come lemon looking things on a vine. "We need fire," he said over his shoulder. I took that as an order to find wood.

With axe in hand I found an old and fallen tree. The width of the trunk offered protection to the ground and under it few plants grew but a lot of debris had collected. Most importantly the leaves and small branches were dry. I gathered an armful of detritus and carried it back to Gabriel, who had started finding stones for a fire pit. I returned to the fallen tree. By poking at the underside with the axe and my knife I managed to peel off sections of dried bark and then dug out sawdust from the rotten interior. By following the tree, I then found a small cliff overhang from a large boulder and a collection of larger dry branches. I carried the smaller of these back to the camp.

Gabriel smiled as I dumped them at our temporary camp. With my helmet on his head, black curls sticking out, he looked cute. It was at least two sizes too big. Shit, he really did look cute. *Fucking hell, stupid time to get romantic.*

"You didn't answer my question." He held his hand out.

I handed over my strike-a-light. "I didn't want to, there's a difference."

"Talk, big man, I want to know your secrets." A black eyebrow rose.

I looked away, already feeling my defences crumble under his dastardly tactics of cuteness and kindness. "They aren't interesting enough for the CIA." Heat crept over my neck and face.

He reached over the, as yet unlit fire, and touched my hand. "Hey, no judgement here. You've seen me hanging bollock naked in an enemy cell. I think I can share your secrets."

Yes, I had seen him naked which is why didn't want to tell him what the problem was with my team. However, we'd be travelling together for who knew how long and trust had to be built. I couldn't afford to be coy. Also, until I'd joined the Regiment, I'd never hidden my sexuality from anyone. A wall inside me, one I'd built the moment Stanton came into my life, collapsed and my shoulders slumped in relief at my silent decision.

"I'm gay, that's the problem with my team." I didn't look at him as I said it. Fuck, when had I become scared of admitting who and what I wanted?

Silence met my statement. Not reassuring. I glanced up, bracing myself for the worst.

Gabriel smiled. "Thank you for looking at me and thank you for telling me."

"That's it?"

He shrugged. "Bit hard to give you a Pride parade in this jungle and I'm on my own."

I laughed. "Twat."

"That's British for kind and compassionate, right?"

"Fuck off."

"So, that's a no then, okay. I'll file it somewhere near fanny."

That really made me laugh and he grinned, which made his dark eyes shine.

"Now you know I'm not a homophobic shit why not tell me the whole story?"

Surprising myself further the words began to tumble out. I'd never talked to anyone about my time in the Regiment, but Gabriel sat, nursing the fire into life and listened while sucking on the strange fruit.

"I joined the Royal Marines when I left college. As a rugby player at school and college I was fit and strong already. I didn't want to go to university, I wanted to travel, I wanted adventure and I wanted to succeed at something. The Marines were recruiting in my area and 42 Commando were based just down the road from where I grew up."

"Where was that?"

"Somerset, edge of Exmoor. Country lad through to me bones," I said laying the accent on thick, like clotted cream on a scone.

He chuckled. "I can't understand a word of that."

"I came out to my mum aged thirteen and she'd always supported me. Being a big lad and a very good rugby player, no one at school or college gave me too much of a hard time over it other than taking the piss, and I never hid it from anyone. When I joined up, I told the recruitment officer and he put it on the form, so the Marines knew from the start and it never became an issue. They also used it as a way to get a cheap laugh but only in the same way they did in rugger." The look of confusion on his face made me smile. "Rugby – rugger."

"Oh, right, sure."

"I spent twelve happy years in the Marines. We went all over the world and I felt secure and safe in my platoon. Then an opportunity came up for me to try for Special Forces. Most Marines go into the SBS – Special Boat Service, like the SEALs – but I thought I'd try for the SAS. After the last lot of mess in Iraq they needed more cannon fodder. The trouble started during selection. They knew I was gay day one and the ruperts – officers – decided not to correct some pretty bad behaviour. It wasn't just me; they targeted a Muslim and a black guy who tried out as well. There is a ninety percent drop-out rate during selection recruitment and I thought about quitting every fucking day, but I didn't. I'd never backed down from a fight and I didn't plan on doing it in front of a bunch of homophobic pricks."

Gabriel handed me a peeled fruit and I sucked on the bitter sweetness. "Guess it didn't stop though, huh?"

"No. When I passed out and found out my new commanding officer was a man called Stanton, I almost requested an RTU."

Gabe cocked his head again.

"Returned to Unit. A shaming thing. Most soldiers opt to resign."

"Fucking armies have more ego than is good for us," he muttered.

I shrugged. "Gets us out of bed in the morning."

He just grunted. I guessed his story about being abandoned in Myanmar wouldn't be comfortable hearing.

"Stanton made it clear he didn't want me in the Regiment. I wanted to make a formal complaint about bullying after six months of being treated like shit," understatement of the millennium, "but one of my few friends talked me out of it. The ruperts knew what he was doing, but they didn't stop him which meant they wouldn't take kindly to my whinging. I've been subjugated to two years of bullying and leaving me in this jungle is just one more thing on a long list of bad practice."

"I thought the UK army would be better than the US," Gabriel said, his voice quiet and gaze thoughtful.

I shook my head. "It's like football –"

"Oh, you mean soccer?"

I laughed at him again. "No, football," I said with deliberate slowness.

"There aren't any gay men in football either. To be honest it's become so bad I just want my career to be over and being here with you is actually the safer option right now. I've never been this badly bullied before, it's exhausting. Low level stuff I'm used to and can handle. I'm so fucking tired of having to prove myself. I'm a damned fine soldier but the constant and needless haranguing has eroded me to the core of my being. I can't even look at a guy I might find attractive in case they notice or find out. I haven't had sex since I left the Marines." Tears pricked at the backs of my eyes as my memory threw up a selection of the 'finer' moments over the last few years. I tried to keep a lid on the emotions but something about Gabriel's quiet and attentive stillness brought the torment buried deep inside to the surface.

He shuffled around the campfire until we were shoulder to shoulder. I looked into his fathomless gaze. "You saved my life rather than leave me in that place. You are my hero, Nick. I need you to understand that – hold onto it and let it repair some of the damage."

I sniffed and nodded. His juice-sticky fingers tangled with mine and he leaned into me. The consequences didn't matter in the moment. I slipped an arm around his shoulders and he nestled against me.

"No one has touched me with kindness for the longest time," he whispered.

We sat together watching our small fire in silence and just let the noise of the forest wash around our little sanctuary. I think we dozed for a bit, but Gabriel shuddered awake, gasping and confused, which woke me. The instant release of my arm had him move away but he didn't try to attack me with anything. He must feel safer in my company.

"Let me make a paste with this bark," he said, busying his fingers so he didn't have to engage with me directly.

I had to hope it wasn't because he thought using me for comfort made him gay – or that I'd assume he was because of the moment we'd shared. I had a bit more self-respect than that, but truth be told, it was a great deal harder to believe in myself than it had been in the past. Besides, he was way out of my league either way. Only my mum, bless her, thought I could pass as handsome.

I watched him take a stone with a small hollow in it, then a smaller one and begin to grind the bark and a little water between the two. He added more bark and asked, "How is the arm feeling?"

"Like I got shot," I said. To be honest, it throbbed in time with my heart which meant a possible infection and I could feel the slick descent of blood down my arm. "How did you learn to do this?"

He glanced up at me for a moment. "Long story, but the basics are this, my father is Venezuelan, and he fled the country as a political and economic refugee back in the eighties. He was arrested by my grandfather at the Mexican border trying to cross the Rio Grande into Arizona. My father was young and strong, and he offered to work for my grandfather for free on his ranch for a year."

I watched Gabriel's face soften at the memories. Listening to him talk about his family made his non-descript American accent become more Spanish and the soft inflection in his voice did strange things to my insides.

"My father is a charming man, educated and intelligent. He is kind, good with animals and handsome. By taking my father into his home my grandfather took in his son-in-law because my mother fell in love very quickly and they were wed. We would go for holidays in the south when the politics calmed down and my fraternal grandfather would teach me all he could. He'd lived with natives of Venezuela as an anthropologist having fled himself from Franco's Spain. I learned much of my jungle training from him and during my time in the US Army I enhanced what I already knew."

"Wow, bit different to growing up on a sheep farm."

He laughed. "I know nothing about sheep, so if we find some and want to eat them, I'm leaving it down to you."

"So long as you deal with the snakes I don't mind."

He grinned. "Deal."

With a sticky goo now on the stone he approached me. The colour, texture and smell did not appeal. "Take your body armour off and your shirt," he ordered.

I huffed, but undid the tough clasps and Velcro pulling the weight off my shoulders for the first time in hours. It felt so good I groaned. Next came the shirt and t-shirt, at which point the usual insecurities started. I couldn't help but watch his eyes as he looked at my chest. I had dark blond chest hair over the large slabs of muscle and wide shoulders with a crow in flight covering my right deltoid, right shoulder and chest, his tail fanning down past my elbow. He studied the tattoo and the rest of my naked torso. Including the nest of very old scars.

When his eyes rose to meet mine, their expression remained unreadable. Like he'd opened a book in a foreign language and knew it said something important but couldn't work out what. He put the goo down at my feet and set about washing the shallow trench in my left arm. When he looked satisfied with his work he placed the goo into the wound and pressed it deep.

"Ouch."

"Baby."

"You say the sweetest things, darling."

He snorted and laughed. "I'm so glad you were the one to find me, Nick."

"Me too, Gabe."

He wrapped the wound in a fresh bandage, and I dressed while he ate more fruit and the goo. The wound stung something fierce but I was a tough soldier so I wouldn't complain – much.

Gabriel looked a little better, more colour in his cheeks and his eyes were a bit brighter but just as I was about to suggest we move on the muffled retort of gunfire stilled us.

"They found the Land Rover," Gabriel whispered, as if they could hear.

"Or the path we took. We need to move out. Give me your poncho, we can carry this fruit and our other supplies more easily."

He handed it over and I rolled up the water bottles, the fruit, and the axe and tied off the ends with the rope. It made a small sausage of the waterproof and a loop to fit across Gabriel's chest. I struggled back into my body armour and webbing, the weight depressing my shoulders and adding concrete blocks to my boots.

Gabriel took a bearing and we headed south, back into the thick secondary jungle.

5

WITH MY GPS GONE AND not having a paper map I worried we'd walk in circles among the dense trees and undergrowth, but Gabriel seemed to have complete confidence in his navigation skills. The same couldn't be said of his strength.

I watched him slow more often. He'd stumble and pant on every incline, slip and lose control on the declines. Gabriel fought his exhaustion, but it ate at him, dragging him down. The afternoon grew thicker and I knew we'd be in for another rainstorm before night. We needed shelter off the forest floor and more food.

If they were following us, I needed to make sure they regretted their decision.

"Wait up." I reached for his arm.

He looked at me, eyes glazed, and I knew I'd made the right choice. "We can't keep moving like this. You can't keep moving like this."

"I can manage." His lips were almost white, skin a horrible shade of grey.

"No, you can't. You know bush craft better than me. I have more energy. Go ahead, make way markers so I can track you. I'm going backwards, I'll lay some traps and move forwards to you when I know it's safe."

His hand gripped my arm. "You want to leave me?"

His wave of need almost buckled my knees and I badly wanted to kiss his fears away. Two or three times in my professional life had I blurred the boundaries with colleagues from other units, but this US Ranger would shatter all my defences in a heartbeat if I let him.

"I'm not leaving you, Gabe. You're going ahead. You are going to make us a camp somewhere safe and you will find us more food and water." I struggled out of my belt, so he had the small first aid kit, the fire starter and all manner of other things he'd need, and I didn't in that moment. Except the C4. I removed the C4, in a military package with the M183 demolition charge assembly. It had everything I wanted to make something go boom.

I handed him my side arm. "Just in case you need it against the Jabberwock I'm sure is out there somewhere ready to bite my face."

"You mean the snakes?"

I shuddered. I also gave into my need to kiss him. I grabbed either side of his face, tilted his head down and planted one on the crown of his head. "Don't get me lost on my way back to you."

"Don't get dead," he said in return.

I nodded, hefted my assault rifle and began tabbing back the way we'd come, following our trail way too easily. Apparently, I can't go anywhere without making a mess with my size twelves. Rather than keep to Gabriel's pace I set the one I'd use if I had to tackle the Pen y Fan on the Brecon Beacons again. The rain and cold I'd endured on those training exercises and punishment routes Stanton forced me to do were easy in comparison to the humidity and tree roots. At least I didn't carry a full Bergen that probably weighed the same as Gabriel did at the moment.

When I stopped, after a forty-five-minute run, I decided I'd gone far enough and had crossed over our temporary camp some time before. Our path was clear to see so they'd be coming this way and I had the perfect location for a trap. An overhanging rock made up of pudding stone – harder rocks smooshed together and held in place by softer rock – with a huge tree on the edge already leaning at an obscene angle.

The forest seemed strange in its stillness while I worked, as if it knew what I had planned, and all the local wildlife had disbursed to safer places. I breathed hard while I formed small sausages of C4 and set the detonators inside it in three places around the rock. When we'd passed earlier in the day, I'd taken note of the location because it represented the perfect place to hinder our trackers' pursuit. Once all the det-cord had been run out, I tied them to the pin of one of my grenades, I carried three in my webbing, and tied that to the bottom of a spikey bush. When the grenade's pin came out, the bush would explode and at least some of the 4-inch spikes would hit something useful. Add in the shrapnel from the grenade, the rock, the tree and its roots, and I had a good weapon's set.

Happy with my results, I placed a thin wire over our track and tied it to another tree's base. They would trigger the grenade to go off – or that was my plan.

I'd take the high ground nearby with my rifle and watch to check for stragglers, then head off to find Gabriel.

With luck the men hunting us would travel close enough together to wipe out the team, but I had no idea if we were dealing with ordinary soldiers, thugs or Special Forces. The latter would spread their men out to avoid just this sort of trap, travelling in groups of two or three at most but with distance between each group to prevent the entire team from being targeted in a single attack.

Once I'd finished, I scrambled up the nearby bank, making sure I stood on stone, not mud or plants and ran along the top, trying to avoid leaving a trail. Gabriel seemed to move through this stuff with disheartening ease, like smoke, but I found myself tangled in vines at such regular intervals I began to think the plants wanted me stripped of weapons so they could feast on my bones.

"Too much bloody imagination," I muttered, while yanking my leg free.

I turned to check the sun, my position, my path down once I'd blown everything up, and my surroundings. I began to hear shouts from my right, so I settled down on the ridgeline I'd chosen to use as my nest and arranged my weapon, sighting on the kill box I'd created.

My only moment of guilt came from destroying a tree or three. I did not feel good about that at all, but I guessed they'd be absorbed into the hungry world of the rainforest sooner rather than later and there would be plenty of blood and bone to feed the soil. I did not feel any sympathy for the men who had held and tortured Gabriel. A part of me wished I could show him evidence of their destruction, but he'd hear the boom.

I waited.

Unlike many soldiers I had no trouble remaining still for extended periods. It made me a good sniper and in the Marines I'd been on over-watch many times while my muckers cleared streets or courtyards in the urban wars zones where we'd been deployed. My current sergeant, Stanton, hadn't been interested in my sniper skills. He hadn't been interested in anything I could do and made it very clear the sooner someone shot me the better. One less *fag* in the world. Which is why he always sent me in first if possible.

I tried not to think about Stanton because it made my body start to tense and I needed to be relaxed if I wanted to be to be accurate. Shooting accurately relies on remaining still and relaxing as much as possible, especially over a distance of more than a few metres. Running and being accurate, despite what the films make it look like, is almost impossible. You run, take up your position, fire, run again, take up your position, fire, rinse and repeat until you reach safety. Running and firing is only really useful for keeping your enemy off balance and denying them the ability to stick a bullseye on your body.

Shouts came down the track. I moved my sights to take in the coming targets. Twenty men, all bunched together, making an insane amount of noise. They must really want Gabriel back to send this many. I could see, even at this distance, at least one with, what I assumed to be, a crack pipe in his mouth. They were high. All of them carried MP5s in various states of disrepair.

A nudge of pity surprised me, they weren't paying any attention to their surroundings and they'd soon be dead or dying. Then I remembered the scarring on Gabriel's body. The state of him when I'd held his weight while unlocking the chains around his wrists. The drugs they were sending to Europe and the kids that would die.

"Fuck 'em," I muttered, setting my sights on the man furthest from the blast site.

The two men in the lead passed through the trees where I'd tied the wire to the grenade.

I counted to five in my head.

The grenade exploded, sending shrapnel in all directions. The detonators for the C4 went off. I covered my head and pressed my face into the dirt. Still the bright white light of the explosion coloured my vision. A boom of immense proportions filled my world and I lost the sense of my body. The vibration from the air, through the ridge I lay on, and the soul of the forest swept away what little understanding I had of my surroundings.

I tried to breathe in, but the firestorm of the initial explosion stole all the oxygen. A landed fish had more chance of breathing in that moment. The surge of panic in my blood helped me locate my limbs in the disorientating tangle of noise and aftershock. In the planning of this trap I might have used more C4 than I needed.

Knowing I still had a job to do I reached with a trembling hand for my weapon and looked over the site for targets.

The size of the crater shocked me.

I'd not just brought down the cliff and toppled a tree. I'd created what could be a large pond when the next lot of rain came down. Scorched earth and burned vegetation registered at last on my nose, the final one of my senses to come back on-line. I couldn't see anything left of the men tracking us, at least not to start with among the debris of the destroyed trees. I did feel bad about that and promised I'd plant more the moment I could afford to go home – back to the farm. Stupid thought but the brain does strange things.

To make certain there were no stragglers in the hunting party I stayed on over-watch for a full fifteen minutes. During that time, I began to pick out bits of body among the wreckage. A 3D jigsaw of a macabre massacre. I needed to get down there to see if I could find anything useful that might have survived. Clothing, weapons, whatever we could use over the coming days through the forest. I had no doubt these guys were just the first attempt at hunting us down. When they failed to report in, whoever controlled them would send more and after this much destruction they'd be prepared for a fight. Gabriel and I needed to run for the border.

6

WHEN I SEARCHED THE GROUND, I found several things of use: some more knives, a torso with MP5 and magazines attached, which I robbed, and some tattered clothing without too many blood stains on it. I took these as well because we'd need to cover our hands and feet and heads to help prevent mosquitoes during the night. I didn't have a huge supply of repellent in my kit. The one true gift I found was a large sheet of heavy plastic someone had tied to their back. I guessed they'd use it as a groundsheet and wrapped inside was some netting. This bounty pleased me more than I could say and even made my rumbling stomach shut the fuck up for a bit.

The sun was now a long way down the sky, and I knew I'd need to run back to find the camp I hoped Gabriel had set up by now. With a sense of purpose, I started to tab back the way we'd come ticking off landmarks along the way. Once I'd reached the place we'd separated, I stopped, drank the rest of my water and watched the sky darken too fast with another rainstorm about to sweep through the area. The heat now pressed down on me and the adrenaline of the victory seeped into the heavy soil. This would be the most dangerous part of the trip, making sure I didn't miss any of Gabriel's way markers.

He didn't seem to leave any evidence of his passing but every 100 metres or so in a southerly direction I saw a small pile of stones and a single one just half a metre away on one side, his direction of travel. When I saw a sign, I destroyed it after me, scattering the pieces. Slowly the forest thinned, and the trees grew taller, we were in primary jungle now. The birds screamed about the approach of night and the storm. Monkeys chattered and laughed at me as I stumbled through their habitat. I lost my directional compass at one point, had to backtrack and found a planted stick with a fork at the top and another stick pointing due south. I jogged on.

The smell of roasting meat and wood smoke hit me just as the first bellow of thunder made me yelp in surprise. By the time I reached the UK I'd be cursed with tinnitus forever at this rate. I followed my nose and found Gabriel, sat on a rock, under the leeward side of another large rock and overhang trying to cook as the heavens opened again.

"Hey," I called out, keeping my hands away from my sides so he could see I wasn't a hostile.

"Nick?" He rose, wobbled and I rushed in to catch him.

His arms went around my neck and he held me. Despite the fact we both stank I buried my face in his neck and hugged him in return. This act of companionship, of mutual comfort after two years of beasting from my Regiment colleagues, meant more to me than I could ever describe in words. A deep and profound sense of belonging settled into my bones. Gabriel, in this moment, became the most important person in my life.

"You're alive," he whispered. To be honest he probably said it in a normal voice, but my hearing really didn't seem to be working very well.

"I said I'd find you."

"I've been so scared."

"Me too, Gabe. Me too."

He continued to hold me, and I let him soak up the warmth of our friendship even as the rain started to pour with real passion.

When he released me the sense of loss didn't come as I'd expected it to, instead the grounding of his physical contact remained, despite the distance between us. A unique experience.

Gabriel looked up at the rain. "I long to be at least a little cleaner than I am now." He glanced at me over his shoulder. "Can you keep an eye on the fire and food for a minute?"

"Sure," I said, a bit confused as to why. "Just don't wander off. Visibility is crap in this storm."

"Not going far," he called out as he yanked off the stolen clothes and boots. Within seconds Gabriel stood naked in the rain, face tilted upwards, mouth open and hair in thick black ribbons over his shoulders. I tried – I really did try – not to let my eyes wander but I couldn't prevent the desire taking control.

From this distance I couldn't see the scarring, but I could see the long lean muscles hugging the slim frame, we were the same height and yet so different. He had almost no chest hair but as he turned in a slow circle, his arms held out with palms up, I could see the dark trail from his belly button and I followed it down to the thick, unkempt black hair around his groin. He started to move, swaying in the rain singing something too quiet for me to hear over the crackle and hiss of the fire and pounding water. I watched him pick a number of leaves, rub them together and fold them up before he started scouring at his skin. With regret I dragged my eyes off his long legs and hard backside while I tended the fire.

"Oh, fuck," I muttered. A snake lay on a sharpened stake over the fire pierced as if the loops were a kebab.

"Don't look at it, just turn it," Gabriel called out.

"Easy for you to say," I growled only for my benefit.

I turned the snake then saw to my mixture of prizes. Gabriel returned, shivering. Feeling like the all-conquering hero I handed him a soft almost clean t-shirt in olive green.

"Whoa, what did you do? Find a 7-11 in the outback?" he asked.

"Better, blew up the bad guys and nicked their kit."

He laughed. "The great British Army." He fussed with the fire.

"Hey, don't knock it. I found socks to go with those boots." I didn't tell him how I'd almost puked as I removed them from the legs, just the legs, of a man.

He went through the other items I'd found. "Christ, we could live here for months with this lot. I heard the explosion, what happened?"

I grinned. "Misjudged the C4. I'm not always the best with those kinds of calculations. I only meant to do something to prevent them following, instead I've blown a huge hole in the ground and I managed to kill twenty men."

Gabriel's mouth dropped open. "Fuck. You think they'll come after us?"

I shrugged. "Don't know, probably when their team don't report in, but we'll be moving on at first light and we'll keep going."

Gabriel smiled at me with such beautiful kindness tears rose in my eyes and I had to look away. No one had ever looked at me like that and it made me naked in a way that had nothing to do with clothes.

"When can we eat?" I asked to divert attention from the half-naked man still dressing.

"Depends on how you like your snake I guess," Gabriel said.

"The same way I like my insects, a long way off while a roast chicken dinner is in my oven."

Gabriel settled beside me, out of the pouring rain, and we were once again shoulder to shoulder. "I'm exhausted. I wanted to make us a sleeping platform off the ground, but I think I've run out of energy."

"I'm not surprised and don't worry – I have a plastic sheet and some netting thanks to our friends. When did you catch dinner?"

"He was sunbathing on a rock. I felt a bit mean ruining his day like that but there you go."

"I feel bad about blowing up the trees," I confessed.

He knocked my shoulder a little with his. "Some bad ass soldiers we are."

We slumped into silence for a bit, just watching the rain, and the fire. I couldn't help but think back to last time I'd been with my Regiment team in a situation like this, and how different things were around the campfire that night.

We'd been in Somalia trying to track down some missing sailors with an SBS team. Stanton had made it clear to everyone I'd been black balled for obvious reasons, but the Special Boat Service stepped up and told him to shut the fuck up. They'd been working with a Covert Ops group called Unit Twelve who were the dog's bollocks apparently and a happy couple called Jacob and Mac had helped out. I knew of Jacob from his days in the SAS, but we'd never done a mission together. Regiment gossip had it that Stanton went for him, like he had me, but Jacob proved the harder man. I'd paid for the loyalty of the SBS team gave to me a few days later when we'd returned to the UK with the hostages, but that night had almost been enjoyable.

This night though, warmed me to my toes, despite the rain. I just needed to know a little more about my companion, something I could use to build a few walls back up before I fell in deeper with a straight man, which was my idea of hell.

"You never said if you were married." I reached for more dried wood while trying to sound nonchalant, I don't think it worked.

"Nope, I haven't said, you're right," Gabriel replied. I glared at him and he grinned. "I'm not married. Was once, a while back, but the job made it difficult and so did other things."

Not one word in those sentences would help me keep him at an emotional distance. I suppressed the need to huff. I wanted to ask more questions, but the man had been subjugated to questions under torture so maybe I ought to leave well enough alone.

I watched the flesh on the snake being to peel back from the bones. "Meat is done."

Gabriel reached out for the snake, the fire now our main source of light despite the rain beginning to ease and the clouds lifting. He peeled off a section of flesh, handing it to me. "Don't think, just eat. It's calories we're after, not a dining experience. We get out of this alive I'll spring for dinner at a restaurant of your choice. Providing they pay me of course."

"If they are anything like the British Army, you'll be docked for going over your holiday allowance."

He laughed and pulled a chunk of meat off, eating it with his eyes closed and a look of bliss on his face. I guess I'd be the same after suffering near starvation for weeks. "I think I might be the happiest man alive right now," he murmured.

I shook my head and stuffed the scran into my mouth. It did not taste of chicken or pork. It tasted of snake. Though it was better than some of the food they gave us in the army, especially when I'd been in the Marines, so I chewed and swallowed like a good boy. The snake was a long one, about four foot, so we ended up eating enough to feel satisfied and Gabriel wrapped the remainder in a few leaves for breakfast.

He yawned. I took the hint and shook out the mosquito net and plastic sheet I'd robbed. The net turned out not to be quite large enough. "Shit, it's meant for one."

"Then I guess you're the big spoon because we both need to be under it," he said.

I stopped moving, trying to see his expression in the firelight. Genuine fear, raced through me and I waited for the cruel joke I knew would come.

"Don't, Nick. I really have no problem with being held all night tucked safely into your body."

"You're not gay," I stated.

He paused for a moment before answering, gathering his thoughts. "No. I might be bi-sexual. I've never had time or the bravery to work it out. But…" I heard the tremor in his voice. "But you need to know something… The torture – it wasn't just beatings and… stuff. They… Um." His voice broke off and his withdrawal from me, without moving his physical body, tore a hole in my heart.

I didn't think. I reached out and took his hand. "Don't. Don't say anything else. Not tonight. Don't think about it. Not now. We can deal with it later. Right now, we live in this moment, not in the past. I'll keep you safe, Gabriel. They won't hurt you."

The rage flaring inside at the inference of what he'd endured almost blinded me. In an effort to keep control I took a few deep breaths and dragged him close. After a moment of resistance, he came.

"Can we talk about something else?" he whispered.

I kissed the crown of his head again, a safe place for now, and told him a story from my early years in the Marines when we'd been given leave in Portsmouth and drunk a pub dry. A stupid nonsense story which explained nothing, but I could make it colourful and use my Somerset accent to add to the silliness. Gabriel laughed in the right places and his hand lay on the inside of my thigh as I talked into the night. I knew then, whether he wanted me or not, I'd fall in love with him.

7

AFTER THE SILLY STORY GABRIEL sat in a slumped heap while I lay out the ground sheet and mosquito net. They weren't big enough for both of us but if we didn't move around too much, they'd keep the bugs at bay. It would be better to sleep off the ground but after the last two days the thought of cutting down enough wood to form a sleeping platform stood to be an impossible task. Despite the heat of the night we would have to remain in our clothes, and I used my NVG, knowing the batteries were dangerously low, to find my small tube of insect repellent.

I hadn't planned on being in the jungle for long so the tube was almost empty, but I took Gabriel's unresisting hands and covered his skin, then his face. I made certain his trousers were tucked into his new socks and removed his boots. I coaxed him to lie down and covered my skin in a much thinner layer of bug love repellent and moved towards the plastic sheet.

Gabriel rolled onto his side, his back to me, so I curled around him and tried not to touch until he reached back and gave my trousers a gentle tug. At that point I gave in, wrapped the mosquito net around our heads having tucked in our feet, and draped my arm over his chest. He pulled my hand upward to cover his heart and tangled our fingers together.

"I don't want to wake up alone," he whispered. We were using my body armour as a pillow and I shifted so my breath ghosted over his neck.

"You won't."

"This day had better not be a dream."

I wanted to kiss the soft skin on his neck so badly I could taste the desire. "It isn't. Though you're going to have to ignore what's happening in my trousers. It's been a while since I last held someone like this, and I think certain parts of me are waking up – sorry."

"Anyone else I'd kill," he murmured, more asleep than awake.

I sensed the moment he lost the battle with consciousness. The fight in him fled and he leaned back into my bigger chest. His body, all bone and hard muscle, fitted against mine with such tender perfection I couldn't sleep despite my exhaustion. I lay on the damp ground, listening to the last of the rain and the rise of the forest noises. The fire crackled a little, helping to keep bugs away and any larger animals, while the air moved with the scent of wet humidity. None of my senses picked up on anything familiar in my surroundings and like so many times in the past when I'd been on combat missions, I thought of home.

The fresh cold air off the moor. The deep scent of thick grass and ancient trees. The smell of the sheep my father loved and the feel of their greasy thick coats under my palms. My mum's cooking and the smell of the farmhouse, full of dog, more damp, and laundry detergent. The noise of the wind and rain against the windows and our waxed coats when we were out working. The slurp of wellies in thick mud. The scream of the crows when we disturbed them in the fields. I also remembered the summers. Endless fields of rich grass, bracken, heather and on the top of the moor the smell of the sea.

I held Gabriel and wondered if I'd be able to show him the home I suddenly wanted to return to with every fibre in my body. Making it back to England with Gabriel was all that mattered to me in that moment.

AN INHUMAN SCREAM WOKE ME with such force I found my hand gripping my side arm and Gabriel pushing back into me. He snatched the netting away from our faces and I held him tight, looking for the enemy.

The culprit let off another scream so brutal it made me want to run in fear despite not having a clue as to what might be wrong.

"There, our two o'clock," Gabriel hissed.

I zeroed in on the threat only to find several small black faces with white tuffs of fur and long tails held high in protest at our invasion of their territory.

"Fuck me, it's a monkey." I huffed out the breath I'd been holding and put the Sig on the ground. "Fuck…"

Gabriel laughed. "They don't seem pleased to share."

"No, they really don't but I wouldn't say no if they started throwing fruit at us. God, what an alarm clock. We should have them in the barracks."

My companion moved away from me but not far and we watched the indignant family – herd – pack...? Whatever their collective noun, the monkeys moved away through the tall trees, babies clinging to their mothers with no effort at all.

"I wish it was going to be that easy for us," Gabriel said.

I rose and stretched. The night had vanished and the sky, what we could see of it through the canopy had painted the world baby pink. After loosening up some painful joints I drank some water, handing the bottle to Gabriel and retrieved our cooked snake. My stomach made some interesting noises at the thought of digesting said snake, but it didn't have a lot of choice, I needed the calories.

When I returned to Gabriel he hadn't moved. "How are you feeling?" I asked, squatting beside him and handing over the meat.

He looked up at me. "Not great."

Those dark eyes were bloodshot and the pallor of his skin worried me. I took hold of his wrist and his pulse felt too fast and light.

"You look like you're going into shock," I said. "Drink more water, take your time. I'm going to see if there is anything I vaguely recognise as food in the area."

"Don't eat anything until you've brought it back to me," he said. "And be careful, Nick. Please."

I squeezed his shoulder and walked into the jungle among the high trees. To be honest I needed a little alone time.

One fearsome pep-talk later about the appropriateness of my ridiculous emotional attachment to a man I didn't really know, and I returned to our small camp. "I struck out on food." I knelt beside Gabriel again and realised my pep-talk had been a waste of time and scant energy.

"The meat is good," he said, handing it to me.

"You haven't eaten enough, Gabe."

He blinked slow and sure. "You need strength, Nick."

I pushed his hand away. "I need you to make it. Eat the fucking meat. That's an order."

"You know I'm a Sergeant 1st Class, right?"

"Not in my army you aren't," I said. "Eat as we move, I want us to travel before it gets too hot to walk."

Gabriel nodded and managed to stand. Whatever energy he'd had the day before from our escape of the camp had vanished and in its place I had a prisoner reminiscent of a survivor from Belsen, despite being slightly better fed, which was saying something. I needed the soldier in him, not the victim or the survivor.

"We need to head to the border."

My companion didn't reply so I backed up our haul of gear and struggled back into my body armour. I strapped the MP5 to my back, carried the HK G36k on my front and handed the machete to Gabriel. Those dark eyes looked at the amount of stuff I carried before they focused on my face.

"I'm sorry I can't be of more use," he mumbled.

I gave him my best smile, trying to stop the lopsided grin I usually used. "Listen to me, Gabe, if you hadn't been here last night I wouldn't have eaten. Find us some more food on the way and trust me, I'll owe you. Come on, let's go home."

He nodded and fell into step beside me. The morning didn't bring any rain; the birds were raucous and competed with the monkeys. I offered to shoot something to get us some meat, but Gabriel made it clear with a single look that bush meat like monkey would not be on the menu. We found some fresh water though that we mixed with my few sterilising tables.

In fact, we found a lot of small streams racing down ancient causeways and Gabriel decided we should follow them despite it turning us towards the west more than I liked. Out of the two of us, he was the senior officer and he had far more jungle experience than me. The going proved easy under the high canopy of primary forest, the only two problems we really faced were hunger and Gabriel's exhaustion. I found him a branch to use as a stick and watched him lean into it more with every step. After a couple of hours at a gentle stroll I called a halt.

"How bad are your feet really?"

"They could be worse."

I stared at him for a long time until he sighed. "These boots don't fit well. I have blisters. On top of that the bruising from the last few months means it hurts to carry my weight. I don't think they are damaged as such, not now, but I feel each step."

"Okay, well, don't hide it from me."

"You want me to tell you every bit of me that hurts? That's a fucking long list, Nick. Let's just keep moving, it's worse when I stand still." He shuffled off and I frowned. We both knew I couldn't carry him for any distance, certainly not the distances we needed to travel, but it also meant he would slow us down to a crawl by the end of the day and there would be no running if the enemy came after us again.

We trudged on. I tried to think about the miles we'd have to travel to the border, then more miles the other side to reach a road. That was a lot of miles. In Britain if you're out in the countryside something like 80% is within a mile of a road. It's hard to get lost in that kind of environment. Out here, the density of the population was so thin we could pass within a mile of habitation or a road and never know it.

The day began to heat up and with it came the roiling clouds. Vast thunderheads of darkness swallowing up the sky. Gabriel stopped and watched them for a bit. He'd been really quiet during the morning, so I had no clue as to the state of his mind.

"We need to take shelter," he said. "Getting caught out in that storm isn't going to be wise."

I looked around. We were in a depression, following a small river that giggled over the rocks. The vegetation was sparse among the boulders and stones dumped by the water during previous monsoon seasons. "Have you seen somewhere sensible?"

"We've time to rig something up using the plastic and the overhang of those tree roots," he said pointing to a huge tree hanging onto the cliff with only half its roots in the soil. The rest dangled over the river.

"Okay. Let's do it but you need to eat as well." I needed to eat and as I was now seventy-two hours into a mission the exhaustion tore at me as well.

Gabriel didn't reply but he moved off again and I watched, wincing, as he struggled to make his brain move his painful feet. We reached the tree and checked it for animals. After clearing out a few rocks we discovered a small cave just large enough for the two of us to fit.

"I'll do a recce, see if there is anything to hunt. I might find a snake."

"Be very careful if you do, Nick. Most of Myanmar's snakes are deadly."

"Good to know," I said dumping all our kit but my rifle and knife. I set off downstream at a better pace than we'd managed together.

A new sound came to me and it took me a moment to realise what I heard. A larger river. I pushed my pace a bit and stopped in my tracks, mostly because I didn't have a choice. The river we followed tumbled some distance into a tumultuous cascade of water.

"Fuck me," I murmured. "We're not getting across that easily."

With the light fading due to the coming storm the bank on the other side of the river wasn't easy to make out but it looked lower than this side and I thought it looked swampy. I knew how hard going it would be for Gabriel through a swamp. Mangrove trees were a tangle of roots designed to trap the unwary and where they stilled, water leeches grew fat on animals and people stupid enough to stray into their territory.

If it was swamp on the other side, it would turn into swamp this side sooner rather than later. Information to store and report but right now I needed food and with the storm coming I had to do something now.

I slid down the steep bank and scrambled over the rocks to reach the edge of the larger river. At this point the water didn't make much noise, what I'd heard were a set of rapids some 100 metres upstream. They made the noise. Knowing more about fishing than I really wanted to thanks to my dad, it didn't take long to find a likely spot to catch some food. I thought about Gabriel's smile if I managed to return with real food.

A still pool of water, in the sun, was the ideal location. Insects hummed and buzzed around me while I squatted on a flattish rock to watch the opaque water. Several sleek trout looking fish swished about under the surface. I checked the coming storm. I'd get wet for certain, but the prize would be worth it, I just had to hope Gabriel had built a fire. Lying flat on my belly I reached out to the water with a patient stillness. The bullet scrape on my arm protested but I ignored the nagging and if it began bleeding it would be worth the risk to bring back such bounty.

Shooting fish didn't work. Apart from the noise alerting all and sundry, bullets didn't behave well in water and fish moved way too fast. This would work though, and it would save me setting up a line and hook from my survival tin. With my arm in the water up to my elbow I waited while bugs feasted on my exposed neck and sweat. The fish swam about my arm and one settled over my wrist and hand. It had been years since I'd last done this, but I'd loved tickling fish as a kid and those waters were far colder than these. With infinite care I lifted my shoulder to draw my hand up just a little. The fish twitched when my fingers brushed his belly, but I cupped him in my palm, not quite touching, and waited for a moment before – snap. My hand closed, the other reached down and I twisted away from the water.

The wet scales slipped in my grip, but I threw the fish onto dry land and scrambled after it. The end was swift. I checked the storm and heard the rumble of thunder while watching the lightning dance through the clouds. They really knew how to make a storm in this part of the world. It didn't look like monsoon rain, this looked far worse. The wind began to rise as well. Returning to the pond I did the same trick a second time and failed. On the third attempt the wind made the trees moan, the sun vanish, and the temperature drop. I caught the fish though. I had a moment of feeling like Gollum needing to return to my precious – in this instance Gabriel.

Not wanting the mess at the camp, I gutted the fish, washed them out and headed back. The storm hit the moment I scrambled up the bank and it tried hard to knock me back. The water from the sky went far beyond a deluge and visibility shrank to 5 metres. I picked up the trail of the tributary we'd followed and fought my way back to the tree with my prizes.

8

GABRIEL HAD RIGGED UP THE groundsheet so it offered more protection than the overhang could alone. He'd started a small fire despite the rain and our shelter kept out the worst of the wind by the looks of things. When I approached, I called out and he looked up with relief and a smile.

"The hunter returns," I said, and I couldn't help the grin of pride as his eyes widened.

Tears shone and spilled over. "You caught me fish."

I knelt and handed them over. "I did. Hey, it's okay you know." I leaned against him for a moment, to offer support. My hands stank of fish and we didn't need that smell on top of all the others.

He took the food with reverence. "I haven't eaten fish in months."

God, I wanted to kiss him. The pang and ache were so intense I turned away and risked a soaking by going to wash my hands. When I returned Gabriel had speared the fish on small stakes and was building up the fire.

I described what I'd found a short way downriver and he nodded. "Makes sense and we need to use it to speed things up."

I shook my head. "I'm not sure, Gabriel. I know from experience these rivers, any rivers, are difficult to navigate and control." The rain and thunder made our conversation halt for a bit. Once the thunder paused the rain smashed around us and instinct made us huddle together.

Gabriel pressed into my side and I placed an arm around his shoulders. He shivered. "I can't keep walking, Nick." He pushed his feet out, nearer to the fire. They were filthy for a start but beyond that I could see the damage. Welts and blisters were everywhere along with open sores.

"Shit." I didn't pause for a moment or think about what I was doing. I grabbed my kit belt, found my survival tin and emptied it out. Then I poured some of the sterilised water into the food container and ripped a sleeve off my t-shirt.

Shifting around, I took Gabriel's unresisting leg and placed a foot in my lap. With care I started to wipe at the muck and blood. Neither of us spoke. The smell of the fire and cooking fish wrapped around us and rain pounded down on the plastic and tree. The river chattered in the background but the world inside our bubble grew still except for my hands and our breaths. The emotional impact of having his consent to such tender and intimate care sent a spiral of longing through me. I could sense the tendrils of it licking out towards him, testing the possibility of his reciprocation. I tried to counsel myself that none of this would give me the connection to another man I craved so badly, but never imagined having for so many reasons. It didn't work. My battered old heart wasn't going to listen to common sense.

The scarring over the tops of his feet, around his ankles from cuffs or chains, and even on the soles, hurt my chest. The new blisters looked like nothing in comparison, but all soldiers knew how pain like a popped blister could nag away until it wore you out and infected feet were the end of more than one army over the centuries.

I finished with the first foot and placed it with care on the sock. After changing the water in my tin, I returned to my task. Gabriel's big brown eyes watched everything. His silence spoke to my need and added fuel to my starved fire.

"The only time I kissed a man was before my marriage," he said into the bubble surrounding us. I glanced at his face. A wry smile twisted his soft lips. "It didn't go well. I was home on leave, drunk and in the one and only gay bar I've ever dared to visit. He wanted far more than I wanted to give, and I scared myself stupid. Sometimes I think that's the only reason I married in the end. It took the decisions away from me, took away the fear of being different and of being in an army who would reject me if I were honest. It made everything go away – does that make sense?"

I nodded and continued to clean the soft skin and fine arch of his foot. He had long toes and dark hair. "I'm not sure I'd have understood if we'd met before I'd been in the Regiment. I've been out and proud since I was a teenager. But being with men who fear or hate me for being gay? I get it now. How people feel they *have* to hide. How they'll do anything to normalise their lives rather than face the truth of what they are, who they are. It's a sad but common way to live a life."

"When did you know you were gay?" he asked.

The memories rushed back, and I smiled. I'd given him the overview but not the details of the event. "I was thirteen and a big lad already. I decided to tell my mum first. It was a Sunday and she was cooking in the farmhouse kitchen – bloody great big room – but she'd have her hands full so I figured she couldn't throttle me."

"You didn't think she'd throw a steak knife at you?" Gabriel asked, half teasing, half worried for thirteen year old me.

I chuckled. "I was thirteen, thinking really didn't happen too often." I patted at a popped blister and Gabriel hissed through his teeth, tensing for a moment. I continued to distract him. "Bold as brass balls I walked into the room, squared my considerable shoulders, coughed to make sure my broken voice didn't squeak and I'd sound like a man and said, 'Mum, I need to tell you something'. She turned, hands full of a roasting tray and a pork joint and said, 'Son, if it's about your porn collection I don't care, can you give me a hand with the spuds my wrists are killing me'."

"Your porn collection?" Gabriel's dark eyes were large.

I nodded. "Yep, it was rural Somerset, so I had a collection of old magazines and a young internet for education. We had a computer in the house but only for my dad's work and smartphones weren't affordable yet. The new millennium took a while to reach the south west of England."

"Go on, what happened?" he asked.

"I said, 'Mum, I'm sorry, but I'm gay. I know you're going to be angry –' She said, 'Nicky, just get the bloody potatoes out of the oven. I've known for years it was likely. No need for a drama, son'. At which point I burst into tears." I chuckled at the memory of my mum pushing the Sunday joint back in the oven and rushing over to give me a cuddle. "I wailed about being gay and how sorry I was and awful everyone was going to be to me while she hushed me. Then I said, 'And Dad's going to be so angry'. He walked in at that moment of course. 'What am I going to be angry about, son? What's he done this time, Maggie? If he's been near that slurry pit or dropped something in it again, then I'll be angry'." I did passable impressions of both parents to add to the drama.

"What's a slurry pit?" asked Gabriel.

I grinned. "You don't want to know but they do kill people, especially drunk people or stupid children, and it's the worst way to die known to man."

Gabriel frowned.

"We had fifty head of cattle at the time and all their shit has to go somewhere after milking twice a day." I left the rest up to his imagination.

"Oh, no... Really?" He understood.

"Yes, sir. Huge pit and I was banned from going near it. Mum said, 'No, Colin, it's about his porn and what we talked about'. To which my dad said, 'Oh, he's finally told you he's a poof then?' My words were, 'You can't use that word, Dad'. He grinned and replied with, 'I know that, son. I'm teasing. I'm just glad you're not hiding anymore'. He came over and gave me a hug. End of drama. I felt like the luckiest boy on the planet that day. Mum even gave me an extra helping of pudding, much to my sister's dismay. They still make me feel like that whenever I go home."

"I have no idea what my mum would have said, and my dad died just before I came on this mission," Gabriel said. The scarring on his ankle this side was worse, he'd been shackled to something.

"Tell me about them?" I couldn't imagine the grief he'd gone through, losing his only parent and having to deal with being captured. Fuck this life.

"I said my mother and father met when my grandfather took my father into his household after catching him crossing the border into Arizona. Well, everything was wonderful for fifteen years. They had me and all was good. Ranching in a desert is hard work, but my father enjoyed the life. Then the politics of Texas changed, and it leaked over the border into Arizona. Some locals came after my father, but he'd gone to Venezuela because his mother was sick. My grandfather tried to stop them, but they wanted me for being a half-breed and my mother for marrying an immigrant. I can't use the words they did. Her high school boyfriend who happened to be the new sheriff was the leader of the lynch mob. When she shot over their heads, he opened fire and didn't miss. The posse disbursed. My grandfather called his old friends at the State police. By the time my father returned the posse were all caught but she was still dead. A few years later my grandfather died. My dad never recovered. I joined the army and rarely go home. I took this job with the CIA to pay for his cancer treatment, but it didn't work, he gave up. He couldn't pay for it and the insurance ran out long ago. I discovered he'd stopped the payments to the hospital from my pay check, left the hospital, left treatment and died on the ranch with a lady friend holding his hand. She wrote to tell me. No happy ending I'm afraid."

His words had tumbled out in a rush and I heard the unshared grief and guilt. My story had come in a well-rehearsed and humorous manner because I'd told the tale countless times. I had the feeling Gabriel didn't share often, if at all. He seemed even more lonely and sad than me, not because of our predicament or his torture, but a long-term sadness I couldn't really understand. My family were all hale and hearty, they loved me. I had sadness, bucket loads of the stuff, but my family were my stalwart against the brutality of the world.

"I'm sorry."

He nodded. "I know. Just as well me and the old man didn't have to have a conversation about sexuality though. Not sure how he'd feel about me wanting to kiss you."

I glanced up at Gabriel's face. His eyes were wide, lips parted a little and I saw colour on his cheekbones. His expression flitted between hope, terror and worry.

"It's probably more important to know how *you* would feel about me kissing you," I said. Smooth I am not. I couldn't breathe very well either. How long had it been since I'd last kissed a man longer than the quick snog necessary before the main event? Years. Lots of years.

"I think I'd feel just fine about it," Gabriel said, switching on the heavy Arizona drawl for the first time.

It made a lot of my blood move south. Probably most of it. Rather than sit on my arse and pull him towards me, which would be ungentlemanly of me, I rose to my knees. It brought us nose to nose. I wanted to remember this moment for the rest of my life, however long that might be, so I cupped his jaw in my right hand and smoothed my thumb over the soft whiskers which had grown during his captivity.

His eyes widened, they were so deep as to be black in this light, and he licked his lips, drawing my predatory instincts downwards to a focus I usually reserved for the shooting range. Lightning flashed and thunder rolled making Gabriel startle.

That was the moment I pressed my lips to his for the first time. A firm claim. In the thunder still rocking around us and the rain hissing I heard my heart whisper, *mine*.

His fingers wrapped around my thick forearms and his kiss shifted from accepting my attentions to demanding them. Those mesmerising lips moved against mine and our roughened skin rubbed, my thicker, longer beard rasping against his much softer hair. He slipped onto his knees, so our chests touched when we moved or breathed. These were still soft kisses, almost chaste but Gabriel wanted more and licked at my mouth. I opened to him and the first brush of his tongue against mine woke all of me, woke every atom of me.

Nothing in all my gay life, which hadn't been much to be honest because of my job, prepared me for this monsoon of sensation. Gabriel didn't let me go, he nosed at my face when he needed to breathe so he didn't lose contact, before returning to tender kisses then sweeping all away in another lightning attack on my heart with his demanding mouth. His arms were around me now, holding me close, and the first time he pushed his groin into my body I almost toppled back into the fire.

I reached back and with care released my body from his arms, kissing his jaw and cheek so he'd know it wasn't a rejection, just a pause.

I needed a breather.

I needed control.

I needed to think.

I needed to never let this man go. Ever.

"Bloody hell, Gabriel. Where'd you learn to kiss?" I asked him, a chuckle escaping.

His hands shook and he kept stroking my face with his fingertips, eyes roving over every millimetre, mapping it and storing just as I was doing. The trouble was Gabriel's face had been touched by the gods. Mine? I was hit by an ugly stick while falling out of the ugly tree. I wanted to pull away from his scrutiny, but he had a right to know.

The noise of the storm faded away while we gazed at each other, our bodies still rubbing together in ways that wouldn't stop my cock from aching with every nudge and rock.

"We need to check the fish." My words were a weak breath of sound and thought even as I ghosted my thumb over his lips and his licked the tip. I may have whimpered.

"I don't think I'm bi," Gabriel whispered. His eyes were black and full of stars and wonder. A child at Christmas couldn't look as amazed.

I laughed and our foreheads bumped together. "Not sure that's a decision to make on the strength of a single kiss, no matter how fucking good."

Gabriel released me enough for us to check on the fish, bits of them were cooked already so we peeled off what we could and ate the steaming meat. It was the best food I'd ever tasted but I vowed never to confess that to my mum. The beautiful man sat next to me hummed in delight and soon settled himself between my knees so he could lean back into my bigger chest and eat at the same time.

"Happy." The word surprised me considering his circumstances. I guessed after everything he'd endured this could be happiness.

I kissed his neck, finally able to sample the soft skin, and he trembled which made me want to explore some more. The storm raged on and we ate our fish, drank our water, collected more from the plastic grown heavy with puddles over our heads, and tried to keep the fire alight. We weren't going to be moving on any time soon and I nestled into the back of the small hollow under the tree with Gabriel still between my thighs. He fell asleep in my arms, his head on my chest, arms tangled through mine and I watched the rain rage against the land and our small river begin to rise.

9

THE SOUND OF BIRDS WOKE me, the sunlight almost blinded me and the weight on my bladder almost finished me off. The weight turned out to be Gabriel who lay half on me and half still between my legs. Moving before he woke up didn't seem wise after his previous reactions. I drew my attention from him and checked our waterlogged surroundings.

"Oh, shit," I muttered.

Gabriel's feet were mere centimetres away from a dunking. The river we'd followed the day before roared through the narrow channel which hadn't looked narrow when we'd settled under the tree to wait out the storm.

"Gabe? I need you to wake up. I need you to wake up now and I need you to remember where you are and who you're with," I tried to whisper in his ear without moving too much. I tensed my body, ready to fight him to stillness if necessary.

He jolted, wriggled against my arms locking around his chest, but grunted and stilled when he heard my voice.

"Nick?"

"Yep." I let him go and he sat up taking deep and calming breaths. I didn't touch him, just allowed him to orientate himself.

"Shit, the river."

"Yep."

He turned and looked at me. "We lost our stuff."

"Yep."

"Fuck."

I drew my knees up and he shifted around looking for his boots. We'd been good soldiers with some of our gear, but everything around the fire had vanished. We still had the plastic but the mosquito net, my body armour and webbing were gone, which meant our spare ammunition had gone with it and the MP5. I still had the G36k and Sig but not enough in either clip to make a difference in a fight. The machete and axe we still had, thank goodness, and my belt kit but nothing in there would be massively useful. We also had some rope.

Gabriel sighed and rubbed his face. He had his boots and socks though he didn't put them on, and I couldn't blame him, they were wet through and wouldn't help the wounds.

"We need to go down to the river you talked about yesterday," he said, not looking at me, but looking at the water tumbling past.

"Gabriel, I know you're desperate to get out of this jungle and so am I, but that river isn't going to be navigable. It's going to be full of things we can't control, rocks, trees, crocodiles, snakes, all kinds of shit that'll drag us under and it'll take time to build a boat able to cope with the flood water."

Gabriel turned to me with a sudden flurry of movement and anger. "Then what the fuck do you suggest? I can't fucking walk any further, Nick. Maybe you should just fucking leave me? Knock me on the head and let the fucking ants eat me." The shouted words were accompanied by flailing arms and when he finished, he panted with the effort. "Sorry."

I couldn't help but grin at him and the paddywack he'd just performed. A three-year-old's tantrum in a grown man is funny. "It's okay. I feel the same. Regardless we need to move, so let's pack what we have left and get our arses to the main river, then make a plan."

"I think I'm a bit stressed," he said wringing his socks out.

Understatement in the circumstances.

"I think you are as well. We'll have a look at the river and make the best of what we see. How much water training do Rangers get?"

He shrugged. "Nowhere near what the SEAL teams have."

"Then we rely on me and what I know as a Royal Marine, agreed?"

He knew what I was asking. The subtext was simple enough; he'd have to follow my orders because I had more experience. He sighed again and nodded. "Agreed. You know more."

"So long as we understand each other we'll be a good team, Gabe. We haven't let each other down yet and I'm not planning on leaving you here to feed the ants."

He smiled and his pale cheeks coloured a little. "That was a dick thing to say."

"Yes, it was." I tried to be annoyed but couldn't help smiling at him.

He covered the distance between us and planted the sweetest kiss I'd ever been given on my cheek. "Thank you for not reacting."

"You're welcome." I'd seen my mother deal with my father's tantrums over computer software more than once and they often ended the same way. He even bought her flowers once after a particularly noisy rant over the VAT returns. It warmed soft places in me to have the same conversation with Gabriel. Dangerous places for a soldier.

Wrapping Gabriel's feet before putting them into his socks and boots wouldn't happen now, we'd lost our spare clothing, so I rolled the socks over his feet while he bit his lip and pushed them into his boots. He gasped a few times but when I helped him stand, he managed. His stick had survived the rainstorm, so he took it and I watched with an aching heart as he stumbled ahead of me up the bank.

The pair of us had fucked up because we'd allowed our emotions and exhaustion to get in the way of SOP, standard operating procedure. I could have kicked myself if I didn't know the day ahead would do it for me. Gabriel's energy ran out long before we reached the river. He puked up what little he hadn't already digested and the water I forced him to drink. His eyes were hollow and whatever light I'd seen in them over the previous few days dimmed to nothing. When I touched him, a fierce tremor raced through his body, as if he were feverish but he didn't feel hot.

The day did though. A fine mist soon wove through the trees as the greedy heat sucked the water from the storm out of the earth. The scent of rotting vegetation filled the air and the mosquitoes were worse than ever. After Gabriel stumbled and his knees hit the ground, I heard him sob, far beyond cursing, he just wanted to give up. I couldn't beast him. I didn't have it in me. Instead, I lifted him, wrapped an arm around him and we walked together.

In such a fashion we made it to the larger river.

"Fucking hell," he said in a breath.

I stared at the swollen artery of water that bisected our piece of jungle. Even I wanted to cry now. Thick, dark water surged and plunged. I knew it would be bad, but this? Looking at it made me feel sea sick and I was a Marine.

I took a deep breath and pushed it out. The promise I'd made to Gabriel, to get him home, meant a great deal to me. Promises were something I didn't make lightly, and I *always* did whatever it took to see them through. This would be no different. My mother would say to me, *'Nicky, you eat an elephant one bite at a time. 'Cept eatin' elephants is bad so don't do it'.* Wise woman my mother.

Eating an elephant right now, good or bad, seemed to be a great idea to be honest. I glanced up at the sky. "There will be more rain before the day's through," I said. "You wait here. I'm going to find us a boat."

Gabriel laughed. "Fuck off. We might as well be on the moon for all the boats we'll find out here. Nick, this is madness. You need to get back to civilisation and then come and find me."

I turned him away from the rushing water and sat him under a huge tree, the roots making a cradle to hold him up and hide him from anything looking to make mince out of a human. "You are going to wait here. At most you're going to find something to turn into a paddle with this," I handed him the axe, "then you are going to remain still and quiet. I am going to find us a boat. You will listen to me and be here when I get back. I might have to tab a few miles so if I'm not back at dark, don't panic. I will be back." I stared into his dark eyes.

He sniffed and nodded. "I've never met anyone like you, Nick." He reached up and touched my face. "Thank you."

I couldn't help it. I leaned in and stole a kiss. He didn't seem to mind. "I'll be back."

He laughed at my terrible impression and I loped off downriver to see what I could find.

The going proved faster without Gabriel and I soon found myself in a different part of the forest. On a long bend in the river the water slowed down enough to form a marshy area on our side. I could see the reeds long before I reached them. The ground became harder going as it started to turn into swamp and it soon filled my boots. The edges of the marshland didn't have reeds tall enough for our purposes, so I ventured further in and sank up to my waist.

The water's temperature made me gasp and breathe hard for a few seconds. I reached down with the machete, grasped the long storks and cut as far down as possible. The machete made quick work of a handful of reeds. I stood straight and managed to lay them flat on the surface of the still water. With diligence I soon had an armful of reeds, but I knew I'd need many more.

In the steaming heat of the jungle, keeping an eye on the gathering clouds I just kept up my work. My stomach tied itself in knots from hunger and thirst made it worse. It didn't take long for my arms to be shaking from the effort, but I pushed the thoughts of fatigue aside. I'd been far more exhausted than this during my time in the SAS and Stanton's bullying. While I worked, I couldn't help my mind wandering over the last few days.

My survival, so far, with Gabriel filled me with a sense of purpose and pride. For two long years every day at work people had made me feel inadequate but working with the US Ranger proved I knew how to succeed under extreme circumstances. This proof made me feel worthy of my status as an elite soldier for the first time in months, maybe the entire time I'd been in the Regiment. I'd endured so much in the recent past that maybe when I had to return, I'd be treated with the same respect as the others because of this mission.

The armful of reeds turned into two, then three. I lashed them together with a length of our rope. When I left the swamp, I dragged the bundle with me and looked down at my chest because something felt a little odd.

"Holy fucking shit balls," I squeaked. An inarticulate sound of dismay tangled with the rising wind and vanished over the water. "Fuck, me, no, anything but leeches…"

I shuddered and closed my eyes. Then I whimpered. From proud squaddie to a total gay queen in one leech infested step. It made my blood surge the same way it did when I trained in the Killing House back in Credenhill. The hardest part was not pulling the nasty little fattening fuckers off my arms, but off more tender places because if they were on my arms, they'd be everywhere else too, including my crown bloody jewels.

Pushing away this torment I forced myself to think. Fire and salt were the only two options. Gabriel had my fire-starting kit and we didn't have any salt handy. I had to get back to camp. Forcing my mind to focus on the important things – like saving our lives – rather than fretting over 'harmless' blood sucking slugs, I relashed the huge pile of rushes. Then I made a sling, knelt and fitted it over my chest. I tried not to think about squashing leeches as I stood or the weight of the reeds trying to topple me over backwards.

I tramped up the shallow hillside that returned me to primary jungle rather than the marshland. The walk back to Gabriel took considerably longer and I had to refashion the carrying method several times to ensure I didn't kill myself in the process. When I reached the spot where I had left him, there was no sign of my companion. Fear shot through me making acid boil in my guts. After the explosion and the storm of last night I didn't think the drug cartel's soldiers would still be coming after us, they must think we'd been lost to the jungle by now and not worth the trouble, but losing Gabriel to them or the forest was unacceptable.

If I shouted what would happen? Would I find Gabe, or would I find a lot of very pissed off Myanmar drug soldiers?

I heaved the reeds off my back and a wave of dizziness blurred my vision for a long time. Once it cleared, I began checking the ground for tracks. The soil might be thin here, but the ground was still wet. I followed the boot marks I could see heading off into the jungle at a forty-five-degree angle to the river. Tiredness made me careless and after fifty paces I returned to the tree where I'd left Gabriel and retrieved my HK G36k carbine. If he had been taken, I'd make them regret it, so with my assault rifle and the machete I set off again.

The tracks were easy to follow and seemed to only belong to one set of boots. I checked the light, we were way past midday, so perhaps the shadows were playing tricks on my brain. I kept the weapon ready in the firing position and allowed my awareness to leak outwards.

10

"MOTHER FUCKER!" CAME FROM THE darkness of a tangle of trees ahead. I also heard monkeys who sounded like they were laughing at something. I followed the shout, scanning my surroundings.

"Gabe?" I called out, doing another sweep of the trees. Relief made my heart soar.

"Nick!"

I didn't move though, merely stood and scanned the area through my scope. "You alone?" I couldn't see anything, anywhere, except a small depression directly ahead.

"No! I'm with the fucking Miami Dolphins!"

I dropped the G36k back on the lanyard around my neck and looked into the small defile. Gabriel sat with his back to me, tugging at a huge forked branch. He cursed and yelled up a storm, but it wouldn't move. Evidence of his journey left a long and deep scar over the rough terrain.

My feet slipped down the shallow bank and I sat beside him. Still he didn't stop tugging. When I looked at his hands, I could see blood from grazes where he'd been fighting the large branch.

"It won't move," he half sobbed.

"Hey, hey, Gabe, come on, stop. Stop, baby. It's okay. It's okay. It's just stuck. We'll move it together." I reached for his hands and caught them in my big paws. He heaved in a breath and the floodgates opened.

Rolling tears tumbled out of him. "I'm so tired. I can't do anything. I just wanted to help. I'm a fucking US Ranger and I'm broken. I'm broken, Nick."

"Whoa, slow down, soldier. Slow down. Take a breath..." I rubbed circles on his back. As much as I might like to wrap him in my arms the emotional meltdown seemed to require something a little less tactile. I knew all too well how physical stress could affect your core emotional strength. Mine had been chipped away for so long I often found it a struggle to keep control.

"It won't move!" he wailed.

Practical, I had to think of a way of solving this problem. I rose and looked at the log. I had to admit it was impressive. How he'd managed to get this far in his state was a miracle in itself. It didn't take long to find the problem.

I lifted the right branch, tipping it a little and pointed. "Gabe, look, it had another branch and the broken end got caught against a rock."

Gabriel sniffed. "It was just a rock?"

"Just a rock, baby."

This set off another wail. "I'm so fucking useless in this state."

I dropped the log and returned to my previous position. This time I put an arm over his shoulders and pulled him close. "It's okay, it'll be okay. We have rope. We have reeds to make this the best raft in the world. We're going to get out of Myanmar, and you will never have to come back, Gabriel."

He clutched my filthy uniform and pressed his face into my chest. "Promise?"

"Promise. Let's get this log back to the reeds I've collected and make our escape."

He sagged against me and I held him while we rocked together. "I just wanted to help you."

"I know," I whispered. "And this is better than anything I could have hoped for. You've made my plan so much better. We'll use the vines you collected. The log you've found, and we'll move. I do need your help though."

"Anything," he said, wiping his face with filthy hands.

"I think I'm covered in leeches. Can you get them off me before I cut my own skin off?"

His eyes widened for a moment and he laughed. "I'm guessing they're in the same box as the snakes?"

"Worse... So much worse." I shook my head with my eyes closed but heard him chuckling.

"Okay. Let's get you de-leeched."

I dropped my head to my chest and something warm slid down my back. "I wish I didn't think that might actually be a medical term."

Gabriel chuckled and struggled to get to his feet without my help. We twisted the log over, freeing the stump that had broken my poor Ranger, and dragged it to the big tree we were using as a base. Within a short time, Gabriel had created a torch using the dry tips of some of the reed leaves and set it alight.

I stood before him naked for the first time and tried not to feel embarrassed by my lack of physical beauty in comparison to others – to him.

"Close your eyes, Nick, the smoke will be unpleasant, and I think you're going to lose some body hair."

One eye opened. "I probably have too much anyway."

A warm palm lay over my heart making it jump against my ribs. Those dark eyes pinned me to stillness. "You look perfect to me, Nick."

I might have whimpered a little in response, and he clearly hadn't spent enough time around other gay men, but Gabriel set to with the torch and I opted not watch as the black slugs began dropping off. He gave me instructions to open my legs, move my arms, and I felt the torch's heat ghost over sensitive skin with great care.

"Um, I think I need bits of you out of the way," Gabriel murmured.

I glanced down and realised he knelt in front of me, face just at the right height. I might be standing in a rainforest, but my mouth currently thought I stood in a desert it was so dry. Despite my desire to be a white knight some filthy things were stirring in my mind. I grabbed a handful of cock and balls, pulling them to the left.

"All clear," Gabriel murmured.

And to the right.

He glanced up at me and I caught the wicked glint in his expression. "All clear, big man."

"Ha, very funny." Heat rushed up my face.

Being naked in front of men had never been a problem until the Regiment. Sharing rooms, tents, showers and life in general with a group of hairy-arsed Marines was normal. The same couldn't be said in the Credenhill barracks. The men in my platoon were not happy about sharing facilities with me on the whole and Stanton just kept making certain it never felt normal for them.

It had left me sad and alone.

Something of this must have communicated itself to Gabriel because he dropped the torch, in the small fire pit he'd built and stepped into my space. "You are beautiful, English. You know that?"

I swallowed and tried to find a smile, a joke. Nothing came and I couldn't move away. I wanted to cry or punch something. I might be many things but being called beautiful by this man only made me aware of his pity. Gabriel placed his hands on my chest and swept them down over my stomach, back to my hips, over my naked arse and up my back.

He made certain we had eye contact. "You are beautiful, Nick. You are the strongest, kindest man I've ever met. I will thank any god listening to me for you coming into my life."

I managed a nod and he placed his lips against mine. We shared a gentle kiss. Nothing too urgent, nothing about desire as such, more a tender acknowledgement and a soft promise of the future.

He moved away from me and I dressed, a sense of shifting emotions, deepening and widening, keeping me silent for a while.

Gabriel changed things up a bit. "Right, we need to find some food."

"Not certain we'll catch anything in the river with it being so high."

I didn't expect a grin in answer. "Come and see what I did."

Together we walked to the river, at least I walked, Gabriel hobbled. He pointed to a branch he'd wedged between two tree roots. "I made a fishing rod from your kit and found some larvae to use as bait."

"You are a genius."

"No, just really hungry and highly motivated to get out," Gabriel said.

With my knees in the dirt I pulled in the line. It was heavy, so we'd either caught a branch under the flood waters, a croc – I didn't want to think about that – or some fish. We'd been so lucky up to now with food, but how much longer would our luck hold?

I kept pulling at the line and gradually we discovered our bounty.

Gabriel whooped in joy, managing to perform the strangest dance I have ever seen, and I've watched my dad dance at weddings.

He'd used all three of my hooks and all three had fish similar to those we'd eaten the day previously. "Holy shit, I don't believe you did this." I grinned at him. "You are a miracle worker."

Thunder chose that moment to announce the coming day's rainfall. "Let's get them back and cook them before the rain kills the fire." He couldn't hide his delight.

I knocked the fish on the head, gutted and washed them. We returned to the tree and Gabriel knelt to start building a rough shelter over the fire using the sheet of plastic and a rope tied around the tree. The fire built up quickly with the aid of some reeds I chose to sacrifice. With the fish making mouth-watering smells I turned my attention to the reeds and the log. The first drops of rain smacked my face.

"Come and sit by the fire, Nick. Don't get wet if you don't have to," Gabriel called.

I glanced over my shoulder. "We'll need more rope to lash this lot into a raft. We are going to have to make some from the leaves." I set to work stripping the large slender leaves. They were rough on the edges as a way to discourage animals from eating them, so my hands were soon sore, but I'd pulled together enough to start work.

Gabriel had a flat rock heating in the fire and had cut up one of the fish so it would cook faster. He handed me a leaf with slices of steaming fish. "Best barbeque ever."

The rain came, the fire hissed and spat, but continued to cook and we ate. I knew we should save some of the fish for the next day's adventure, but I didn't have the heart to deny Gabriel. He licked every flake off his fingers, and I had to stop him licking the stone. Afterwards we sat, shoulders pressed together and began braiding the leaves into rough rope. Not an easy task but necessary.

We then gathered reeds together, about all I could hold in two hands, and began lashing them into bundles. Most of the time we used the reeds we'd turned into rope and the vine we'd gathered at the beginning of the journey.

We worked in silence, intent on our task and happy to just let the rain fall, fill our plastic to give us clean water, and be together. Gabriel did ask one question, "When we start cutting our rope there's no going back is there?"

I shook my head. "No, I don't think so. This is do or die, Gabriel. I think

I'm getting sick, the wound on my arm is a problem and we have no way of redressing it."

"Yeah, I know. I should have been changing the dressing every few hours. It's been two days."

My fingers reached for his, both our hands raw with our efforts. "Hey, we're doing okay but if I get too weak, we're fucked. So tomorrow we launch and drift out of here."

Gabriel looked up at the plastic over our head and dug around his pockets. He found the two plastic bags we'd robbed from the Land Rover. They had holes so we couldn't use them to collect water but neither of us wanted to throw them away.

"We can make paddles with these," he said.

I grinned and nodded. "If we find some thinner branches with forks, we can attach the plastic to make webbing."

"Guess not all throwaway plastic is bad."

"Guess not." Before it became dark, I went in search of more branches while Gabriel went to check the re-baited fish hooks. Without a precise location we weren't certain which river course we'd be following so we didn't know if this one ran into the river marking the border between Myanmar and Thailand or if this was the river. We could only travel by day, night would be far too dangerous, and even a hint of bumpy water meant we would have to carry our raft or drag it through the shallows while we walked and tried to avoid all the inherent dangers of being in the water.

By the time I returned with two branches that might function as paddles with some whittling, Gabriel had two more fish on the fire. He already looked better for the protein and his success. We had found a small shoal of edible fish and we were wise by making the most out of our bounty. I couldn't remember the last time I'd worked with someone so easily. We were a team already, able to help each other with few words.

When night began to fall, we did all we could to protect ourselves from the bugs and we curled up, me as the big spoon. Moments before I drifted off Gabriel tangled his fingers amongst mine and sighed in contentment. I tried to use the downtime to visualise how to get the raft into the water but didn't succeed before I too slipped from the world.

II

IN THE MORNING WE ROSE before dawn. I had enough mosquito bites to form a new café brand called 'BitesOnUs', but we had other more important things to do than sit and scratch. We dragged the raft to the edge of the small cliff I'd scrambled down two days previously for our first fish and studied the river.

It had risen further during the night. Good for us because we wouldn't have to drop the raft far to reach the water, bad because its speed scared the shit out of me. We would have almost no control.

As if reading my mind, Gabriel touched my arm. "It'll be okay, Nick. We'll get out of this. We've come too far to fail now."

I wanted to point out that plenty of people failed at the final point, you just didn't hear about it because they didn't survive to tell the tale but figured it wouldn't help.

"If I get into the water, I can hold the raft steady. I'm heavier than you so it makes sense." Which meant I didn't want any arguments from him.

Gabriel didn't look happy but understood and conceded. Everything we had left was wrapped and strapped to the raft. The pointy end would go first and between the forks we'd lashed the bundles of reeds to create a bed we could kneel on for paddling. Under no illusions about my emergency boat building skills I wanted Gabriel prepared for the possibility it would fall apart and we'd be using the forked log as a buoyancy aid to drift in the water. He understood. If that happened though, in our weakened state, the sheer quantity of bacteria and animals able to kill us in the water, made survival a slim chance. If the raft remained whole after launch our odds of finding habitation that would be friendly rose to a definite possibility.

I lowered myself into the water. The cold shocked me for a few minutes and I worked with my booted feet until I felt steady against the current. It was strong and fast against the confines of the bank. The day was just dawning, and I realised we'd be heading south-east to start with, and I couldn't see any sign of more monsoon rains. I took both of these as good omens for a launch.

Gabriel pushed and I pulled on the bow of the raft. It seemed eager to fulfil its destiny and lurched towards me so fast I toppled into the water. I could hear Gabriel's panic and felt the raft tugging and twisting on the current, trying to break free. Coming up from the water I grinned and watched as the raft floated and pulled at my arms where I held a short piece of rope we used as an anchor just for the launch and any emergencies where we needed to tow the craft behind us.

The reeds remained in place. "All aboard," I said looking up at Gabriel.

He smiled, the one that made my heart falter, and with great care, lowered himself into the middle of the raft. His weight didn't make it drop down too far and it remained intact. The paddles and our meagre supplies were in the centre with him and he took them both, to make certain we wouldn't lose them as I walked us out into the stream of water.

"It seems strong and steady. I'm not getting much in the way of water coming through the reeds." He kept twisting to check all around the raft.

I worried what my weight would do to the chances of our small craft remaining whole, but I had to climb on board at some point. The back end of the raft swung around and pointed downstream. Gabriel knelt and tried to turn us but the current and design made it impossible. The cold began to leech under the surface of my skin, and I was now almost chest deep.

"Okay, I'm coming aboard," I said. "You can't fight what's about to happen and if I get this wrong, I'm going to have to swim after you. Do not lunge for me, Gabe. You need to stay aboard, and I'll catch you. I'm a very strong swimmer."

"Don't get this wrong," he told me, his face grim once again at the possibility of failure at this point in our mission.

I clung to the sides of the raft, fighting to keep it still in the water, and once at the stern, which currently acted as the bow, I pushed off the riverbed. The raft made a sudden and stomach dropping spin, righting itself through 180 degrees. I clung on in silence and Gabriel watched me with wide eyes.

We were already travelling downstream too fast for my liking. I just stayed where I was, legs in the water, the back of the raft dipping and rising under my belly.

Gabriel shuffled to the bow and acted as a counterweight. It worked and when we reached the reed bed area and the other side of the river turned into a mangrove swamp, the raft slowed. I wriggled up the reeds and the boat sank a little but held and no water rose through the reeds.

We both whooped in glee, disturbing birds and monkeys in the process.

By the time the sun rose in the east we were in the centre of the river, paddling only to keep straight, and making very good time.

The humidity gathered in a sticky morass but being on the river, not in the jungle, made it easier to bear because of the breeze. We watched the first few basks, which turned out to be my word of the day thanks to Gabriel, of crocodiles because they made us nervous but apparently we weren't seen as dinner by dinosaur brains.

I had the feeling that it would be different if we were in the water. Our combined ingenuity and determination had made this possible and my heart filled with pride. I'd been a different creature when I'd met Gabriel. Uncertain, lacking faith and confidence in my skills, but I would leave this jungle a new man and I wasn't going to take shit from Stanton or any of the rest of the Regiment.

"Fuck 'em," I muttered.

Gabriel, kneeling on the side with the smaller branch, looked at me. "Fuck who?"

"The Regiment. Fuck the SAS. I thought I'd always be proud of serving with them but I'm not. I'm not proud. I'm proud of what we are doing here but what I've endured for the last two years, just to wear a fucking badge that says, 'He Who Dares Wins', isn't worth it."

Gabriel's dark eyes softened. "You are a damn fine soldier, Nick. I'm proud of you. We wouldn't have survived without your skills."

I nodded to confirm his compliment but knowing it was sliding off my skin and into the murky depths below. "I'm going to request a return to the Royal Marines, I think." As I said that I realised something awful... When we left this jungle Gabriel would return to America and I'd go back to the UK.

The same thought hit Gabriel and I watched the light die in his eyes. "Yeah, no shame in being somewhere that makes you happy."

"No, I guess not," I mumbled.

The thought of Gabriel and I separating hurt far more than it should. We hadn't even done a week in each other's company, but I knew losing him would create a hole I didn't know how to fill.

We were quiet for a while, drifting and trying to prevent the raft turning in circles. It left us exposed to the sun but after what we'd already endured a little sunburn on the few exposed bits of me didn't matter too much. I watched the banks of the river, looking out for any possible settlements or evidence we were in Thailand, not Myanmar. The entire time the humidity rose and so did the clouds overhead.

"I don't know what I'll do if I get back to the States. Maybe the ranch, I guess. Depends on the state of it as I haven't been back for years." Gabriel's musings didn't sound happy and I couldn't help but notice the strange cadence in his voice. I had the uncomfortable feeling I didn't really know much about Gabriel Cabrera.

I needed to keep things light between us for now. "Will you keep the ranch on?"

Gabriel shook his head. "I'm not a rancher."

"I'm not a farmer," I agreed. "It takes a special kind of person to do a job like that." Though the pull of home was also undeniable. Maybe I could learn to be a farmer? I wasn't a natural soldier, the army made me one.

"It's a lifestyle, not a job. I just don't know anything other than ranching and fighting." He stopped paddling for a bit and seemed to stare down into the murky water. "I have nothing left to give."

That sounded far too bleak to me. "You're a clever man with some mad skill, Gabe. You'll find something if you retrain."

He managed a sad smile. "I'm over forty, Nick. The US isn't kind to men like me and who knows what damage has been done to me while I've been incarcerated? I could have any number of health problems."

"Equally, you could be fine," I told him. "Not everyone who goes through what you have comes out with diseases like HIV or hepatitis. I bet you had all the jabs before coming out here, right?"

He nodded but his mood continued to darken, which surprised and worried me. We drifted on until I noticed a change in the wind direction. It began to come from our backs and the raft moved more quickly. I twisted around and looked at the sky. My mouth dropped open.

"Oh no," I whispered on a breath.

Gabriel twisted and looked up as well, following my eye line. "Oh, shit."

Even though we couldn't hear the thunder we could see the lightning striking down into the forest below. Vast black clouds rolled over the landscape and the speed with which the storm travelled left me in awe. The temperature dropped, and the air started to smell of ozone and rain.

"We need to get off the river," I said.

"And go where?" Gabriel asked, waving his plastic bag paddle at the shoreline. We were surrounded by mangrove swamp and I could see the crocodiles on either side sliding into the water as if in anticipation of our doom-laden future. Not even the storm would make us foolish enough to risk the mangrove trees.

"Maybe if we move faster we can stay ahead?"

Gabriel looked at me as if I was mad. "Seriously? You think we can race a tropical storm?"

I closed my eyes. The hunger, thirst, wounds, exhaustion, the number of decisions and responsibilities, all turned to rocks and sat on my back. It bowed under the pressure and I pressed my head to the rough bark of the tree too tired to figure out this latest crisis.

"No way," Gabriel said.

"I don't want to know." Tears pricked my eyes.

If we were caught out here in the middle of the river during a tropical storm on a raft, we'd be dead. I couldn't get us to shore with two plastic bags as paddles and the raft would breakup in any kind of rough weather. The joints were already wearing thin and we were making the odd repair on the move. I really was going to fail. Just as so many Englishmen had done before me, I would die in the jungles of Burma trying to cross a fucking river. I'd kill for a bridge about now.

Gabriel brushed my arm. "Nick, look up. Please, trust me."

The overwhelming sense of failure that sucked at my soul tore away all the positives I'd accomplished over the last few days. All I could think about was the humiliation of being left by my team, left to die in this fucking jungle because I wanted to save a man's life. Left because I was weak, soft in the heart and the head. On top of all of that, I'd take Gabriel down with me.

"Nick, please, look up," Gabriel whispered.

I managed to raise my head.

"No way," I echoed Gabriel's words.

He laughed. "Yep."

A string of very colourful and English expletives followed. I knelt on a raft, built by our sore and torn hands while gazing at the shiny hull of a large ship. A proper ship. With radio masts, engines, water bilges, cabin on the top and a name in glorious English written down the side. *Serendipity*. And something underneath about a computer mogul and his desire to save the world.

We started to laugh. Then started to shout and move our arms making the raft wobble in the water. The storm built its tempo behind us and the thunder rolled while the river began to form waves from the wind pressure.

"Oh, no," I yelled. "They are hauling in the ropes." They were tied to a large tree and although we couldn't see who or what they were moving on and off the boat, they were preparing to leave the area. "Gabriel, keep yelling, I'll paddle."

I moved to the front of the raft and began paddling with every ounce of strength I had left in my shoulders. My entire body, every muscle, worked to its limit with each stroke and the small raft shot forwards.

Gabriel sat behind me, yelling and screaming for all he was worth over the noise of the coming storm. Rain began to fall; the wind rose more. "The raft is breaking up," he shouted.

"Hold on," I growled.

More, I dug deeper, deeper, deeper into the water with each stroke until – snap. The paddle broke and the plastic bag bobbed to the surface. I reached for Gabriel's, but he'd taken the bag off and was waving it over his head.

"Fuck it," I said. I drew my side arm, chambered a round and sent a swift prayer up to anyone listening that the P226 would still fire having been drowned more than once over the last few days.

I squeezed the trigger and released a round into the riverbank. I kept firing. Still nothing from the boat that made it appear as if they'd seen us.

Gabriel grabbed the HK G36k. The raft was now in tatters at the back and he half sat in the water and half gripped the log as he let off a volley of rounds from the magazine. When it clicked empty we had nothing left to give and now we were both in the water, clinging to the wood. He dropped my weapon.

"Hey, hey, you there!" a woman's face appeared at the gunwale.

"Help!" we screamed at the same time, then Gabriel slipped and went under the rising water.

I didn't have the time to check what was happening on the boat. I pushed the log away and dropped under the surface, turning in frantic circles trying to see in the murky water. I found him by touch. My finger brushed his arm, at least I hoped it was his arm and not a croc's leg or a snake, and my fist closed tight. I felt his hand grip my arm in turn and I pushed up. We broke the surface with a gasp.

A small rubber boat came towards us. I rolled onto my back, dragged Gabriel up my chest and floated. Tears mixed with rainwater as hands and voices filled my world, dragging us up and out.

12

TWO MEN WERE IN THE small rigid inflatable and we lay in the bottom while they yelled at each other over the thunder and pounding rain. I held Gabriel to my chest and checked his pulse. It beat, too fast but his chest rose and fell under my palm. The shouting turned out to be in French and I couldn't understand a word but just hearing a European language made me feel at home.

We made it to the yacht in no time and I saw a ladder against the gleaming hull. The craft rocked in the choppy river water and the engine fought the current to remain still. The men tied off the small boat.

"Is your friend alive?" asked one of the men. He looked like a fuzzy brown bear with blue eyes and I wanted to laugh.

I nodded. "Yes, but he can't climb that ladder without help. I'll make it though."

"Okay, we'll find the harness and lower it down. You know how to use a harness?" he asked in accented English. I nodded again. Without another word he scampered up the ladder as if it were as easy as climbing stairs.

"What's your name?" asked the second man. He looked and indeed sounded, American. Bright teeth in a tanned face, all too perfect for my tastes. A nest of sun bleached dark blond hair and hazel eyes marked him more surfer than scientist.

"Nick, Nick Wilde. This is Gabriel Cabrera."

"What the hell were you doing in the water?" surfer dude asked.

"We seemed to have gotten a little turned around. Should have gone left at the Himalayas not right."

Gabriel stirred against me. "Ignore him," he croaked. "He thinks he's funny because he's English."

I hugged him tight. "Welcome back." Gabriel grunted and wiped rainwater out of his eyes. A small seat appeared over the gunwale and bounced off the hull in the wind.

Gabriel helped slide his arse onto the rubber seat and clung on. It unnerved me watching him rise out of my reach, I didn't want to let him go in case something happened in the few metres separating us. We'd become welded to each other over the ordeal and having other humans in the mix began affecting my self-control.

Once they had Gabriel aboard, I grabbed the rope ladder and realised my arms had turned into rubber bands during the intervening minutes. I really struggled to hold onto the slick metal and only years of training as a Marine made it possible to reach the gunwale where more hands pulled me over. I landed on the shiny wet deck in a heap. Gabriel crawled into my lap and we just rested there while a dozen people stared down at us.

"What the hell happened to you two?" asked a young woman. She looked like a scientist.

"Doesn't matter," said the bear man. "Get them below. Those not on duty; get them clean, dry, fed and start seeing to their wounds. I need all hands not dealing with our guests to help get this lady back in front of the storm." The captain.

Everyone jumped to and two women, both a little older, tried to help Gabriel up. He stiffened against me.

"Might be wise to let me help him," I said, collecting his hands as they began to push the women away.

"You sure you can manage?" asked the darker of the two. Her African American accent sounded like something from the Deep South.

"I can manage," I said and raised a smile.

With legs made of jelly beans I hauled Gabriel off the deck, and he hobbled beside me, the rain still pounding down on our heads and backs. The women shepherded us under the canopy of the large cabin, and I saw the steps down to the galley. Muddy footprints covered them but everything else looked clean and shipshape. Gabriel went first and I could tell he'd begun to lose control as the adrenaline started to seep away. The ship started to change direction and he lost his balance until I grabbed him and held him while we slithered down the last few steps.

He clutched my arm. "Nick, I'm in trouble." His breathing sounded more laboured than it should, and he shook, not just trembled, actually shook.

The women appeared in my eye line. "I'm a medic and she's a nurse," said the American. "Let me help," she spoke to Gabriel.

He held out his hand to her. "Thank you."

"That's it, sugar, just let us help. We'll get you squared away. You're from the US?" she asked. Her questions were just meant to ease his mind. All the times I'd been in Accident and Emergency over the years I'd heard similar things from similar professionals.

Gabriel nodded.

"I'm British."

She glanced at me as the two women held Gabriel's elbows and helped him walk to a large dining area. "No kidding I wouldn't have known."

Her deadpan delivery made me chuckle. She reminded me of my mum, and I had the urge to drop to my knees in gratitude, trouble being – I'd never get up again if I tried it.

The blonde lady came back for me. "Hey, it's okay, you're safe here." She spoke in English but sounded Greek maybe and her tone sounded strange.

"It's been a tough week," I muttered. With a small arm around my waist I moved after Gabriel, joints stiffening and muscles cracking. They sat us side by side and Gabriel wove his fingers through mine, seeming not to care what anyone thought of the intimate gesture. A flurry of activity from the two women followed.

Blankets were placed around our shoulders. Heat pads were stuffed against our bellies. Water under our noses and with gentle compassion, bowls of hot noddle soup. Tears rolled down my cheeks and Gabriel openly wept.

"I'm Anna, by the way, and this is Grace." Anna sat beside Gabriel and wiped his face with a clean cloth then his torn and grazed hand so he could feed himself. Grace passed me a cloth and nodded with a sweet smile.

"She's almost deaf so doesn't speak much, just look at her when you talk, and she'll understand."

"Thank you."

She smiled and nodded in return before going to rummage in a cupboard.

"What the hell happened to you?" Anna asked.

Gabriel spoke, "I was part of a trade delegation and the Myanmar Army kidnapped me. They found out I used to be a US Army Ranger and thought they could get intel from me. They've been holding me prisoner for three months. Nick was part of the rescue mission. We were separated from his team and had to make our own way out of the jungle."

Okay, we were going with that – suited me. Talking about blowing up shipments of drugs and the pair of us working on black ops didn't sound like a good idea.

"Oh my God, you poor thing," Anna murmured. She repeated the story to Grace in sign language. Grace's eyes widened and she patted my shoulder.

Gabriel spilled more soup than he managed to get into his mouth, so Anna gave him some bread and broke it up so he could soak it in the soup.

"We need to get you both cleaned up. We have a bathroom with a shower, you can use that, then I can clean your wounds."

"I got shot," I said.

"I have antibiotics and I can deal with most wounds of the body," she said, frowning at Gabriel's bent head while he continued to fight the soup. "I can't do complex blood tests on board, but I can check for most things and we're a long way from a city hospital I'd trust. Our phones are down right now because of the storm."

"Where are we?" I asked.

"We're south of Mongpan."

"So, we're still in Myanmar?" asked Gabriel, his voice weak.

"Yes, we have permission, more or less, from what I can gather but things are so changeable at the moment the captain wants to head back to safer parts of the river. Are you two going to be a problem? We couldn't help but notice the guns…"

"If we are found by Myanmar soldiers, we are going to be a problem," I said deciding honesty might help us in the long run. "Gabriel was an important political prisoner, so we cannot afford to be caught."

Anna nodded. "Alright, I'll explain to the others. Some of them weren't too happy because of your weapons, we're not supposed to be armed."

Gabriel glanced up at her. "You came into Myanmar on this floating goldmine without an armed escort?"

Anna nodded and I could see the tension in her face. "Personally, I didn't think it wise either. We were supposed to remain south of the border with Thailand, but the research led us north, so we're here."

Gabriel reached out a shaking hand. "Get them south, quickly. This area is dangerous for all of you, not just us. This is bandit country. Get south – fast."

Anna relayed the conversation to Grace who vanished from the galley. "Alright, forewarned and all that, I'm just glad we were here to pick the two of you out of the water."

"So am I," I said.

Gabriel put his spoon down. He'd managed a third of the soup and a slice of bread. "Can I get clean?" He turned those big dark eyes onto Anna, and I watched her cheeks colour. He had the same effect on me so I couldn't complain.

"Of course." She left his side by sliding around the curved bench seat. "We have the most amazing shower facilities. You can take as long as you need. Though I wouldn't lock the door because you don't seem well enough to be left alone."

"Nick will come with me," Gabriel said.

I opened my mouth to make a comment about it not being appropriate when Anna nodded and smiled. She bustled away to find us towels and fresh clothes.

"You sure you want to make it look like we're a couple?" I asked him the moment we were alone.

"Why wouldn't I, Nick? Isn't that what we are? Or are you intending to leave me the moment this is over?"

I opened my mouth and snapped it shut. "I hadn't thought that far ahead." Not quite a lie. I hadn't imagined what it might be like to introduce him to the family while he'd been asleep in my arms... honest.

He tugged his hand out of my grip. "If it's not what you want –"

"Whoa there, fella. I never said it wasn't what I wanted." I grabbed his hand again. "I'm just not used to men being this – um – kind to me." A sad truth. The few times I'd been officially attached to someone hadn't gone well. They liked the uniform, the muscles but I'd been arm candy or a novelty and nowhere near pretty enough in the end.

"Don't fuck this up by presuming I'm like every other bastard out there," Gabriel said, almost snapping at me. "I need a shower, Nick, and I need it now. Please help me."

I took his beautiful face in my hands. "It would be my pleasure and my honour."

It took a while for Gabriel to co-ordinate his limbs and slide out from the table. I wrapped my arm around his shoulder, and we shuffled down the narrow passage to where Anna waited with a smile. "Here we go, use as much water as you need and when you're finished, we can take you to the lab to draw blood and get you both on a drip."

"Can't I just sleep?" Gabriel asked.

"Not until I get an IV into you and some antibiotics," Anna told him with a firm glare. I bet she had sons somewhere in the world; she used the same tone as my mother.

We walked into the bathroom and Gabriel whimpered. The shower was already running, and steam gushed through the wet room. We had stainless steel in place of plastic and porcelain. Everything shone with cleanliness. Gabriel left my arms and shuffled forwards, but I grabbed him to halt his progress.

"We don't want dirty clothes in there with us. Come on. Naked time."

I took hold of his filthy, torn, stolen off a corpse, t-shirt and shirt before lifting it over his head. He groaned with the effort of raising his arms. He looked at me as my fingers brushed the button of his trousers. We'd never touched like this before and the moment confused me. The soldier just saw a job to be done. The gay man saw his potential lover. I froze, the two world colliding in an exhausted tangled mess.

Gabriel, his soft lips forming a gentle smile, took hold of my equally foul shirt and started to undo the buttons. It took too long because he couldn't organise his fingers. I chuckled and started to help. Once the shirt was off, we stood. He brushed his fingers, ghost-light, over my skin and I shivered.

"Take my trousers off," Gabriel ordered in a soft voice I couldn't deny.

I knelt before him and gazed up at his torn and battered body while he stroked my face and ran his fingers through my short hair. I popped the button of his stolen fatigues and they dropped off his narrow hips. For the first time I saw the extensive damage done to him over the months. Scars littered his body. Some the size of cigarettes, small and round, others much larger and flatter. The devil's confetti.

"Oh, Gabriel." I mourned for what must have been flawless skin just a few short months ago. The nest of thick black hair around his genitals had been scorched and healing wounds were embedded among the tangle of darkness.

Gabriel trembled under my examination and I looked up. The vulnerability in his dark eyes made it hard to comprehend how he could stand here before me. "Can you really deal with all this?" he asked in the same soft voice. "It's not just the scarring on the outside, Nick."

I studied him and while I knelt, the close proximity of my mouth encouraged an already well-endowed man the opportunity to intimidate me. "I know it's not just the scarring on the outside, Gabriel." A wall of sadness rushed up to meet the joy of having Gabriel in my arms and naked. This might be the only time I held him, when we returned to civilisation he would go back to his life in the US and I'd have to make a decision about my future.

I wanted to scream at the injustice. In the foul and fetid darkness of a Myanmar prison I had found my angel.

Such thoughts shouldn't haunt this moment. I needed to banish the sadness. My strong legs pushed me up, and I unclipped my belt and my fatigues dropped off my slimmer hips. I'd lost a lot of weight over the last few days. Gabriel cast his eyes down over my torso and further. I couldn't hide my excitement at having him so close.

His fingers tickled over scarring I'd sustained in the Middle East while in the Marines, and much older more faded scars, but my time with the SAS had yet to produce much physical damage beyond the wounds I'd sustained saving Gabriel. He brushed his fingers down my chest and I shivered, a low growl grumbling through the room.

If I didn't do something soon, we'd never get clean. I took Gabriel's hand and drew him into the water streaming out of a huge rose above a drain. He made a strange sound like the water hurt and I realised he hadn't experienced this kind of heat in a long time. I turned down the temperature a little and he started to relax. Filth sluiced off our bodies. I grabbed a large bar of soap, but Gabriel chose that moment to sink into my body and place his forehead against my chest. I tried not to focus on the terrible marks spread over his back and started to wash him with a soapy flannel.

In silence I worked, the depth of our intimacy growing but I did not allow it to become sexual. Gabriel needed care. I needed care. I coaxed Gabriel into turning and I worked the cloth and soap over his backside and down his long slim legs. Each corded muscle glinted in the soft light.

"You should clean your – um…"

He took the soap out of my hand and set to; I grabbed another flannel and started on my limbs. The bandage around my arm came away for the first time in days and I pulled a face as the goo Gabriel made vanished under the stream of water. "Damn me, it worked," I muttered, pulling at the wound. It looked clean and had a thick crust of goo and blood. I guessed I didn't have a brewing infection.

"Clean it gently," Gabriel managed to say. I focused on him because he didn't sound right. The cloth and soap were being used in a scouring manner on sensitive parts of his body.

"Hey, slow down. You're not made of cast iron and that's not wire wool." I pointed to the cloth in his hand that he was using to take off several layers of skin.

"I'm dirty." The words were pure distress. Layers of pain, shame, confusion, hurt… Too many emotions wrapped up in a two-word sentence.

I didn't know if touching him was the best course of action, especially because I stood before him with nothing on but water, but those hands needed controlling. When we were children and I'd fall out with my sister and one or the other would be hysterical over something, mum would use distraction rather than pity.

"Can you touch your elbow with your tongue?" I asked, feeling like a complete idiot.

"What?" he glanced up and the hands slowed their assault.

"Can you?" I asked, and to complete my idiot award I tried to do just that. To be fair, when I was small, just about anything my mum did that was silly made me laugh.

"Nick?" the look of utter bewilderment on Gabriel's face made it a moment of amusement and sadness.

"It might work better for your mind than rubbing yourself raw," I added in a gentle voice.

He drew in a mighty breath full of steam and huffed it out, dropping the cloth and the soap. I took that as a small victory for this meltdown and grabbed the moveable showerhead. "Can I get rid of the soap?" I asked him.

He shut his eyes, tilted his head back and refused to look at me, but held still while I rinsed him off without touching him with my hands. I knew falling in love with a man so damaged presented me with an ocean to swim but I couldn't help it, his broken heart called to me – a siren song even with all the inherent dangers.

I switched off the water and handed him a towel. After I dried myself, I opened the door a crack and found two sets of simple clothing outside on the floor. When I turned back, Gabriel remained standing with his towel in the rapidly cooling room. The engines rumbled and vibrated under my feet and the storm raged outside the hull.

Removing his towel from unresisting fingers I dried him, again trying not to make it sexual which proved to be easy under the circumstances and pulled a black t-shirt over his head. "Jogging bottoms," I said handing them over. Gabriel took them and put them on, but he felt like a shadow, a ghost of the man I'd fought the jungle and river to save.

"We need to go and see Anna, the medic lady. You need an IV."

"No." He gave me no eye contact.

"Gabriel –"

"I said, no. I don't want to be messed about with."

A hardness in his voice reminded me that Gabriel was in fact a Sergeant First Class, not a grunt like me. "Okay. I'll let her know. You want to wait here?"

"I'll be in the galley." He left the bathroom and I released my breath. Riding a roller-coaster with a blindfold on would be more predictable than Gabriel's emotions.

13

IT DIDN'T TAKE LONG TO find Anna. A deck below the living quarters had been turned into a series of research labs, one of which doubled as the medical bay. "Ah, where's my patient?" she asked the moment I darkened her doorway.

"He won't come down," I said. "I don't think he's in the right frame of mind to be fiddled with."

Anna put down the IV bag she held in her hand. "Oh. How badly tortured was he?" her question caught me off guard, but she hadn't meant it to be nosey.

"Bad."

She nodded. "I've some experience dealing with soldiers in some terrible states of mind. We'll get the two of you squared away in a cabin and I can rig something up in there. You've had training on how to insert an IV?"

"Basic but yes. He'll have done more than me." I qualified the statement so she's understand, "The Rangers receive a lot more training in emergency battlefield techniques than most grunts, me included."

"Alright, Nick. We'll do that."

"I'm sorry."

Her dark eyes were sharp when she looked at me. "Don't be sorry, son. You're protecting your shield brother, I understand that."

I smiled, surprised by her turn of phrase. "That's a very Viking thing to say."

"I read far too many history books," she said with a wink. "Come on, let's find Mister Grumpy and put you to bed. I've managed to convince someone to surrender their bunk, so you have a double while you're with us. That okay? You seem close enough."

"It was okay half an hour ago, not quite sure about how he feels now, but we'll give it a go. Thank you."

She patted my arm without further comment and filled my hands with medical supplies.

"GABE?" I CALLED OUT IN warning as we approached the galley. "Anna's found us a room if you're okay going twos-up. She can rig the IV as well so you can get some fluids in you and if you want, you can put the cannula in your hand." I kept my voice bright, breezy and full of assumptions, I was also rambling from nervousness.

"I'm sorry," he whispered. His hands were in fists under the table and he still didn't look up. In fact, he looked ready to rip his skin off. So much distress swirled around those broad shoulders I should have been able to see the sparks.

Daring a fight, I reached out for his shoulder. "It's okay, mucker. Better the poison is drawn now rather than later. That's all it is, poison. You'll draw a bit at a time until there's nothing left."

He lifted his eyes to mine and I almost backed away at the awful horror scrawled across his face. "What if there is nothing but poison inside me, Nick?"

I crouched beside him. "But we know there is so much more, Gabe. They didn't break you. They might have made you talk but that's a different kind of break. You are alive. We've survived thanks to your skills. You want to know the best bit?" I asked him.

He sniffed and nodded.

"Whatever happens next we will face it together. You aren't alone anymore, Ranger."

The tension fled and he almost collapsed into me, pressing his head into my neck and shoulder. I stroked his soft black curls.

"Did you think I was going to leave you?" I whispered.

He nodded against my neck sending shivers down my spine.

"Never." I ached to say, *my love*, at the end but I dared not confess what I knew to be true. My tongue stuck to the roof of my mouth.

Together we followed Anna who kept quiet and small while she showed us the room we'd be using. "It's mine, I'm bunking in with Grace, so you can use whatever you find. The clothes are from a couple of the lads, we'll find something more appropriate when we reach civilisation."

I thanked her and she explained the IV to me. It had been doctored with antibiotics and a high dose of multi-vitamins and minerals. She then handed me a second one and said I'd need to replace the bag if I woke up and it was empty. I nodded a lot and she left without looking at or speaking to Gabriel. He had crawled onto the small double bunk and dragged his knees to his chest as if he couldn't believe he sat on a real bed.

The door closed and I studied the huddled figure. He looked forlorn staring into the middle distance as if it held answers to question he didn't yet understand and those answers or maybe their questions, might cut him off even further from humanity and the normal world we'd soon be entering.

"Hey, you alright to help me fit this?" I asked him, holding up the IV bag and cannula.

Those big brown eyes turned to me and he held out his hand. I sat beside him, careful not to crowd him despite the size of the room and took an antiseptic swab to the back of his left hand. With a level of precision any nurse would envy I wiped his skin.

"I've only done this a few times in the past. Maybe you should it?" I asked him. The Ranger medical skills covered far more than my basic training.

"I trust you," he said.

Removing the cover from the cannula betrayed my nerves. I almost dropped the damned thing in an effort to hide my trembling hands. Gabriel's diet and dehydration meant seeing the veins in his hands wasn't difficult but stabbing one proved hard. I made several botched attempts before sliding the needle into his skin, but he didn't so much as wince. I taped it in place and attached the tubing before fixing the bag to the hook on the back of the door, which I could touch while lying on the edge of the bed.

"Lie down, Gabe." I pushed him a little to make him move and he complied without a word. Too tired myself to comprehend his state of mind I lay on my back beside him without touching him.

He rolled over, giving me his back and whispered, "Hold me."

My heart ached with the soft request and I struggled onto my right side, slid an arm around his chest and fitted my body around his. The wind, rain and river battered at the hull. We could hear the distant shouts of the crew dealing with the storm, and the room smelt of soap and female. I reached for the light switch over our heads.

"Wait. I don't want to wake up in the dark."

I dropped my arm back down to hold him. "You're safe, Gabriel. Try to relax, try to sleep."

He nestled back and by increments the taut lines of exhausted muscles started to find peace. When his breathing slowed and deepened, I allowed a small smile of victory to be my last act before chasing him into surrender.

I woke several times because of his dreams but he stayed under and I realised Anna had put a sedative in his IV bag. He also woke at one point but remained out of it while I helped him to the small bathroom so he could take a piss. I changed his bag and when I returned to the bed he'd already slipped back into sleep. This time he opted to lie almost on top of me and I cradled him.

My stomach began to protest that I'd probably slept long enough, and I found Gabriel curled around my back and still gone to the land of the fairies. It took some doing but I managed to untangle myself and scoot out of bed.

"Blimey," I muttered when I checked my watch. We'd been asleep over thirteen hours. I peed again and opened the door to the room in silence before padding up the gangway to the galley.

A few low lights were on and Anna sat drinking something at the table while reading a book. She smiled as I approached. "Hello."

"Hi, where is everyone?" I asked. "I thought there would be a watch."

"There is, I'm it. I'm not much use as crew so once the storm had passed and we'd tied up for the night I offered to take watch. Would you like hot chocolate and a drop of something stronger?"

She chuckled at my astonished expression and made me sit while food appeared and the heavenly offer of chocolate with a drop of brandy.

"You drugged Gabriel," I said, hoping it didn't sound like an accusation.

"I did," she said, making me a sandwich with chicken breast. Actual chicken not snake. "His stress levels made it clear that despite his exhaustion he'd keep fighting to remain awake. He needs time for the subconscious to catch-up with the present. Once that happens, he'll begin to relax."

"Thank you," I said. "For helping him."

"Can I ask you a question, Nick?"

"You can ask."

A small smile flickered around her mouth. "What actually happened to the two of you? I know a cover story when I hear one and that was about as thin a sheet of rice paper."

I opened a packet of crisps she'd taken from stores and we both picked at them while I tried to think through my options. In the end I went with the 'fuck it' approach and chose the truth. "I can't tell you most of it, live operations and all that, but I was part of a small team sent to a suspected drug camp. We were supposed to destroy the shipment bound for Europe. I found Gabriel in a locked cell hanging by his wrists in the tunnels. I still don't really know what he was doing there or how he was caught, but he had to take the life of a fellow prisoner to save her from a fate even worse than death. Neither of us can afford to be found on this ship, Anna."

"We are heading back to Thailand. We have the evidence we need of the hunting and rainforest destruction and our supplies are running low. We have no wish to be stuck on the border by the Myanmar Government and their soldiers. It's not likely they'll stop us, but you can never be certain. The others aren't terribly happy at having two fugitives aboard."

"We aren't criminals. We're soldiers."

"Same thing in some people's minds."

"Then they are stupid people," I muttered.

She opted to change the subject and we chatted for a while. Somehow it felt strange. The last few days had been so intense, Gabriel and I battling the environment together, that sitting and eating sandwiches while drinking hot chocolate with a lovely American nurse struck me as odd. More surreal than building a boat from nothing but our wits and what we could find in the jungle.

It didn't take long for me to need to sleep again so I excused myself and returned to Gabriel. The second IV bag was now empty, so I removed the line, taped up the cannula more securely and snuggled back into the bed.

Gabriel's moaning and thrashing woke me. I managed to struggle out from under him before an elbow cracked either a rib or my nose. "Hey, wake up, Gabe," I called while trying not to touch him. The heat in the cabin pressed down on us and we were both sweaty.

When his eyes popped open, he looked around in a confused state until he located me, pressed against the doorway. "Nick."

I relaxed. "Morning." I switched off the light and the interior dimmed, the porthole now giving a little daylight and a lot of jungle on the banks of the river.

"What happened?" Gabriel rubbed his face with his hands.

"Nothing," I said.

He glanced at me. "I feel terrible."

"Anna slipped a sedative in your IV. You've been out cold for almost twenty-four hours."

I thought he'd be angry, but he seemed unconcerned by the revelation. "You alright?" he asked.

"Yeah, I think so. Little unnerved still but I'm okay."

"We need to talk to the captain."

"You need to eat something."

He slid off the bed and went to the small bathroom. "Nick?" he asked through the closed door. "I don't want them to call the US Embassy in Bangkok."

"Gabriel, you've been missing for months. I think they'll want to hear from you. Why don't you want to talk them? Surely you need to go home?" And leave me.

I heard the tap running and he came out shaking his hands dry.

A hardness in his face took me by surprise. "I can't go home."

"I think I need a bit more information, Gabe."

He stared off over my shoulder. "Sit down for a minute. I have to tell you a bit more about why I'm here, who I work for, because I need to trust someone, and I need help."

I sat on the bed and Gabriel leaned against the wall arms folded over his chest. "If I return to US soil the people I work for will find me and throw me into a hole darker than the one where you found me."

This was news. "You didn't think to mention this before?"

He studied the soft carpet under his naked feet. "I wanted to, but I've been keeping secrets so long I didn't know how. Things are complicated at the best of times and this has hardly been the best of times."

"Get to the point."

His gaze shifted to mine in surprise at the sharpness in my voice. I'd been left out in the cold in the Regiment for so long the thought he'd been lying to me burned more deeply than it should. Ultimately, Gabriel didn't really owe me anything. Other than a few passionate kisses and some nights of comfort I couldn't call what we had a romantic relationship where he owed me the truth. It didn't stop me wishing he hadn't lied though.

He chewed his bottom lip for a moment before relenting the tough guy persona and joining me on the bed.

"You got any food?" he asked.

"If this is going to be a long chat, then let me go get us coffee and something eat."

He nodded and I did just that, returning from the empty galley – I had no idea where the others were – with coffee and pastries. Pastries! Gabriel moaned in a way that went straight to my dick and colour flooded my cheeks, making him laugh. He licked his lips and I refused to watch any more Gabriel and food-based porn.

"Bastard," I muttered. "Talk now I've fed you."

He put down the food and sighed. "I started working for the CIA after sustaining a serious back injury in the Rangers. During a parachute drop over Yemen the chute didn't fully deploy, and I hit the landing zone too hard. I could no longer take the weights necessary to continue active service in the field. The CIA came calling because of my language skills and ethnic background. I'm so fluent in Spanish I'm not considered American by outsiders."

"Makes it easier to be accepted."

He nodded. "I thought I'd be working in a South American office, in the field maybe, but mainly behind a desk. What I didn't know at the time was the group recruiting me are called Jupiter Section."

"Jupiter? As in the Roman God?"

Again, he nodded and picked at the food. "Jupiter, the planet, is also the shepherd of our galaxy. Did you know that?"

"Sure, its gravity pulls in stray space debris protecting the inner rocky planets."

"That's the principle they work on. They eradicate problems heading towards the US before they reach the US."

"Eradicate?"

He tugged at the pastry, dirt still ground into the skin of his fingers. "I killed a lot of people, Nick. I thought they all deserved it until they sent me after a political activist in Guatemala who wanted the regime changed so they could start protecting the environment. It meant the US companies would be thrown out."

"Did you kill him?" After what he'd told me he'd done to the Chinese hostage he'd been taken with, I had no doubt as to his skills in that department. It also made more sense; I suddenly understood why he could do it and see it as the better option for her.

"No. I made it look like he'd accidentally been blown up in a gas leak in his home, when actually, I managed to get him out of the country. My handler was suspicious, but I smoothed it over. Or thought I had. That's when I started to figure out I wasn't working for the White House." He pushed the food away and sipped his coffee.

"Who were you working for? Who runs Jupiter Section?"

"A faction within the CIA. They are black ops, Nick. Covert. They have massive resources, but it doesn't just come from the federal government. Jupiter Section is controlled by a group of men and a few women, one of whom is my direct boss, she's called Maddox. They work for the interests of right-wing religious groups and their business interests. I have the evidence stashed away, but if they catch me, I'll go somewhere that makes Guantanamo look like Disney Land." He studied his hands and I wondered if he was taking a trip down memory lane – Guantanamo, not Disney Land.

"They know you have this evidence?"

"I think they suspect. I think I was supposed to die in Myanmar. I think the Myanmar Government, those that knew where I was, kept me alive to use me against the Jupiter Section but it backfired because Jupiter want me dead."

"And the US Embassy know you're alive?"

He nodded. "And they'll come after me the minute my name appears on a computer screen."

I leaned back against the bulkhead of the ship. "Shit."

"I should have told you."

I shrugged. "What reason did you have for telling me? None. You didn't know we'd make it out of the jungle alive. Did you tell your captors about Jupiter Section?" I stole his pastry.

"I broke, Nick. I told them everything in the end. But Jupiter keep their operatives separated so I didn't know any operational intel the Myanmar interrogators could use. That's when I was sold to the drug cartels."

Jesus... Just the thought of all this was enough to give me a headache.

The ramifications of his past were too much for me to unpack in a moment. I needed to consider our options in the present and the near future; the rest would come with time. He needed my continued protection now.

"What do you want me to do to help?" I asked.

He cocked his head, the tangle of black curls touching his shoulder. "That's it? You're not angry with me?"

"What's the point? Gabriel, up until a week ago we had no idea the other existed. The only thing we have between us right now is some of the most intense survival time I've ever endured. You had no reason to tell me and you certainly don't owe me anything. I'm not wasting energy being angry about something that's not your fault. What I want to do is help solve this problem."

"Why?" he asked.

"What?"

"Why do you want to help?"

Oh, I don't know, because you're the most beautiful and fucked up man I've ever met?

I said, "Because although we've only known each other a few days I care a great deal about you, and I don't believe you're one of the bad guys in this world."

"I killed a woman to stop her being raped to death," he said. "I'm hardly going to win the Nobel Peace Prize."

"We're in Myanmar, Gabe, I think it's safe to say that analogy has had its day." I tried to think of a way to convince him of my intentions without sharing too much of my emotional turmoil. "This group are killing people who oppose business and religious interests of a privileged percentage of the American machine, right?"

"Yes."

"And you have evidence that can be used against them?"

"Yes."

"Then it's my duty as a soldier of an allied country that depends on the integrity of the US Government, to take this to people I can trust to help keep you alive so you have a chance to stop the enemy within your State."

He looked away from me and plucked at the bedsheets before a small nod made the light catch on his dark hair. "If that's the reason then that's enough, I guess."

I pushed myself away from the bed because I wanted to touch him too much and I didn't know where we stood – intimately speaking – now our parameters had changed. Since he'd woken there hadn't been any intimate interaction and I didn't know if there would be again – I had to leave it in Gabriel's hands for a list of reasons too long to contemplate.

"Are you okay here? I'll get some more definite intel from the captain about who has been contacted and we'll come up with a plan."

"Sure," he said, looking more defeated and unhappy than he had any right to considering the circumstances.

Feeling lost and confused myself, I left the room.

14

I FOUND OUR FORMIDABLE LOOKING captain at the controls of his ship. He turned to watch as I climbed the steps.

"Good afternoon," he said in an accent more French than English.

"Captain, good afternoon and thank you for everything."

The weathered and bearded face broke out into a smile. Several teeth seemed to be missing and the crinkles made it a little alarming. His face seemed to be part accordion. "It is what we do, is it not? Save the stranded?"

"I guess so, but you endangered yourselves to save us and have given us a good berth." I shook his hand, large, strong and callouses so thick you could mistake it for elephant hide. "Anna said you have contacted the embassies?"

"Oui, we thought it would be a good idea for them to know we were on our way. If they can meet us on the river, it would save complications with paperwork, would it not?"

"Yes."

He waved his hand. "Then all is good. You can continue to enjoy our hospitality until we reach Phop Phra. It will take another day maybe two, the river is difficult this time of year. Get rest, see Anna and eat."

"I wondered if I might be able to speak to the UK Embassy? I'm a soldier, they need to inform my people."

"Sat phone isn't working well. We only have emergency calls most of the time out here. It's why we are heading back to Phop Phra. We cannot be out here without good communication. These jungles are dangerous."

He didn't have to explain that to me. Unfortunately, it meant I couldn't communicate with the Head Shed back in England, which meant I had no way of gaining their help in protecting Gabriel. Not that I thought they would, helping stray American servicemen in the jungle they might forgive me for, but starting an international incident because the CIA or Jupiter Section wanted him dead, would be a step over the line they wouldn't countenance.

"Can I send email?" I asked.

"Oui, speak to Anna. Sometimes it works."

Not a statement to fill me with confidence. If I could use email, I could use internet calls. Perhaps we'd have a way to stop Gabriel disappearing down a satanic rabbit hole. I returned to the kitchen and found Anna with Grace; they were deep in conversation using sign language but looked up when I approached.

"You're up, Nick."

"I am. Listen, Anna, the captain said the sat phone is out of service again, but you have internet?"

She shook her head and grimmaced. "Our beloved captain is very good at some things and not so good at others. We can't move any heavy data packets off the ship and email is a bust right now. There's something wrong with the satellite receiver. Short of catching a parrot and training it to speak there's not much you can do. I guess you need to touch base with your commanding officer?"

"Something like that," I muttered. "Oh, and we ate some pastries, is that okay?"

She nodded. "You need more for Gabriel. How is he?"

"Awake and okay," I said.

"Drop by the medical bay and I'll re-dress your wounds, check him over and give him another dose of vitamins." She rose from the bench around the table and began pulling food out to give me. Fruit mostly and more, easy to digest starch with a couple of bottles of water.

I retreated like a teenager to my room and found Gabriel had managed to shower again. His wet hair was combed back and his face free of beard for the first time. He smiled when I came in with more food. Feeling a little stunned at the new look I stood watching as he rescued various items from my arms.

"God, you're beautiful," I muttered. The scar over his cheek to his nose was now clearer to see but added to his rakish charm rather than ruined his handsome face.

He looked up and grinned. "I do polish up better than a turd."

My sharp intake of breath as his fingers brushed the front of my t-shirt turned the grin into a shy smile. "What did you find out from the captain?" he asked, distracting me from the growing intensity filling the room.

"Internet and phone are patchy at best. We won't be contacting anyone easily. They might be meeting us at somewhere called Phop Phra."

"Shit."

"What are the chances of Jupiter Section reaching you before the British reach me?"

He crawled back into the bunk, hands full of food. "Have you ever tasted anything like this apple?" he asked, holding it for me.

"Gabe –" We needed a grown-up conversation.

"I'm serious, Nick. It's amazing. Sharp and sweet and juicy…" He took another bite and groaned, long and low.

Giving up I sat beside him and he offered me the apple. "You're a wicked man," I murmured.

"Maybe? Maybe I just want to find out a little more about you, Nick. Not soldier, survival Nick, but happy gay man Nick."

I couldn't hold his gaze with those words strung between us. "Not sure happy gay Nick exists anymore."

"Then I shall do more than Adam ever did by biting the apple, I shall raise your Gay Pride from the grave."

I couldn't help the smile and he responded with a wicked glint I'd never seen on his face before. He held out the apple to my mouth and I took the hint. I bit down on the hard almost white flesh and yes, it did taste good but I hadn't been in a prison for months so what made it special was Gabriel's fascination. He watched me lick the juice off my lips.

"Why don't you think you're good enough for me?" he asked. Both his voice and eyes were soft, but the words hit me with the power of a poison dart.

The suddenness of the question almost made me choke. "What?"

"I can see it in your eyes. You really don't believe I find you attractive."

"Gabe, can we not discuss my shortcomings right now?"

He chewed on more of the apple, thoughtful for a moment. When he finished the tasty morsel, core included, he relaxed against the bedhead. "Come and sit beside me."

I did as instructed. He shifted with his usual fluid grace and slung a leg over my lap before sitting again, on my thighs. My hands went to his hips without conscious thought, but I held him gently, wanting to reinforce he could move away at any time. The position made him much taller than me and he brushed back my hair.

"You have such a strong face, Nick. But your real beauty comes from your heart. I don't know how you came to be what you are now, a soldier trained to kill –"

"I trained to save those weaker than me. It seemed wise to be able to kill those stronger than the weak as the most effective form of protection."

"See," he said tapping my chest, "a big heart. It makes your strength that much more noble." I looked away from him, unable to stand the scrutiny but he took hold of my face and made me meet his eyes. "Teach me how to give us pleasure, Nick."

My breathing ramped up alongside my heart rate and things south went even harder than before. The loose-fitting jogging trousers didn't hide very much. Gabriel leaned down for a kiss and I obliged. I kept my hands on his hips and his gentle kisses turned into something more serious, darker and full of need. His tongue brushed mine and I moaned. I could do this and not fall further in love – couldn't I?

He pulled away for a moment. "Don't be afraid to touch me, Nick. I'll let you know in plenty of time if we need to slow down or stop."

Or maybe not. "Make sure you do." The words were almost low enough to be a growl of sound and he rocked forward, nudging against the head of my straining cock. "Fuck, I can't remember the last time I came."

Gabriel set to work on my mouth, jaw and neck. I let him have full rein because in return I could explore his back, waist, chest and when my fingers brushed against the waistband of his trousers he moaned in approval. I dipped my fingers down and began exploring the taut muscle of his backside and thighs.

Every atom of his being seemed to vibrate under my questing fingers and his rocking hips moved harder and faster against me. For my part I began trying to push back but with his full weight on my thighs I had some limits. I wanted to turn us over so I could be on top but I had the feeling that would be a hard no right now so instead I took a handful of his hair and tugged it gently to move his mouth from my neck.

The position gave me access to that sweet spot I'd found in the jungle. I licked the tender flesh and he whispered something in Spanish. I kissed the spot and realised he didn't speak English when aroused, his soft murmurs whispered into my heart even though I could not understand the words. I held his hip and his hair then bit down hard on his neck. Somehow, he shifted enough to give his cock friction against my belly, and we fed off each other. Me doing my best impression of a vampire and him trying to be a lap dancer. The heat between us grew.

"Fuck, Nick, I need more. Please."

We didn't have lubrication and I already knew Gabriel was circumcised. I pulled his t-shirt over his head and he shifted off me enough to yank his trousers down before removing mine. When I sprang free, he looked a little alarmed.

I had no such fears. Taking his thick full length might hurt at first and it would certainly be a challenge learning to swallow that much, but damn it would make me feel good.

"Gabe, look at me."

"I am."

"Not that bit, baby."

He glanced up at my face. I stroked the sweaty hair from his face. "I'm not a natural top, Gabe." The look of mystification made me chuckle. "I like to be fucked. Men usually want me on top because of my size but… To be honest, I just want to be held and loved and when it comes to penetration it's not the be all and end all for me and if it comes to that, I would far rather have you doing all the work."

Those big dark eyes were soft and a little too wet. He kissed my mouth, unable to find words but allowing his body to tell me what he understood and how much he appreciated my candour.

Perhaps if we all talked about sex before we did it, maybe we'd all enjoy it a bit more.

Gabriel opted to lie down on his side, and I lay beside him, our noses almost touching, our chests brushing with every breath and the rest of our bodies lining up in perfect harmony.

I licked my palm a few times. "Best option we have right now."

He nodded. "Just make me feel good about myself, Nick."

We kissed and I pulled his leg over my hips, so he remained in the dominant position. I slid my hand between us and soon realised I wouldn't need much extra help to lubricate the pair of us lustful boys.

The moment my hand brushed his cock his body stilled for the first time and a shudder passed through him. I held still. He took a few deep breaths and screwed his eyes shut trying to fight memories.

"Look at me," I whispered the demand.

He opened his eyes and locked onto me. I tumbled head first into his black gaze and almost drowned until he touched that magic spot on my chest again, just over my heart, grounding me to the present – to him. Those delicate fingers traced the wing of my crow tattoo and he gave me a small nod. I bent my brow to his, breaking the contact.

"Don't be afraid, Nick, I'm not going to break your heart," he whispered against my lips.

I wished I could find the strength to argue against him, to maybe say: I didn't have to equate sex with love, I didn't need his protection, I wasn't falling in love with him. They would have all been lies and, in that moment, we had no room for lies between us.

He kissed me, trailed his fingers down my arm until he could coax us both into holding our cocks. When I had us in a firm, rough grip, he returned his hand to my cheek and stroked while we kissed and rocked through my fist.

It wasn't the physical act drawing my balls tight and making them ache. It had to be the incredible connection we shared. The heady scent of us in combination. The beauty of our dance together. The murmured broken words and phrases. The skin on skin contact. His so smooth and mine so rough with a tangle of dark blond hair.

"*Oh, si, mi diablo, si,*" he whispered against my lips. We moved faster and his fingers dug into my arse trying to draw us tighter together.

"Fuck, Gabe, I can't hold on."

"Don't, want, need… *mas… amore… mas…*"

He shuddered and groaned long and low, lips pressed against mine and I soon tumbled down the hill with him. The scolding heat of our union graced our bellies and my hand. It felt so good to finally have him give me this gift I couldn't control the emotional effects. He hushed me, sobbed with me while he stroked my face and we kissed tears off each other's cheeks. Naked and wrapped in a sticky mess we fell back into sleep.

15

THE SHIP'S BRIDGE DIDN'T FEEL large enough as we came towards the wooden dock in Phop Phra. In the end it had taken another full day to reach and boys being boys, Gabriel and I had made the most of the time together. We were still at the 'getting used to having a man handle my cock' stage but I had hope that blowjobs might be on the menu soon. To be honest the level of emotional intensity between us left me reeling. I'd never experienced anything close to how Gabriel touched my body and through that medium every atom of my being.

It scared the crap out of me.

The present moment scared me as well. Even at our current distance we could see the black SUVs with tinted windows parked beside a wooden dock sticking out into the river. Big men with black suits, sunglasses and bulges under their arms stood near the vehicles keeping the locals at bay with their aggressive vibes.

They didn't have flags on them, but they screamed American. As we watched, another vehicle pulled up, a battered old Nissan Navarra. "Bet that's the British contingent," I said. Gabriel snorted.

The ship docked. I had my uniform back, or what was left of it and my trusty boots, while Gabriel looked far too vulnerable in ill-fitting jeans and shirt. The captain brought the ship into the dock with hardly a bump and the crew tied us off.

"They are here for you? Oui?" he asked, pointing at the opening doors. You could almost see the people shudder as the heat hit their air-conditioned arses. More men in suits exited and a woman.

"Unfortunately," I said. They weren't likely to try anything too terrible while we were in public, so we left the ship with Anna and Grace as security.

I'd asked them to accompany us as representatives of the organisation to rescue our pretty backsides out of the frying pan. Even if they were helping us into the fire.

It took a few minutes to give our final farewells and thanks to the men and women who had saved us but before we knew it, we walked up the dock towards Thailand.

We were both tense, but we had a plan of sorts because Gabriel held dual citizenship to a country with refugees spilling out of it at a rate of knots. The heat didn't seem so bad this far from the jungle and among a farming township. The Thai people were smiling, and everything seemed relaxed. The air smelt a little too much of human mixed with dead fish, but if that was the cost of returning to civilisation then we'd pay it.

Now we faced a woman in heels, surrounded by the men in black suits with white t-shirts on and those give away bulges under their left arms.

"Maddox?" I asked.

"Yep," Gabriel said. "They aren't going to let me get to the embassy."

"Fuck that," I muttered. "We'll swim for it if we have to."

Our fingers brushed.

The woman removed her sunglasses. She looked like Starbucks had made her out of latte and spite. I didn't know humans came in so many shades of dun colouring.

"Gabriel Cabrera. It is good to have you home."

Gabriel didn't move or speak.

I stepped forwards. "Ma'am. My name is Private Nick Wilde of the British Special Air Service and this man is in my custody as he is a person of interest in an ongoing operation sanctioned by my government. He states he is a Venezuelan citizen and therefore you have no extradition rights. He is claiming political asylum with us."

She laughed. A hard bark of sound. Movement to my right caught my attention and I flicked a glance at the Nissan. Three people were climbing out. A small woman in full fatigues and two big men with assault rifles in their arms. One of them looked vaguely familiar.

"Really? That's the best you can do, Sergeant?" she asked Gabriel, who remained mute. "A British bull dog barks and you expect me to hand you over?" She laughed again. I didn't like the sound and it seemed to me she hadn't enough practice to make it sound natural. "Get in the SUV, we'll discuss your operational fuck ups on the way home."

Gabriel opened his mouth but the approaching woman from our right shouted, "I don't think so, Charlotte."

Maddox turned, frowned, then I swear she snarled. "Elizabeth."

Brant approached and nodded at me. "Well done, Wilde, thank you for bringing him in. The paperwork is in the truck. You've done Unit Twelve proud."

I glanced at the man I thought I knew. He lifted his sunglasses and removed the baseball cap. "Jacob Hayes?"

He nodded. "Good to see you, Nick. Go get in the truck and we'll get you back to the FOB."

I glanced at Gabriel; we were confused. However, I knew of Jacob Hayes. He'd been deployed so long I hadn't seen him much over the two years I'd been in the Regiment and we'd never worked together but as the only other gay man I had hoped our paths might cross, for nothing more than solidarity of course. I also knew Stanton hated him and feared him in equal measure.

Maddox chuckled. "You really think I'm going to let you take Cabrera?"

Brant's eyes narrowed. Maddox, stood in 4-inch heels that dug holes in the dirt of Thailand. Brant, diminutive in her army issue boots, carried the pips on her shoulders with far more authority.

"I sent one of my team in with an SAS deployment to find and retrieve a Venezuelan citizen who requested our help before he dropped off the face of the earth. It took a while for us to find him, but we did."

"You expect me to believe this horse shit? You had no idea –"

Brant stepped forwards, the men behind her fanned out and became 'weapons ready', not quite pointing them at Maddox but making it clear they would given any kind of excuse. Her team reached into their jackets until she waved them to stillness.

"Jupiter's days are numbered. Remember that, Maddox. You're a leaky boat."

"And Unit Twelve are a fucking joke."

"Unit Twelve are small enough for me to have direct operational control over every member of my team. We don't resemble a sieve with dementia.

You lost Snow, you lost control of the North Koreans and now you've lost Cabrera."

Maddox's rose-tinted lips formed a smile and I expected Colonel Brant to vanish in a melting puddle of goo at her well-heeled feet. "Show me the fucking paperwork."

Brant raised her hand and the driver's door opened. A young man stepped out with a thick folder in his hands. "Ma'am," he said with terse military perfection as he handed over the file.

"You can keep these. I have the originals. They show how long Wilde has been working for me, how long we've been looking for Cabrera, when he first made contact as a citizen of his native country –"

"He was born in fucking Arizona."

"The son of an immigrant whose mother was murdered by racist thugs I believe. Would you like the file to show to your bosses?" Brant asked with a smile so sharp I was surprised it didn't draw blood.

Maddox turned on her heels and the posse fell in behind her but when she reached the open door of her SUV, she turned to look at Gabriel. "This isn't done, Cabrera. I'm coming for you. You belong to me."

Gabriel kept his mouth shut but I could feel his fear and his rage. He didn't move either and I realised he'd retreated to whatever safe place had kept him alive during his incarceration. Without Gabriel putting up a fight Maddox had no target, doubtless his intention, and she climbed into the air-conditioned dark interior of her carriage to be carried off to whatever circle of Hell spat her out.

When I focused on Colonel Brant I also took in her escort. Both men had raised their assault rifles pinning Gabriel and I to the spot. "Time to talk, gentlemen," she said.

Gabriel lifted his hands and Jacob dropped his weapon only to find a pair of plasticuffs. I was about to explain that wasn't a good idea when Gabriel said, "It's okay, Nick. It'll be okay. Right, Colonel?" He looked at Brant and I could see how he fought his panic at the feel of the cuffs on his wrists. To outsiders all they would see was a tightening around his eyes and mouth, but I saw it in every breath and the stiffening of his usually graceful limbs.

"I hope so, Sergeant. This is just a precaution. I don't trust Maddox as far as I can throw her and right now, I have a bad back so throwing her anywhere isn't really an option. Shall we leave the town now? I think we've given the locals enough of a show. Lydia, you're driving."

"Yes, ma'am," said the young man.

Brant looked at him and dropped her head to her chest. "Sorry, Corporal Lancing."

"That's okay, ma'am. I know it's confusing having a different wingman." He said it with a straight face.

The older of the two with weapons hot, chuckled, "He's got you there, boss."

"Fuck off, Mac." Brant strode away.

"I don't understand," I said.

"Lydia Greenbrook is her aide-de-camp, but she was shot and she's still not ready for field work. Our lovely Richard Lancing used to be Brant's secretary in the UK. She's having a hard time adjusting," Mac clarified.

"Right," I muttered and followed in her considerable wake despite her diminutive size.

We piled into the truck, Mac and Jacob in the back of the flatbed, Gabriel and I inside in the back seats of the large cabin and Brant up front. The air conditioning didn't work very well, and I looked longingly at the ship already leaving the dock.

"How the hell did you know about me?" Gabriel asked the moment the doors were closed. I returned my focus to our current predicament.

Brant ordered Lancing to drive north, then turned to Gabriel. Her warm brown eyes were sharp and the smattering of freckles over her small nose didn't make her look cute – more like a tabby cat turned leopard. "You two were lucky we were in-country already and at the British Embassy in Bangkok when the call came through."

"That didn't answer my question," Gabriel stated. At moments like this I saw the Ranger training take over. The jacket covering on a NATO round had more weaknesses. With his hands still in plasticuffs I didn't see him relaxing in the colonel's company.

"Why don't we take these off and perhaps we can talk somewhere with a little more civility?" I suggested.

Brant's gaze flickered over me and narrowed. "Nick Wilde. Why did your team leave you in the jungle?"

"Because I'm gay," I stated with a flat lack of emotion. "If you want any more details on that you can ask them. I stayed because Gabriel needed my help. They left me because they don't believe I'm worth helping."

"Your orders were clear. Retrieve some hard drives. Lay charges on the drug shipments. Get out without engaging if possible," she said.

I gritted my teeth. "I could not leave him hanging in that fucking cell, ma'am."

"So, you decided to go against a direct order from your superior officer?"

Gabriel snorted. "Sounds like the SAS need to re-evaluate what it means to be a superior officer."

I glanced at him but said, "Yes, ma'am."

"They'll bounce you for it."

"Hopefully, ma'am. Being RTUed is the least of my problems in the Regiment."

She tilted her head a little. "Being returned to your unit is preferable?" Although her face didn't show any emotions, I could see her mind working behind her eyes. Was I being tested?

Perhaps, and if so, I was tired of having to prove myself to the British Army. "Yes. I didn't join the Special Air Service to be treated like a fucking outcast and I'm sick of it. I can't go back after this; I don't trust them. After getting out of that jungle with Gabriel I'm done. I'm worth more."

I had to believe it, I *had* to, or my entire life had no value. There would be no point to any of the work I'd done if I didn't take a stand at some point. I'd spent a lot of the time on the ship, time I didn't spend kissing Gabriel or eating, thinking about my future and it might just look like a small farm in the backwaters of Somerset.

I felt Gabriel's fingers seek mine out. "You are worth it," he whispered.

Brant's eyes strayed to our contact. "Christ, aren't any of you straight anymore? I swear I'm the only person I work with who is in a conventional relationship."

"I'm straight, ma'am," said Lancing.

"Not exactly reassuring," she muttered. "And you," she stared at Gabriel, "I want everything you have on Jupiter Section."

"How do you know so much about me?" he asked again.

"This isn't a trade, soldier."

"Right now, I'm not anyone's soldier, Colonel. The US would sooner disavow me than admit I exist. They aren't going to want me back after this stunt. Only Maddox is going to want me back and it won't be to pin a medal on my chest."

Brant studied Gabriel for a while, then she looked at me. "Do you trust him?"

"Yes."

"Is that because you're sleeping with him or your professional opinion?"

I frowned. "Who I am sleeping with isn't any business of yours, ma'am."

Her mouth twisted to fight what might be a smile. "You're right, it's not. But my Bravo team are gay and living together. My Alpha team were gay and are now married. And I need a Charlie team to help bring down Jupiter. I like to know if I can trust the grand passions involved or if they are going to be a hindrance. Relationships between soldiers, male or female, are frowned on because it changes priorities. I need to know I can trust you two to make the right decisions when they need to be made. I need to know you have each other's backs, but the job comes first. Does that help if we're playing trust exercises?"

"Yes," Gabriel said. I nodded.

"Good. So, now tell me what I need to know so I can finally move against Maddox and prove I'm the better fucking soldier."

Gabriel chuckled. "I can safely say, ma'am, you're already the better soldier."

Brant grinned at him and finally the atmosphere in the truck relaxed. She handed me a knife. "Cut him free."

16

THE MOMENT GABRIEL'S HANDS WERE rid of the cuffs he started talking. "Jupiter Section is a black ops unit under the CIA umbrella. It's isolated from the rest of the CIA, outside the usual oversight. The operatives are kept separated from each other unless we need to work together. Under those circumstances we are given a call sign and only use the call sign."

"What was yours?" Brant asked.

Gabriel's cheeks coloured. "Angel." He glared at me as if daring me to laugh.

I managed to fight the grin but couldn't prevent the words, "Aw, sweet."

He scowled but Brant's eyes lit up. "I knew it. The chatter we've been following talks of *Angel*. They've been sloppy, which is how we found you."

"Who found me?"

Brant smiled. "I have some very good white hats working for me and they've been following the thinnest of ribbons to bring me intel on the group."

"They must be very good."

"They've found your cyber safe box, or traces of it, before you and it vanished. I feared we'd lost you completely, that they had decided you were a security risk. When you popped up on the radar, we had the perfect plan already in place to execute. I just had to make certain you ended up in my clutches not Maddox's."

"Should I be honoured by being the baby in Solomon's choice?" he asked, sounding a little faint at the prospect.

"Don't worry, I won't let anybody cut you in half," Brant said, dismissing his fears.

"You know I've been collecting evidence?"

"As I said, it's very hard to hide things in cyberspace if someone finds a ribbon to follow. Think of my people as bloodhounds."

"More like Rottweilers," Lancing muttered under his breath.

I didn't bother to hide my smirk. It felt strange though, to be among people again, my people. I had no idea how Gabriel might be coping. He'd been a prisoner and isolated in every sense of the word for months. All this organised chaos and interaction with the world must be causing him more stress. Our time on the ship was already fading as a quiet oasis of calm among the madness.

Brant ignored Lancing. "One of our operatives, Mac," she nodded to the men outside the cab who sat beside each other chatting on the flatbed, "tried a similar move with the UK branch of Jupiter Section. He left his intel on the cloud in the dark net, assuming it would be safe, it wasn't. They removed his evidence and bounced him from the Regiment. When he ran into Jacob in the DRC, Unit Twelve were brought on board. We've been trying to find more evidence since. I can see the ghosts of the operations that are sanctioned but I cannot see the full imprint. I need more insight. I need your intelligence."

"There's a UK branch of Jupiter Section?" Gabriel asked. The undercurrent of fear in his voice surprised me.

"You didn't know?" Brant's expression shifted to concern.

Gabriel shook his head. "As I said, we were mostly kept like mushrooms. So, the UK has the same problem with big business using government resources, like the CIA, to do its dirty work?"

Brant's expression softened. "Yes. But it's nothing new, the East India Company was doing it in the 19th century. This is what happens when companies, like oil or tech, get so huge they don't have to listen to government oversight. They are above the law. They cannot be brought to heel and they know it. Then they recruit the best of the best inside agencies all over the world, to further their own ends. We've dealt with any number of these issues recently. The threats aren't coming from central governments, the threats are coming from business – Russians, North Koreans, Chinese... It's always about the money in the end."

Gabriel stared out of the window for a while before he whispered, "All those lives I took..."

"It's not your fault, Sergeant, and I think you've paid a heavy enough price," the colonel said.

I appreciated her compassion, but Gabriel didn't seem to hear the words and I wondered if he'd ever be able to internalise such sentiments.

He spoke again but the quiet distance in his voice worried me. "I have the intel on a USB drive. A 3TB one. I had the feeling Maddox knew I'd been stealing information and hiding it, so before they sent me to Myanmar, I downloaded the lot."

"Where is it?" Brant asked. I could see the internal battle she fought with the need to wring the location from Gabriel and the need to treat him fairly. Her better nature won out and she remained patient. I guessed this was why she bred such loyalty in her people.

"With it being air walled Maddox might know I had the intel, but she couldn't retrieve it. Maybe that's why they kept me alive?" Gabriel muttered.

I gave up trying to be professional and reached for his hand, lacing his inert fingers between mine. "It doesn't matter, Gabe, none of that matters. You just have to move forwards."

He looked at me. "But I need to understand. I need to understand why they left me in that hole. Why all this happened to me. Was it because they knew about the intel or was it because I really didn't matter to them?"

I didn't know what to say. My team had left me, left us, to die. Stanton had done it because of my gender preferences when it came to sex. If I'd been caught and held like Gabriel what damage would that have done to my mind over the weeks and months? The time I'd spent serving under Stanton had eroded my self-confidence so much I'd begun to second guess my every decision. Not something an elite soldier could or should do, especially in the field when the lives of his team mates lay on the line. What Gabriel had been through had to be so much worse.

"The choice is simple, Gabriel. It comes down to three things: priorities, trust and what you want for the future."

"Maybe." He studied our hands.

"Listen to me. We've both been royally shafted by our people. For different reasons maybe but shafted, nonetheless. So, together we move forwards. We place our trust in these people. We fall back on our training, on our original values, those we held when we signed our lives away to our respective armies, and we move forwards. Always forwards."

He managed a weak smile and his eyes shone. "You have such a gentle soul, Nick. How the hell did you end up a soldier?"

The heat in my face made Brant chuckle. "All armies need soldiers with a heart in their ranks. Without heart there is no conscience."

Gabriel gave a small nod. "I stuck the USB stick in the post to a friend with a note attached."

Brant blinked several times, her mouth opened and closed. She took a deep breath and the colour rose in her face. "You trusted the US Postal Service with your evidence?" Horror etched her expression.

Gabriel shrugged. "I made sure he'd have to sign for it. Providing he's still alive that is."

"Who? I thought your father died?" I asked surprised. Maddox would be monitoring everything to do with Gabriel's family.

He shook his head. "No, a friend. Someone I served with when I first joined the 75th Ranger Unit. My old CO. He's in Alaska."

"Alaska?" Lancing chipped in for the first time. "Frozen north type Alaska?"

"You did say it was June now, right?" Gabriel asked me.

"Um, yes, monsoon season started early here, but yes, it's June," I said.

"Then Alaska won't be quite so frozen," Gabriel said.

Lancing muttered under his breath. Brant looked at him. "Want to share with the group, Corporal?"

"No, ma'am. I'm just not a great fan of the cold."

She grinned, a wolfish creature which scared me and didn't seem to help Corporal Lancing's peace of mind either. "Wishing you hadn't decided to get out from behind a desk?" The sweet tone didn't fool any of us.

"Erm, no, ma'am. Alaska sounds exciting, ma'am. Can't wait. I'll arrange travel the moment we stop."

"Good, Corporal. Very good. You wouldn't want to disappoint Sergeant Greenbrook's faith in you, would you?"

"No, ma'am."

Her attention returned to Gabriel. "I'll need an address or GPS location."

"GPS is better. He's out in the forests. Keeps to himself."

"My next question is important, Sergeant 1st Class. Are you able to do this?"

Gabriel's jaw clenched and they assessed each other. "I can get us to its location. He won't hand it over if I'm not there to vouch for you and you won't get through his defences without it costing lives. After that, I'm out. I'll need to vanish because of Maddox. Even with the evidence I have, it is going to be difficult if not impossible to eradicate her quickly."

Ouch, the pain in my chest expanded exponentially as his words echoed through my head. Gabriel would be leaving, he'd be disappearing. I hadn't realised how stupidly romantic I'd become, but during our quiet time on the ship, motoring down the river, I'd begun to daydream about us on my dad's farm in Somerset. Long hot summer days bringing in the silage and hay. Milking the few cows and helping with lambing. Walks in the woodlands and combes. What a fucking idiot. Why would he try to plan for a future with this hanging over him? Why would he consider a future with me at all?

I clenched my jaw to keep the implosion in my chest quiet, but it just made the hurt travel that much further. "The sooner we do this, the sooner we can all move forwards." I seemed to be stuck on that word, *forwards*. There were worse ones to choose but in that moment, it left a bitter taste in my mouth.

"I will need a plan of attack once I've seen the evidence," Brant said, focusing on her future. "I have support within the US and UK governments, factions that want to move against Jupiter Section, but we don't have enough power yet."

Choosing to zone out of her machinations wasn't difficult. I didn't have a political bone inside me and didn't intend to find one. I didn't really see the point of concentrating. I'd go where I was told, do what I had to for the survival of my team and get us out. Beyond that I could no longer predict my life. I wouldn't be returning to the SAS. If you can't trust the Brotherhood to have your back, what was the point? Perhaps, I needed to leave the Armed Forces altogether. Did I really want to continue with a military life when I felt so betrayed? Or should I go back to the farm and start again? Though it shamed me to think I'd wasted so many years and failed to make a life for myself in my chosen career.

Brant and Lancing were discussing logistics in the front of the truck when

Gabriel tugged on my hand to draw my attention from the window. "You're quiet."

I shrugged. "Just thinking."

"Anything I need to worry about? It looks serious."

I managed a smile. "Nothing to worry about, Gabe. Just concentrate on getting us to Alaska without you being caught by US immigration." I raised my voice a little. "Which is a good point, ma'am. I don't have any travel documents any longer."

"All in hand, Wilde, all in hand," she said.

Once more the window provided me with the entertainment I needed. At some point Gabriel untangled his hand from mine and stared out at his version of the world.

17

I DOZED AND LANCING PULLED over with a quiet, "We're here."

I roused and saw we were parked in a hotel car park near Mae Fah Luang – Chiang Rai International Airport.

"How long have we been on the road?" I asked.

"About eight hours," Lancing said, glancing at us. "You guys were asleep most of the time. The colonel is getting us some rooms."

I didn't feel like checking how Gabriel might react to this nugget of information. The gulf between us made my mind buzz with low level anxiety. We were back in the real world and everything would be different. He had to make the rules for me to understand and follow. Climbing out of the truck I found Mac and Jacob chatting quietly together, their body language making it more than clear the conversation should remain private. I envied them the easy union they seemed to share and wondered how long they'd been lovers. It looked like forever, but no one had talked about Jacob Hayes being in a relationship with a man while we served for the same Regiment.

I sighed and tried to take an interest in my surroundings. Not easy as it looked like every hotel airport the world over, though the trees in the green patches around the concrete and glass faceless monolith were tropical.

A shadow fell over mine on the wet tarmac of the car park. "Can we talk?" Gabriel asked.

Here we go...

"I asked Brant to get us separate rooms."

Air huffed out of me and my stomach clenched. "You don't pull your punches."

"I figured it would give us some much-needed space, Nick." He studied the ground between our feet, rather than look at me. "Brant's given me some cash so I can buy some clothes for Alaska. She said you can use it as well. There's a shopping mall in the airport."

"Sounds delightful," I said. "Not much point going shopping together. Give me some and I'll find my own way." I held out my hand and caught Mac studying us while Jacob now chatted with Corporal Lancing.

Gabriel stepped back a little. "I thought space might be a good idea, Nick, there's no reason to be angry with me."

"I'm not angry, I'm hurt, there's a difference. Give me the cash because you're right. I need some fucking space." The anger caught me by surprise and due to its nature, it flared hot and bright, more than a little out of control and catching the hurt in Gabriel's dark eyes just made it worse. He had no right to be hurt and the petrol of that unhappiness fuelled my temper.

Feeling the muscles in my jaw bounce with tension I watched Gabriel count out and hand over a pile of notes. Without really paying any attention to my direction, I stomped off, away from the dusty truck and towards the shopping mall, lights bright and full of horrific welcome.

AFTER TWO HOURS I'D SIMMERED down, had more carrier bags than I ever thought possible and a belly full of good food and a few beers. Finding clothes to fit someone my size in Thailand hadn't been easy but when I found familiar brands like Levis it began to work for me.

"Nick, there you are." Jacob strode towards me through the crowd of evening shopaholics.

"Not exactly hard to miss in Thailand," I said. I towered over most of the locals.

He grinned. A good-looking bloke, Jacob. The few times I'd seen him in Hereford I'd had my interest piqued but he never allowed anyone close and to be honest I hadn't made an effort. Stanton had already eroded my self-confidence.

"It's good to see you, I'm glad we were the ones to find you," Jacob said. "Listen, do you want to grab a drink? You looked like you needed to off-load and the colonel likes her ducklings to be all squared away when we're on a mission."

"You a therapist now?" The walls were coming up so fast I almost gave myself vertigo.

The grin turned into a half smile. "Hardly, I usually leave Mac to deal with the emotional stuff, which is saying something, but he's taken on Gabriel as his mission. So, you're stuck with me."

"To be honest, mate, I'm not interested in a gay heart to heart." The words came out with a touch more savagery than I'd intended.

"Fair enough, but you and I are going to sit and talk whether you want to or not, because Mac and I have to leave and you're going to be our colonel's back-up. That means you need to be focused and on mission."

My fists clenched around the handles of the bags. "Despite what you might have heard, I'm not a bad fucking soldier. Stanton's just a fucking prick and that's not me making excuses."

Jacob reached out and placed a hand on my shoulder. "I know that, fella. I'm here to listen and help. You need to off-load. When was the last time you could be honest with someone?"

That brought me up short. Then tension washed out of me leaving behind a miasma of sadness. "I don't remember. I can't even talk to my family about what's happening in the Regiment."

"Come on, beer time."

I followed along behind Jacob and he found an 'Irish' pub. Two pints of Guinness were ordered and while we waited for them to settle into the black and cream liquid heaven, Jacob gave me a potted history of his time with Mac, the Regiment and how they came to be working for Unit Twelve.

"What I'm saying is this, you can trust Brant. Gabriel can trust her, but we need to trust you with someone who means a lot to us."

I nodded and sipped the black gold of Ireland. "Fair enough."

"Christ, you really don't open up easily do you?" he muttered.

I snorted. "Not anymore, no."

I contemplated all the different aspects of my current life which made talking to Jacob hard work. I never used to be this closed to those who offered friendship. Most of it boiled down to the bullying, which meant Stanton lay at the heart of my emotional black hole. That pissed me off enough to force a change in behaviour.

"I've been in C Company for two years under Stanton and he's been a bastard." The moment I began to think about it a sickening wave of anger and tears threatened to unman me. I breathed out, nice and slow, and my hands shook. "I've run up the Pen Y Fan so many times I've lost count. All weathers he's ordered me up there. All times of the day and night. Every opportunity, humiliations have been piled on."

Jacob's face was serious. "Why didn't you go to the ruperts? That's what commanding officers are for, you could have gone over his head."

"Oh, yeah, as the third openly gay man the Regiment has had, I go and tell the higher-ups I'm being bullied – good move."

Jacob grunted. "Maybe you have a point. Luke and I were already serving when we came out."

"The effect of all this has been me doubting every fucking decision I've made. Every action." I shook my head. "You can't function at the top of your game if you can't make a decision and trust it. The rest of the team knew it. I became a Jonah."

"I'm sorry, Nick. That's shitty. I've read your file – you could have done well in the SAS."

It felt odd hearing that in the past tense, but he was right and we both knew it, I wasn't going back.

"Brant will have Stanton bounced and facing charges if you want?"

A tempting thought. "I'll think about it." The consequences could be more than I was willing to pay.

"You did the right thing by Gabriel though," Jacob said.

"Yeah, I did do right there."

Jacob drew circles on the bar from the condensation off the glass. "What about Gabriel Cabrera? Can he really endure three months of torture and go back out into the field?"

"Ha, no." I didn't mean it unkindly. "But he's a Ranger first and everything else comes second. He'll manage. I'll back him up and we'll get the job done. I can't imagine Alaska being too much of a problem. I think it'll do him good in the long run. He needs to get out of his own space a bit and back into the world."

"What about you and him?"

"If you're expecting a romance story then forget it. I have no fucking idea where I stand, or what he wants. He's experimenting because he thinks he might be gay. How that manifests outside the jungle I have no idea. He wants separate rooms, so I guess that's clear enough, I'm just trying hard to accept it."

A bowl of peanuts appeared in front of us and we both started picking at the salty fatness. "You care about him though?"

I growled something even I couldn't understand. Jacob tapped me on the head. "Hey, Nick. Be honest. It'll help. Trust me on this. Mac and I wasted years I wish I could have back. And from what Luke and Sam have said, they wasted even more time tearing each other to pieces. Being soldiers shouldn't make us emotional cripples unable to talk."

"I thought it came with the Soldier's Pocket Book?"

He laughed and held his fingers a few millimetres apart. "Swallow this pill on day one and you'll never have to think or discuss your feelings again."

I smiled, thinking of my battered copy of the essential book we all used as new recruits to understand the great British Army and all her quirky ways. "God, I wish." I thought about how to phrase things then gave up trying to find dancing metaphors. They wouldn't help. "I'm falling in love with him and I have no idea how to deal with someone that damaged, in that much pain, or sexually flexible."

"I like that, 'sexually flexible'. It's better than most terms."

"Life would be so much easier if I could be," I muttered.

Jacob grunted. "It really wouldn't be, Nick. Trust me on this, being bi-sexual is a bloody minefield of bad decisions, confusion and unhappiness. At least that's my experience up until Mac finally pulled his head out of his arse. Life became a lot simpler for me when I decided to opt for the gender preference I leaned towards most – male."

"I never even considered being anything other than gay."

"Then I'd count that as a win, fella. You need to talk to Gabriel though. You need to tell him and if you're emotionally entangled then either back off and get out if you think he's going to leave you at the end of this, or..." Jacob shrugged.

"Or fall all in and hope I don't get burned."

We finished our pints and returned to the hotel. Jacob handed me an electric key card and I continued to ponder my options as we reached the floor we were all staying on. I wondered if Gabriel knew which room I was staying in, then decided it probably didn't matter. Just admitting to Jacob aloud that my connections to Gabriel were far deeper than they should be after just a week, created a swirling hole of ever deepening thoughts and a sense of disquiet I didn't understand and couldn't control.

The room looked out over a small parkland but had triple glazing to keep the noise, pollution and heat out, and the air conditioning in. I had a very nice king-sized bed and an even nicer bathroom. It looked like every stock hotel room I'd ever been in and left me even more depressed because I was alone. As I showered, I continued to think about the future, and returning to Somerset to the farm didn't seem like such a bad idea, but it would also be lonely. Rural England wasn't known for its hedonistic gay nightlife and besides, I'd never been a 'fuck 'em and chuck 'em' kinda guy. I wanted a partner, a friend. I wanted to laugh, cry and make love to the same man year after year. I wanted forever.

The more I thought about returning home without Gabriel and trying to find someone else, the more my heart ached until I had to put the whole idea on a very cold block of ice and park it at the back of my brain. If I didn't, I'd slump to the floor of the shower and never stop weeping.

I turned the water off and left the shower. Acting on autopilot I dried the cuts and bruises before looking for a pair of scissors or a razor.

"Give him time," I muttered into the mirror as I tried to tidy my beard. "He's been back in the world for a matter of hours. Can you really blame him for wanting some space?"

Of course I couldn't blame him, but it didn't stop it from feeling like a massive rejection. I wrapped a towel around my waist and decided to empty the minibar. I'd just opened the tiny bottle of scotch and settled down to a book I'd bought, when a knock came on the door.

"It's open," I called out.

Gabriel walked in. He'd had a haircut. The tangled curls were now a soft black halo and he wore a soft black shirt and black jeans with good quality boots on his feet. My heart may have stopped beating.

"Hi," I managed. "You look better."

He didn't say a word, just stared at me for a long time. I couldn't interpret the gaze at all or his body language. Everything screamed neutral but a charge gathered in the room, a zapping static ready to shock the unwary.

"Gabe? What's wrong?" I asked. I began to feel unnerved.

He did seem to be breathing and to say he looked like a dark angel in that moment wouldn't be an exaggeration. The natural swarthiness of his skin had warmed over the days we'd been travelling and as the tension rose his eyes became darker. Christ, yes, the dark angel I wanted to make mine.

"I'm sorry," he said.

"Okay."

"The colonel took me to an actual spa in the hotel, then Mac took me for a drink."

"Okay." I had no idea where this was going and moving off the bed didn't seem like a good idea, but I needed to change the atmosphere. "What can I do to help, Gabe?"

"We need to talk." He didn't move.

"We are talking." I didn't move.

"I thought it would be best to give myself some time to get used to being in the world again. I thought I needed to readjust without help. I thought it would give us time to figure out if we'd made the right decisions in the jungle and on the boat."

"I figured as much," I said.

He moved. A creature of pent-up darkness striding across the utilitarian carpet, turning and striding back to the corner of the bed. "You are beautiful lying there."

I snorted. "There are many ways to describe me: big, strong, bearish, not beautiful. You are beautiful." And he was, it left me breathless.

"Why don't you like yourself?" he asked and sat on the bed, on the edge, a long way from my legs.

The question floored me. "I don't have an answer."

"I need one."

"Why?"

He studied me and licked those lovely lips. "Because you've seen me at my most vulnerable, Nick. You've seen me in ways no other human being ever has or will again. That vulnerability, the breakdowns you've witnessed, make me want to fight what's happening between us and that's not fair."

"You want to see me vulnerable?"

"I need to. I'm a warrior but you've seen me naked, broken, sobbing because I couldn't move a fucking branch or cope with the ship. I'm not used to being weak."

Without realising it I had pulled my knees up to my chest and wrapped my arms around them. I didn't know what to say, because I didn't explore what made me vulnerable.

18

I THOUGHT ABOUT WHAT HE needed from me. If I gave him what he wanted I'd find it even harder *if* or *when* he walked away. If I began exploring the damage in my head what other locked boxes would spring open and how would I cope? As a soldier I was lucky. All the horrors I'd seen as a Royal Marine I'd had my brothers and my family to help me deal with the experiences. Even in the SAS Stanton was worse than anything I faced in the field. I didn't have PTSD. I had memories that haunted me, we all did, but they didn't steal my life, didn't make me react strangely to stress, I didn't have nightmares or insomnia.

There were reasons why I'd never been in a committed relationship though.

The sad thing about what Gabriel proposed came down to trust and that's a peculiar creature at the best of times. If you're caught in a fire in a house, you trust the fire officer to save you, even though you're strangers. The same thing in hospitals or the coast guard, maybe even the police. So, when something goes wrong in those organisations, that bond of trust is broken with the public.

As a soldier I had to trust the men and women around me all the time. I would trust them with my life in many, many different scenarios and on the whole, I had no reason not to trust them when I'd been in the Marines. Things in the Regiment were different and the stress of having to watch my back took a toll, I knew that it made me paranoid and led to mistakes.

The trust a child, even an adult one, has in their parents is different again and changes frequently over the years. If that is broken it might well be one of the most damaging kinds of destruction because it touches on something deep inside.

Gabriel wanted me to trust him. I did. When it came to fighting for our lives – but…

The truth now stretched before me and I didn't like the colour of it, a nasty sickly yellowy-green. I had to trust him with a part of myself I'd never, ever, shared with anyone. No one in my family, no one at work, no lover, no friend. He wanted me to give away the only part of my heart I'd hidden from the world forever.

He sensed something deep inside me shifting and seemed to understand my internal struggled to break free of my fear or retreat into the shadows. He moved up the bed to sit beside me. He wore black socks over his torn feet. I hadn't noticed him remove his boots.

"Do you understand why I'm asking this?"

I nodded. "I get it." I turned to look at him, that beautiful face, full of patience and compassion. How could I tell him what burned in my heart? "I have to decide if you're worth it."

"Yes," he whispered, reaching out and tracing the line of my ear with his fingertip. "I am rather hoping I am."

Tears pricked my eyes and I sniffed. "I'm falling in love with you." I blurted the words. A simultaneous explosion of emotions collided with the confession. I dreaded his contempt and laughter. However, I felt relief at not holding the words back any longer.

"I know. That's why I need to hear what you're working so hard to hide, Nick."

"I'm handing you a weapon to destroy me."

"You might be handing me the tools I need to help you heal." He grasped my naked arm which held my knees so tight to my chest breathing only happened with great effort. His thumb stroked circles, moving the rough dark hair. "Give me your trust, Nick." Those big dark eyes were so full of compassion how could I deny his soft request?

Unfortunately, it wasn't that simple. How could I love him if I didn't have an inclination on how to love myself? Isn't that what we're supposed to do? Love ourselves so others can love us in return, and we can love them without demands? How the *fuck* does that happen?

"It's so stupid, Gabriel. In comparison to what you have endured over the last few months, it's fucking nothing." It shamed me to be talking to this man, this beautiful creature who had suffered so much, about something so petty.

"Nick, I have the feeling that the poison inside you has been there for a very long time and what Stanton has done just made it worse. What I've gone through is nothing. I know what I am: I'm clever, I'm very good at my job, I know what I look like and I know how I sound. What happened to me in Myanmar is an aberration in a life that's been somewhat blessed. I may have lost my mother to something horrible. I may have lost my father to cancer. Those things are tragic, and they hurt, but an accident of genetics and my hard work has made life just a little easier for me than for most. I will recover from what Myanmar has done because I have to, because I want my life to go on, because I want to make love to you and I want you to make love to me – without fear or flashbacks."

I lost control of the tears, they rolled in silence down my cheeks and I sniffed some more. Gabriel fished the free tissues off the bedside and handed them over. His last statement broke my self-isolation. He wanted to make love to me. He didn't want to fuck me. If he felt the same way I did then I needed to trust him, and love couldn't be in the same bed as us if we didn't have trust sharing the space as well.

One deep breath in and I forced my legs back down the bed. Gabriel stretched out beside me and I rubbed my hands over my face. "Okay, you want the hidden bits of me, but I warn you now, Gabe, they are just a series of sad stories. Nothing dramatic. Nothing unusual. Just normal human shit."

He took my hand and laced our fingers together. "I'll take normal human bullshit over torture and humiliation."

I managed a sort of chuckle. "You've got me there. Okay, it's really unglamorous but here it goes. When I was about five, before my sister was born, I was in the hay barn playing with the puppies and I climbed up high. I wasn't supposed to be there at all, but Mum and Dad were busy in the house. I climbed all the way to the top, about 10 metres and looked out over the farm and hills. I'd never been so high on my own before and I felt very grownup. The trouble with hay though, is that sometimes the baling doesn't happen very well and the string holding the bale in place comes loose."

"Oh no…"

Gabriel came from a ranch; he knew what came next.

"The bale collapsed under me and I tumbled out of the barn. On the way down I hit several more bales slowing me down, but I landed face first on a roll of barbed wire my dad was taking up to the top sheep field. I also hit the wood it was wrapped around, which knocked me out, fortunately." I rubbed the spot just above my right eye on the soft area below the temple. "Mum found me. I don't remember much after that, except being driven very fast to the nearest town and being in Mum's arms not the car seat."

I sipped at the small bottle of whiskey.

"No one let me near a mirror for months." I traced some of the faint scars a good tan still brought to the surface. "The damage to the nerve running down the side of my face is permanent. That's why my right eye and the side of my mouth droop sometimes, especially when I'm tired."

"Doesn't stop you from being a damned good shot though and I've only noticed it occasionally."

I managed my strange half smile, more conscious of it than ever. "No, it doesn't. The Regiment almost didn't take me because of the scars, makes me too memorable, that and my size but with a beard they aren't so visible these days. Other than those things my face is entirely forgettable. I am forgettable. I'm completely average. I'm clever, I'm not sharp. I am big and strong, like my old man but where he is a good-looking bloke, someone hit me with the ugly stick on the way out of the womb." The heat in my face would turn my skin a nasty red colour and I couldn't look at Gabriel.

"School made it really obvious. The scars were bad in those days. My droopy eye, sometimes I'd drool because of my mouth. I wore braces on my teeth until I was seventeen. They never really straightened the way it was hoped they would. I grew big fast, so I stood out even more among the rest of the class. My only saving grace was my ability to run fast, and it meant I did well at rugby. It stopped me being a complete outcast, so I managed."

"Go on, Nick."

"This is all very dull, Gabe."

"No, it's you and I want to know you."

I huffed but continued. "The bullying was constant. Even my friends and family. They thought they were poking gentle fun, but it added to the erosion. The constant fuelling of my sense of self in the negative. I knew I wasn't handsome, but I was kind and I held on to that. Being on the farm helped too because every day I was useful, every day I made a difference to the lives depending on us – to the sheep and the cattle. The dogs and cats. It gave me something back. So, I wouldn't be a catwalk model, but someone would see inside and love me one day. When I came out as gay at home mum worried. Then others in school found out a year later when my sister blurted it to a friend at primary school who told her older sister in my year at school. That was rough, but it was all the same as the other stuff. A drip, drip, drip…"

More whiskey, Gabriel finished the bottle and went to find another.

"The Royal Marines was more of the same. I followed orders, worked very hard and it made me a good soldier, a good Marine. I had friends, but you know what young men are like in a pack. Being gay didn't help. All sorts of things happened over the years. We'd be on leave, we'd go to a club, and they would spot a good-looking bloke in the crowd who was obviously gay. They'd try to set me up and he'd turn me down because – well – to be honest gay men can be fucking judgy."

Gabriel laughed. "Really? They can be that bad?"

He clearly didn't watch enough reality TV. "They would look at me and..." I shook my head, unable to use words to describe the memories. "I can't begin to tell you some of the horrible put downs I've endured. Much to the amusement of the guys I worked with all day, every day. I think people look at my size and assume I must be tough, that I have skin made of bloody Teflon."

"But you don't."

"No. I don't. The few times I met blokes interested in me it never came to much and to be fair I'm not very good at the one-night stand thing. I'm not witty, I'm not well read. I like films and TV, I love stories, but not literature. I like adventures, thrillers, fantasy, you know?"

"I know."

I began fiddling with my fingers in my lap. "I'm just average. Normal. I'm completely average."

"You're an elite soldier. That's not average."

I shrugged. "My team hate me enough to leave me in a foreign country under fire."

"Your team are going to pay a heavy price for that, Brant told me."

A grunt was my only response. I couldn't think about them. All our fates were sealed that day one way or another. "Being an elite soldier, in my case, happened because I am good at following orders, most of the time, you were the exception to that rule. I work very hard. I am loyal. I pay attention to what's happening around me and I go where I'm needed without question. I keep my head down and I'm just clever enough. I made it to lance-corporal in the Marines and I might have made it to the same grade in the SAS without Stanton being there, but I'll never be more than that in the UK army and I've never risen above private in the SAS."

"And what has Stanton done? Exactly."

I glanced at Gabriel. Those dark eyes studied me, and I couldn't hide my shame. "I don't want to talk about it."

"Nick –"

"No. The things I did – dirty, disgusting, humiliating… the beasting I could handle. The endless press-ups, extra runs, time trials, the gay bashing and that was bad, but I could cope. But some of the other stuff he and a couple of the guys did – that was wrong."

"It was all wrong, Nick."

I felt my mouth twist. "Hmm. The trouble is I don't fit anywhere. I'm gay, but I'm not pretty enough and I don't have time to build friendships in the community so no one had a chance to get to know me. I'm gay so even my mates in the Marines have a reason to take the piss – all the fucking time. I have no friends in the Regiment for obvious reasons and I've been really lonely, for a really long time. And I look at you and I know you could do so much better out there, in the big world of Pride and handsome men and I know I'll lose you. Because I'm not pretty, I'm not handsome, I'm average to look at, average to talk to, I'm just a normal bloke with a cool job but it won't last."

Gabriel sat in silence, his legs folded under him so he could face me, and I tried to meet his solemn gaze.

19

THE SILENCE HELD FOR A while and I broke it first, the feelings of discomfort too great. "Pathetic right? A grown-arsed man still whining about being bullied as a kid. Letting his boss humiliate him."

"How can you ever think you're average?" Gabriel asked. I looked at him and a tear slid down his cheek. "I feel humiliated because every time I look in a mirror and every day for the rest of my life, I'm going to see where those bastards stubbed cigarettes out on my body and they used me as an ashtray and worse for days. But only for days. What you've gone through has been your entire life. Low level misery every day, every time you saw your so-called mates. Every time you shave you hear their voices in your head, right?"

"Only when I'm feeling down or tired."

"You're a fucking SAS soldier, you're always tired."

I shrugged. He seemed to be angry and was agitated. It made me uncomfortable, but I didn't know why. "It's just life, Gabe. Everyone gets shit for something."

"Maybe, but they have a safe place where it doesn't happen. Even your family takes the piss."

"They don't mean any harm by it." I wasn't about to paint my family as the bad guys.

"No, but it doesn't help. Not with all the other crap building up and not having anyone to talk to. Nick, you said it yourself, you're lonely."

Again with the shrug, what did he want me to say?

Apparently, he didn't need me to say anything at all because he was on a mission. "You are beautiful, Nick. Do you know why?" He placed his hand on my naked chest. It felt warm and his fingers were strong. I wished it felt safe, but I didn't feel safe. I felt ripped open, ragged and more vulnerable than I'd been in my entire adult life.

"You are beautiful because you have the biggest heart of anyone I have ever met. You are the very definition of soulful. Those sweet, kind, moss green eyes. That quirky soft smile. These hands," he picked them up, "these hands saved my life while placing yours in terrible danger. Nothing would have made you abandon me. Nothing. A sweet kind man from a small farm in a place called Somerset saved my life and I will always love you for it." He let the tears fall down his perfect cheekbones as he stroked my damaged face. "How can you think I wouldn't be proud to be by your side?"

"You're an angel," I mumbled, feeling foolish under his scrutiny and thinking of his call sign.

"I am a flawed man and I do not have your heart. I would be guided by it though. I want to learn to have a soul as beautiful as yours. Nick, I look at you and I see a butterfly. Others might think of a moth, if what you tell me about the gay community is true, but I see a creature as delicate as gossamer who needs sheltering and protecting to reach his full potential. I want to offer that shelter while I learn from you how to be a better man. The one thing my incarceration taught me about myself is this: I am not a good man, but I want to be."

I wriggled my fingers back between his. "Can we draw a line under all this sharing bollocks now?"

He chuckled. "Only if we make one promise to each other." I looked at him. "Promise we can talk about this again."

"Gabe…"

"I'm serious, Nick. Your self-confidence is on the floor picking up dust bunnies it has been down there so long. You need to believe in yourself a bit more. From what I've seen you are not average at all, in any way. You excelled in that jungle and if I were your senior officer, I would be proud to have a man like you in my unit."

That surprised me. Gabriel's rank of Sergeant 1st Class went above Stanton's rank. "Thank you, that means a great deal."

"Thank you for sharing so much of yourself and for trusting me."

"Big thing trust."

"The biggest."

"Still want to sleep alone?" I asked, looking up at him through my lashes.

He smiled and managed to look coy. "I'm an idiot."

"Is that a no?"

"It's a no."

"Good."

I reached for his jaw with both hands and drew him towards me. The kiss began a gentle and tender exploration. My fingers worked his buttons free and I pushed the soft shirt off his shoulders, only to make him shiver as I kissed his neck and went further, biting and sucking at sensitive spots. He lay back and I moved over him, the towel vanishing as he yanked it away.

"And you can't tell me that's average," he murmured when he grasped my cock.

I gasped. "Bastard."

With his other hand he carded his fingers through my hair. "Can this be real, Nick? Am I still in that cell waiting to die? How can you be real?"

He was asking me? "It's real."

"What you're feeling – I need you to know – you aren't alone and it's scaring the crap out of me. Nothing like this has ever happened to me before. Not even with the woman I married."

I had no more words to share and he seemed to understand because when I kissed him again our bodies pressed together as if they should never come apart.

Facing each other we stroked skin while we kissed, Gabriel pushed his thigh between my knees and pushed up against my balls just enough to make me whimper. He nosed at my mouth, asking me to take just a little pain for him. The husky words proved my need to be subordinate to him in bed and it further heated my desire. I rocked, feeling the rough hair against the soft surface of my balls. Gabriel moaned in pleasure as I made use of his body.

"I want more this time, Nick. I'm ready for more," he whispered.

I rubbed my beard against his smooth cheek making him growl. "Whatever you want."

He pulled back enough to look at me. "Can we try a 69?"

That surprised me enough to stop me rutting against him. "Um, yeah, but are you sure? It can be a bit intense and I might not have the greatest control."

"We can do it like this, though, right? On our sides?" He sounded so hopeful I had to grin.

"Yeah, we can do it like this."

All bashful worries about my physical body vanished under the look of lust that made Gabriel's eyes almost black. He moved before I did and scooted around so I could reach his straining cock. And, my God, it was straining. I'd never seen anything so perfect though and my mouth watered.

"Hey, Nick?"

"Huh?" I managed to lift my eyes up his body.

"Go gentle with me?"

I managed to nod, then licked the soft tip with my tongue and Gabriel jolted, his cock bouncing on my nose making him giggle. Sex should be fun.

Before doing anything, I wanted to breathe in his musky scent. I'd never been this close to his scars and unruly hair despite wishing for it more than once on the boat. A soft nip of his thigh and I glanced up to see him trapped between staring at my face and my groin.

"Hey, if this is too much, just let me know." I twisted my hips back just a little to give him some space.

He didn't say anything, just grabbed my hips and rolled me back to my original position. Then he opened his mouth and pushed me inside the soft wet heat of his body.

"Fuck!"

He hummed and sucked hard.

"Wow, slowly, sweetheart. Gently." I stroked his back and I tried to remember what I was doing. Oh, right, getting revenge.

While I tried to detach a little from what was happening in my nether regions, I placed a hand on Gabriel's muscular backside and swiped my tongue over his glans. Gabriel's movements stopped. I grinned, knowing far more about being able to give him pleasure and did what I loved the most. I lowered my mouth over him and closed my lips, feeling him pressing down on my tongue. I pushed against his backside and his cock slid further inside hitting the back of my mouth. Deep throating is hard to do and takes practice, patience and isn't really necessary. I'd never managed it before and didn't plan on starting right now, but I could take him a little further back and add a few extra tricks to give him pleasure.

I hummed, long and low, the rumble in my chest and Gabriel keened. "You bastard."

With slow movements I rose and dropped repeatedly before sliding off and burrowing into his groin with my nose. Body wash and his heavy spicy scent filled me. Rather than return to his cock I took one side of his scrotum in my mouth and rolled the soft ball with my tongue.

He returned to my cock and soon we were sucking and licking and kissing and nibbling each other. With tender, slow movements Gabriel explored his new territory until he said, "Fuck, I thought my favourite thing was going down on a woman, but this? This is great." His voice sounded even more husky than usual from his attention to my needs.

"Glad you approve."

The feelings being produced in my heart with every soft stroke he made to my back, thighs and arse, as well as all the work on my cock made me want to cry and explode all at once. Totally overwhelmed I had to stop and rest my forehead against his thick thigh.

"Nick?"

"Just give me a minute." I couldn't look at him. I couldn't do anything but remember how to breathe. My chest hurt from the effort of holding in all the emotions tumbling through me and I couldn't stop them or control them. I just couldn't...

Gabriel, attuned to me like no other human being I'd ever met, rolled away and turned around. We were nose to nose again. He brushed his fingers against my head, the stiff bristles of the shorn sides moving. "Look at me?" A gentle suggestion.

I couldn't.

I didn't want to humiliate myself – not in front of him – not now.

"Nick, look at me." An order this time.

I tried to meet his gaze and the moment I did our eyes locked. "I love you, Nick. I love you."

I whimpered, torn and shredded inside my heart.

"Say it, my love," he murmured against my lips.

If I admitted it in this moment, with us naked and physically vulnerable, it would pierce my shields for all time and I'd never be the same person again. I had never said it to another man before I met Gabriel. I had never admitted I even cared for someone. I always waited for the axe to fall and it always did, over my neck and that would be it. They would move on and I'd be left struggling to understand why I was never good enough.

"Trust me." His eyes were pools of dark, unfathomable oceans of patience and kindness.

"I love you too." The words came out with such strength and dignity it surprised us both and he grinned at me.

"There, another hurdle crossed. We can do this together. We can do anything together." He traced some of the faded scars over my cheek.

I leaned in and kissed him. The kiss soon turned heated and he groaned as he rolled me over onto my back pressing me into the soft mattress. Turning his attention to my neck I gasped and bucked, reaching for my cock to finish off, but he slapped my hand away and kept it pinned to the bed. Gabriel then worked his way down my body, licking and sucking hard on my nipples, biting my ribs and hip bone.

Then he returned to my straining cock and took charge. It took no time at all for my balls to tighten further as he sucked, licked and moved up and down my cock. I tried really hard not to thrust up, but it was impossible not to as every time I groaned or moved, he moaned in approval sending small shockwaves through me.

The tension inside me continued to grow and then the bastard went and added his hand to the mix. He rolled my balls before grasping my shaft and moving it up and down in union to his mouth. I looked down and watched his dark eyes focus on me, the wicked glint enough to make me throw my head back and curse him.

I couldn't help it. I grabbed his soft curls in my big fist and thrust up, but he kept control and the fire in my belly tightened, tightened, tightened before exploding outward, upward, expanding through my entire body.

I felt him swallow, choke a little then lick hard over the head.

"Oh, no, don't," I begged, way too sensitive now.

He chuckled and came back up my body with soft kisses.

"You?" I managed, barely able to form a sentence.

"Done. I came with you, baby. God, that was hot. You're hot." He kissed me, deep and I tasted the earthy flavours on his tongue. We kept kissing, stroking, making our way up the bed, before curling into each other.

"Love you," I breathed into his ear.

"Hmm, love you as well," he rumbled. "Sleep now."

20

ALASKA BURNED MY BONES WITH cold, even in June. Colonel Brant and Corporal Lancing were with us, Mac and Jacob were in London helping Sergeant Greenbrook with the UK branch of Jupiter Section. They'd be working closely with the domestic branch of the Secret Intelligence Service, MI5. Brant didn't seem too happy about it because she needed the evidence from Gabriel's USB drive to know for certain who in the SIS worked for Jupiter Section.

"Damn it's nice to be cold," Gabriel announced as we walked over the tarmac from the small Cessna which had flown us north from Anchorage to Rampart, a small town on the Yukon River.

We were in the middle of bum-fuck-nowhere.

"You're weird," I announced, and he laughed.

Things with Gabriel, over the last few days of intense travel, had been wonderful. The look of panic had dimmed in his dark eyes. He responded to the colonel's orders as if he'd been following them all his working life and he answered all Lancing's questions about the US Rangers with great patience. He never stopped being demonstrative with me in public, despite people's obvious confusion of the whole beauty and the beast thing we had going on, and he behaved as if we'd be together forever.

It all left me happy but a little confused and troubled to be honest. We'd see what happened when crunch time came, and I handed in my resignation to the colonel. I hoped Brant would make some noise and get me out of Credenhill and the Regiment fast, so I didn't need to work my notice. I wanted to leave Hereford a long way behind me. Gabriel had yet to mention his future plans and I didn't want to push – too bloody scared of what he might say.

"We need a vehicle to take us up the Eureka-Rampart road to where Little Minook Creek joins its big sister. We'll have to walk from there," Gabriel said.

"Corporal?" Brant said.

"On it, ma'am."

She watched the young soldier stomp off through the fine drizzle to talk to a huge man who must be part bear because he made me feel small, about hiring a vehicle of some kind.

"He's growing on me," Brant muttered.

"He's a good lad," Gabriel agreed. "If a bit green."

Lancing hurried back. "We have a problem."

"What?" Brant asked.

"We've been compromised."

The colour in Gabriel's face drained away. "What do you mean?"

"The guy over there said the only new trucks they have here are already on hire. A group of men, led by a blonde woman, came through three hours ago and took both trucks. They looked military and they had weapons."

"Maddox," Gabriel hissed and seemed to deflate as I watched. I gripped his shoulder and he turned into me for a hug.

"It's okay."

"How is this okay, Nick?"

Brant cursed. "Does she know the location of your friend?"

"If she does, I don't know how. It doesn't make any sense. How could she know we were coming here? We went through multiple airports. Nick and I don't have our original passports, you've given us aliases, you aren't using your real name... How?" Gabriel sounded desperate.

"Can she find any communication between you and your old CO?" Brant asked. "Anything electronic?"

Gabriel mulled this over for a few seconds and his eyes grew colder than the wind dancing icy fingers under my clothes. "She's been to my father's ranch. Bitch."

"What was there?" I asked.

He turned a bleak expression in my direction. "Everything necessary to find this place. Fuck! How could I be so stupid?" He turned on his heel and walked away from us, exasperation and anger in every defined line of his body. "It didn't even occur to me. There's an old address book, an actual book, where I keep important contact details for people I care about because technology fails and can be hacked."

"So, they have an exact location?"

Gabriel's eyes lit up. "No. No they don't. They have the postal address."

"Which is different?" Brant asked.

"It'll take them directly into town and the people here aren't in love with the Federal Government, so the chances of them finding out more are slim."

Brant rubbed her hands together, the wind cold and the airfield way to open to the elements to be standing around talking. "Right, let's find a vehicle and get ahead of them. We'll need to think about E and E up here. You're not strong enough to survive the elements for long, Sergeant."

Escape and evasion? In Alaska? That didn't sound like fun to me, not after Myanmar. While I pondered this, I stared out over the open ground and caught sight of a truck heading in our direction at speed. "Ma'am?"

"Wilde?"

I nodded in the direction of the incoming vehicle. "Hostiles?"

"Could just be a local. Keep it light, gentlemen." Despite her words I could feel the tension in the colonel ramp up a few dozen notches. We were on open ground, with little cover except the Cessna and too far to run to reach the safety of a tree line or a building.

Lancing came up beside me and handed over the heaviest of our equipment. On a stopover in Canada we'd gone shopping with a contact from Brant's 'who to call in an emergency' list of people. They managed to supply us with weapons. I removed the Heckler and Koch G36, a tough polymer fibre plastic assault rifle that I loved to use. I clicked the magazine in place and took point. The others removed weapons from the bag. We spread out to make harder targets.

The truck grew closer and slowed on the wet grass at the edge of my effective range. I kept the muzzle of the gun down, but the weapon felt alive in my hands and against my body.

A window opened and something white fluttered in the wind.

"Lower your weapon, Wilde," Brant ordered.

I stood down.

The truck approached. A young woman with dark hair climbed out. "One of you Gabriel Cabrera?" Her accent was strong and her face sharp, knowing, a small falcon of a woman.

"Yes, ma'am," he called out.

"Thank God," she said, coming closer. "We need your help."

The four of us exchanged glances. "What's happened?" asked Brant, stepping forwards.

"My name is Angie, I'm from the town and we have a whole bunch of government men looking for Vulture."

We all looked at Gabriel. "Shit."

"Vulture?" Brant asked, as if a little scared of the answer that would be forthcoming.

"Yeah, Roger Davis's old call sign." Gabriel rubbed his face. "There will be too many of them for a direct confrontation. Rampart is small, we'll never be able to hide well enough to pick them off one at a time. Too many opportunities for mistakes to happen."

"We need to give them a reason to follow us into the mountains," Brant said. "Get them away from the civilians."

Gabriel looked at me. "Up for some idiotic behaviour?"

I grinned. Playing soldiers with Gabriel sounded like something I really needed to do. "Ma'am, if you and Corporal Lancing can find a crow's nest, we can drive the enemy to your position."

In a matter of minutes Gabriel and I were fitted with the H4855 Personal Role Radio, PRR, a small UHF transmitter-receiver with full headset and microphone. We donned body armour, webbing with magazines filled with 30 standard NATO rounds. Between us we had almost 300 rounds, 4 fragmentation grenades, and a couple of flash-bangs but we left the partridge in the pear tree…

By the time I'd finished dressing the familiar weight gave me a reassuring boost in confidence. Angie opted to come with us and spent the time finding a vehicle for Brant and Lancing. They had mortars and their firearms so we were confident we could slow the enemy down.

"Rules of engagement, ma'am? We're going up against allied soldiers I don't want to be hauled up on charges because of accusations of murder or unlawful killing." Too many Special Forces personnel were subject to the vagaries of law because of following badly given orders.

Brant's face grew serious. "Don't engage unless they fire first. Shoot to wound if necessary. Kill when you have no other choice. Most of the people working for Jupiter don't realise they aren't working for the US Government. They don't deserve to die."

I nodded. Her orders were clear enough for me.

"Are you certain you want to come back into town?" Gabriel asked Angie.

"You need to know who is local and who isn't. I don't want you shooting my friends." Being an all-American girl in hostile territory she wore body armour and carried a hunting rifle and side arm.

We climbed into her truck with Gabriel driving. "What about law enforcement in the area?"

"We have a sheriff, Tommy D, but he's about as much use as a handbrake on a canoe. We have one bar in town and that's where he'll be until all this goes away," Angie said with such depressing inevitability I couldn't help but chuckle.

"How did you know I would be here?" Gabriel asked, not seeing the funny side of anything.

"Vulture. He's always said I need to keep an eye out for you because if you arrived in town then trouble would be on your coat tails. We look after our own and those that belong to us. I was told you were important to Vulture, so you're important to me. We've been struggling to keep the town alive since the government stopped funding the airport in 2016, but we're still a community, those of us what's left."

I understood that predicament all too well being the son of a farmer in a small rural community. Whether you needed public transport by bus or plane, losing funding could be the death knell of small villages and towns.

Gabriel hit the road leading to a small community on the banks of the Yukon River.

"Give me the geography of the place," he said.

"One major road, if you could call it that, which runs parallel to the river. Then the town stretches back to form a kinda triangle. There's only thirty of us that live here full time and we have a small school. We just act as a base for the odd prospector who still thinks there might be gold in Minook and the loggers mostly." Angie pointed through the windscreen. "We're almost there."

I could see a handful of low-lying buildings clinging to the flat land around the river. It looked sad, desperate, defiant and impermanent. As if nature had decided to bide her time before sweeping in and reclaiming the homes of the upstart humans and returning everything to wilderness. From the river I gazed to the endless sweep of mountains, trees and scrubby grass, the boundless blue sky and scudding clouds. Isolated and lonely – Rampart looked like a place Clint Eastwood should ride into before taking a stand against a bad guy.

Gabriel slowed the truck down. I chambered a round into the G36 and wound down the window.

Angie, sat in the back, leaned between us and pointed. "He's one of them."

A dark shape stood outside a building that looked like it was made from a timber frame and corrugated sheet metal. We were 150 metres away and closing. I glanced to our three o'clock, the river only – a wide strip of dark and rushing water. Our six o'clock – trees, mountains, wildness. Our nine o'clock – spread out houses, no people. If my rounds went astray, they'd punch through the walls too easily. I needed to be accurate.

"You sure it's them?" I wound down the window. The fresh air, almost artic cold this far north, rushed in and made Gabriel shiver.

"I'm sure," Angie said.

Gabriel glanced at me. "Ready?"

I nodded.

He gunned the engine. The truck roared, the tyres bit the asphalt and jumped into action. We covered half the distance in a few seconds.

"Now," I said, raising the G36 and lining up the ZF 3×4° dual optical sight. The man was in my target. My finger added a pound of pressure to the trigger mechanism.

Gabriel yanked on the handbrake and pulled the steering wheel around, dropping the clutch. The truck slew around giving me a perfect broadside. The target, dressed in black fatigues with full body armour and assault rifle over his chest, turned to face us. His eyes widened as he took in the image of me, half out of the window, HK rifle live and ready in my arms. He lifted his weapon. I squeezed the trigger, my sights on his upper thigh, and the G36 barked in my arms, recoil easy to absorb.

A cloud of blood filled the air around the man's knee and groin. He screamed and, as the truck did a full one-eighty, he collapsed.

"I'm impressed, English," Gabriel said, wrestling with the recalcitrant truck.

"Fuck me," Angie murmured.

"Not likely, honey. He's all mine," Gabriel murmured.

Wide eyed Angie said, "What a fucking waste."

"Not for me." I grinned at them both.

"Way to make a girl feel good," she said, sitting back.

We were returning to the airport, the road crossing the bottom of the landing strip.

"Did they take the bait?" I asked.

Gabriel glanced in the mirror. "We've upset the hornets' nest that's for certain."

I turned and saw two trucks beginning to pull out from the side of the building. Two men were with the downed soldier, so he'd live, and it took three of them out of the fight. Not bad for a single bullet.

"Sit rep, Charlie One," Brant said over the comm's unit.

I pressed the pressel attached to my webbing. "Zero, this is Charlie Two. They've taken the hint."

"Roger that, Charlie Two. How far away are they from your six?"

I glanced behind me; it would be a truer estimation than Gabriel looking in the rear-view mirror. "I'd say 200 metres and closing, Zero. Their trucks are faster."

"I'm doing the best this pile can manage," Gabriel growled.

"Hey, I love this truck." Angie defended her truck like others would an ugly puppy – if such a thing existed.

"Best if you make it more, Charlie Two."

"Roger that, out."

Gabriel knocked the truck down a gear to gain more speed. It sort of worked. We turned around a vicious ninety-degree bend and shot off up the road.

One hundred and fifty metres from the end of the runway on our right we could see another shift in the direction of the road. "Take the first corner and be ready for the explosion, Charlie One," Brant said to Gabriel.

"Roger that, Zero." He slung the truck around the corner making the tyres squeal in protest and the entire vehicle shudder. Our speed picked up just as we hit the second corner in the strange dog leg the road builders of Alaska had decided to create rather than building a bridge.

I turned and watched the lead vehicle, now less than 75 metres from our position, hit the corner and the world lit up just half a breath before the sound smacked into my head.

"Fuck!" Angie screamed in my ear.

"God, damn it," Gabriel muttered, wrestling us around another corner as the shockwave bounced the truck around. I saw the large SUV leap off the tarmac, yaw to the left and crash down. The second vehicle, still rounding the corner, swerved, lost control and ran off the road and into rough terrain. Not enough to stop them for long. Brant had laid a trap with mortars.

"She's good that colonel," Gabriel muttered.

"Thank you, Charlie One," Brant said in my ear.

21

"WE ARE HALF A CLICK ahead of you, Charlie team, preparing to go mobile into the forest. We'll never outrun them on these roads." Brant sounded controlled and efficient. It felt strange to have such confidence in a CO again after all I'd been through with Stanton. She just inspired utter faith in those surrounding her – I wondered how often that resulted in her people losing their lives.

We reached the meeting spot and Angie left the truck first. We came out, my knees a little weak after the intensity of the last few minutes and gathered around Brant. She stood in full battle kit, her SA80 slung across her chest. Lancing stood beside her, his innocence a bright halo around him but he'd gone through the training I had, so he knew his stuff, just lacked experience.

"You have GPS, Cabrera?" she asked Gabriel.

"All programmed in," he said.

"You won't find the right route without me," Angie said. She stood with assault rifle, webbing, DPM clothing suitable for cold climates and a stubborn set to her small jaw. "I'm serious, you won't find Vulture without me."

"Thoughts?" Brant asked, looking at Gabriel again.

"I have the location but not the best route to take. I've only been here a few times and always with Vulture to show me the way. I haven't been here in years and he could have changed any manner of things. It might be for the best, Colonel."

Brant looked at Angie. "You follow orders. If something happens to me, Cabrera is next in line. Do you understand?"

"Yes, ma'am." Angie's eyes were bright with adventure. I wondered if my sister would do the same thing or if this was a purely American excitement – going up against armed men in the wilderness.

"They'll be able to see which direction we left the road," Gabriel said, and I had an odd flashback to the jungle and our old Land Rover.

"Then we better hustle and find a way to throw them off as we move," Brant said.

We set off into the wilderness of Alaska.

The going proved tough. Angie led us down to Minook Creek and we worked hard bouncing from rock to rock so we didn't leave easy tracks to follow. Brant and Angie found the going hard because they were smaller but once both women acknowledged that longer legs and arms gave me an advantage, they allowed us to help. Gabriel also suffered but I knew better than to help until he asked. His feet were still a mess and there was no way on this earth he had recovered enough to endure a rough trail walk, never mind the run we were doing.

He slipped behind and I waited, watching Lancing haul the women up a shallow cliff.

"Let me take your weapon," I said when Gabriel caught up.

He nodded and without comment or argument, I took his weapon. "I don't know how long I can do this," he murmured. "I'm in no fit state for an escape and evasion exercise." His breath came out in explosions. The temperature had started to drop. Despite it being just past midsummer and the nights hardly existing this far north, it wouldn't be warm.

We turned as one unit to catch up with the others, but I already knew they wouldn't be able to keep up the pace necessary to find safety from the highly trained operatives chasing us. We needed to delay them, whittle them down, discourage the chase or divert them.

As a team we made it up Minook Creek to a rope bridge strung over the tumbling and chaotic river. Angie scrambled up, put her hand on the wooden upright to step onto the bridge and a *crack* filled the air a second after I saw splinters of wood shower her arm and chest. I hit the ground. No one made a sound.

"Report, Angie," Brant said after a moment's silence.

"I'm okay."

"Charlie Two, lay down covering fire."

I handed Gabriel his rifle, he took it with a nod.

"Yes, ma'am." I rose to a crouch, checked my surroundings and found a good boulder I could lie on and snipe at our pursuers.

"I'll take the bridge," Gabriel said, scrambling after Angie and setting up his position.

The two of us were laid flat with the sun at our backs; we'd be hard to see. The enemy were dressed in black and showed up well in my sights. There were ten men and one woman coming up the riverbed. I heard Brant giving quiet orders to the others to run on command over the rope bridge. I didn't think running over it would be an option; it consisted of wide spaced wooden slats tied in place with thick rope.

I thumbed the pressel to be able to speak to Gabriel. "The moment you can, get after them."

"I'm not leaving you here. Stick with correct formation, Charlie Two. I lay down covering fire, you move. It's the only option. You try to move alone from there and you'll be taken down."

I knew he was right, but it didn't make me feel any better. "Roger that, Charlie One."

"Good, remember that. Me sergeant, you grunt."

"Thanks, babe."

Brant cut in. "Just stop them, boys."

I focused on my target, the lead man, probably the one to shoot at Angie. My heart and lungs calmed to the perfect Zen space I always found when holding a weapon and taking a bead on my enemy. My trigger finger took up the pressure and I squeezed. The man's leg vanished in a haze of blood spray while I took aim at the man behind him, now clear, and tried for another leg shot. I missed. I fired again and hit the target. Gabriel released two rounds and took out numbers three and four before the others managed to find suitable cover. I didn't turn but I heard Brant giving orders over the comms system to move the others over the bridge. All we needed to do now was force the enemy to keep their heads down.

To do this I began taking pot shots at small rocks, exploding them into shards to force the enemy to keep their heads below the ridgeline sheltering them.

"Charlie Two, we are clear of the bridge," Brant said in my ear.

"Roger that, Zero. Charlie One, move out." I gave the order hoping Gabriel would do as he was told.

"Negative, Charlie Two. Move towards me, take my position."

I sighed. He had a point but still, it would have been nice to be listened to for a change. Changing magazines took no thought and no time, the action so ingrained it felt like a breath. I laid down a longer burst of automatic fire, rather than single shots I'd been releasing previously, and raced to Gabriel's position by the bridge.

"Hi," he said, not moving his head from the sights and following my example of exploding rocks.

"Hi. Couldn't save yourself then."

He grinned at me as I settled in, took aim from the new position and released rounds. He toggled the pressel for the comms unit. "Zero, I'm moving, lay down covering fire if possible."

"Roger that, Charlie One. Move," Lancing said in our ears. Three separate retorts came from further up the hillside, among the trees. Brant had moved them into the safest place possible. How they'd found a spot that far away which gave them a view into the gully I didn't know but I wasn't going to argue.

Gabriel rose from beside me, changed magazines, and raced for the bridge. I heard it clatter and some poor sod poked his head and rifle over the boulder to take a shot at Gabriel. The shot clipped the wood near his feet making him curse, but Lancing, Brant or Angie fired, and the gun shattered in the man's hands. Shards of metal went everywhere, and I could hear the screams.

"Charlie Two, I have you, move," came the terse command from Gabriel.

"Roger that, moving," I said. I lifted my rifle, held it close to my body, ran in crouch, and climbed onto the bridge. It swayed. It groaned. Bullets cracked from barrels, shrapnel flew, and the wooden structure didn't hold under my weight. My left foot snapped a board and I tumbled after it, unable to keep my balance. I couldn't drop my weapon, so twisted and landed heavily facing downriver.

"Nick!" Gabriel screamed.

"I'm okay." Hands slick inside the tightfitting gloves I wore, I managed to regain my knees, then my feet. A sharp and intense pain in my left ankle made me curse but it had to move, so I pushed on. The stupid joint screamed so loudly in my head nausea rose. I pushed that back as well. When I reached the other side of the river, I pulled a grenade from my webbing, yanked out the pin and tossed it onto the bridge.

Scrambling for cover, I landed on Gabriel just as the world lit up with a flash, bang and pieces of bridge.

"I should just toss the rest in the gully." I turned my left foot in experimental circles. The pain became more manageable.

"Brant said, no dead if we could avoid it." Gabriel released a series of rounds. "Ready to move to the tree line?"

"I've damaged my ankle."

"Can you manage?" he asked, looking at me, then my foot.

I grinned at him. "Race you?"

"Dickhead."

I toggled the pressel. "Zero, we're coming to you."

"We have you in our sights, Charlie team. Move out." Brant's voice remained calm and focused. She impressed me, few ruperts were that centred under live fire in the field.

As one unit, Gabriel and I changed magazines once more, rose, turned and raced towards the woods. Under normal circumstances I had no doubt Gabriel's leaner frame would give him more speed, but we both struggled up the steep incline. My ankle made every step hard work because my knee wanted to collapse under the pressure and Gabriel's physical endurance seemed to be nearing its end.

"We go this way," Angie said, pointing into a forest of pine trees with little foliage close to the ground.

"Can you give us a minute?" My protest fell on deaf ears, the others moved out. Gabriel and I took the rear, Lancing point with Angie giving instructions covered by Brant.

We could hear the commotion below as they began trying to cross the freezing, rushing water of Minook Creek.

Running through the woodland, uphill, over the soft collection of countless pine needles I struggled to keep going on my ankle. Gabriel struggled full stop and more than once, I grabbed his webbing and hauled him along with me.

When we reached another ridge line Brant stilled. Her hands were on her knees and she was taking deep, pine scented breaths that heaved in and out of her small body. "Fuck, that's a good way to shed a few pounds," she muttered.

Lancing, the youngest and fittest among us, dropped to the ground and took up position, resting his weapon's bipod stand on the soft ground. "No sign of pursuit, ma'am."

"If we lead them to Vulture's there is no guarantee we'll get off this mountain with the evidence. Maddox could call in the big guns whenever she likes." Gabriel managed this through gasps that sounded almost asthmatic.

"Why hasn't she already?" I asked.

"I've been thinking about that," Brant said, opting to sit for a moment. "She's showed up with two smallish, for American, teams to take Cabrera down. I don't think she has official sanction even from Jupiter Section to do this."

"So, if we take her out now then we'd be done with this fight?" Gabriel asked.

Brant squeezed his shoulder. "I don't know, soldier. We can hope."

He studied the terrain around us. "Angie, are there more rivers between us here and Vulture's?"

"No, sir."

"A straight run through the trees?" he asked.

"There's a natural meadow to cross. He uses it as a kill box. To get around it takes a long time and he's laid traps with flash bangs if you don't know where to go."

I watched Gabriel's mind work up a plan, his eyes bright and focused. "We tab in a straight line to the meadow, Nick and I will take up position at the lower tree line. We'll give covering fire from there as you cross the meadow with Angie. Vulture will know we are here after Nick's desire to blow things up decimated the bridge. Then we'll come after you."

"If something should happen to you?" Brant asked. "How do I get the information from Vulture?"

Code for – *even if you are dead, I need to continue the mission.*

"Tell him, the Angel sends hope for the future, that should make him

~ 154 ~

trust you enough to give you the intel." Gabriel knew this meant Brant had no reason to keep him alive. She could go for the intel without him.

"Thank you, Sergeant 1st Class Cabrera."

Gabriel and Brant shared a long and silent moment of communication. The final gesture between them, Gabriel nodding his assent, meaning he trusted Brant to protect us if possible and she would retrieve the intel Vulture possessed.

"I can see movement, Colonel," Lancing said from his place on the ground.

"Let's move out. Angie, you take point. The rest of us fan out, usual formation."

This meant we were too far apart for a sniper to set up and take us out as a group. It also meant Gabriel would be out of arm's reach. An unpleasant sensation. I took the left flank, leaving Gabriel and Brant in the middle, with Lancing on the right. We were 25 metres apart and moving at a jog through the trees. The slope down from the ridge made my ankle scream but it didn't last long, and we were soon going up a steady incline. The air around us smelt so clean it intoxicated me and the huge lungful's made my head buzz.

22

WE REACHED THE MEADOW WITH surprising ease and Gabriel gave the others final directions to give to Vulture in case they needed it.

"Ma'am," Lancing said. "I should remain with Wilde, and Cabrera should go with you. I am expendable and a damn fine shot."

"You are also stronger and fitter," Brant replied. "That means we might need you on the way out. Even if Cabrera makes it over the meadow we might be running out of here as fast as we came in, I'll need you for that, Lancing."

The young man held my gaze for a moment, possibly to seek a second opinion from an experienced soldier. "She's right."

"Understood." He turned away with Angie. They were going to travel over the meadow, the grass tall and full of flowers, in single file, twenty paces between them. The moment they left the cover of the trees Gabriel and I separated to wait for the enemy's approach. The tension between us a thin wire buzzing with anticipation of the coming attack and fear we might not make it out alive.

"I'm sorry you're involved with this, Nick," Gabriel said from behind a tree 10 metres from my position.

I glanced at him, but he kept his eye to his sight. "Don't be. I wouldn't be anywhere else."

"This isn't your job."

"Apparently, saving US Army personnel is my job now."

He finally turned those dark eyes in my direction at last and my heart warmed. "I am so grateful for you, Nick. Never forget that. Without you, none of this would have meaning. I want us to move forwards after this is done. I mean it when I say I love you."

I grinned at him, even as we heard the enemy's approach. "You asking me out on a date, Sergeant?"

He managed a soft chuckle. "I am."

"Accepted." I smiled as I pressed my eye to my scope and saw three men coming up the slope towards us through the shadowy trees. "I have multiple inbound targets," I murmured.

Five men and one woman were making their way towards us. They moved with skilled precision through the trees and created almost impossible targets for us and the moment we did fire they'd know our position in the gloom because the muzzle flash would be impossible to hide. Unless we could take out all five at once then we'd be just as pinned down as them with the open meadow at our backs. We could hold them, pin them to this point, but it would limit our options and our survival.

There would be no cavalry coming over the hill to save us. UK Armed Forces were not meant to operate on US soil.

"Choose your targets with care, Charlie Two," Gabriel said in my ear, using our comms unit.

"Roger that, Charlie One," I said.

We waited, remaining still, watching the shadows of the opposing force moving in silence, advancing on our position. I'd take my lead from Gabriel, his experience exceeding mine.

A flash of pain so bright and hard stole all but my hearing which caught the loud crack of gunfire from my right.

The rifle, pressed into my right shoulder, fell onto the lanyard around my neck and banged against the body armour over my belly.

The world tilted as wave after crashing wave of pain radiated, pooled and rolled back in on itself repeating the loop until I dropped to my knees. From my knees I listed to the right, the blood spilling from me dark, staining the pine needles – so many needles.

Training kicked in. "Contact, multiple shots fired." The report came from someone else, but it sounded just like my voice. Deep, rumbly, full of something alien.

"Nick!" Gabriel bellowed.

One of the enemy must have raced through the forest ahead of the others and come in on our position to the east. I heard more shots fired and a yell of pain some way off to my right. I struggled to keep my mouth shut so I didn't betray our location as Gabriel fired round after round into the on-coming soldiers.

He had to get out of here.

I looked at my right arm, it needed to pick up my weapon, not just hang there being useless. I didn't have time to fuck about, we had enemy inbound. Multiple targets, shots fired.

I tried to focus, my eyes and brain seemed to be giving me some strange information. There had never been a mess this dramatic. From the elbow down all I could see was torn flesh, stark white bone and blood. Lots of it, all over the pine needles and making a right mess of my uniform.

"Nick!"

I blinked and swayed, leaning into the tree trunk, the bark rough under my palm and cheek. I needed to stop my life gushing onto the ground. Being right-handed my brain tried to make my fingers move towards my webbing, but nothing happened. Weird.

"Think, Nick." Muttered words, thick and almost silent in the noise from the gun battle happening without me. Rounds punched into the tree trunk and I flinched away, trying to protect my vision.

Left-handed now, I fished into my webbing and drew out the tourniquet we all had as standard issue. Giving myself verbal instructions, I wrapped it above the wound. The pain became a distant hum for a few seconds. A feeling of being very drunk or really stoned hovered around me, through me and I wanted to giggle. I managed to figure out the thick band of the tourniquet and yanked.

The agony roared back, and I blacked out.

A shape bent over me and the loud retort of a weapon sounded very close to my head. Gabriel knelt at my side and fired in short, controlled bursts.

"Fuck, I'm in a shit state. You need to run," I managed, uncertain of what he heard over the sound of gunshots.

"Fuck you."

I forced my left hand under me and pressed myself back into the tree trunk. With waves of blackness accompanying the pain I managed to lever myself upright. It took so long, and this gun battle had to have been going on since the dawn of time.

I scrabbled at my weapon, tucked the barrel between my raised knees and loosed off a couple of random shots down the hill.

"Run. Maddox doesn't need me, she needs you. If she captures you all this is for nothing, Gabe. Run. Get help. Come fetch me."

Gabriel gazed at me for a long time. I could see every word he wanted to utter in those dark eyes, and I managed a nod in return, hoping he would read the same in mine.

"Stay alive, Nick. Do whatever she wants, just stay alive. I will find you." Gabriel rummaged through his webbing, tugging equipment out. He pulled the lid off something with his teeth and jammed it into my shoulder. I didn't feel a damned thing. More rummaging before turning and firing back into the trees.

"Fucking, fuck, hell," he cursed. He tugged at me and as the world began to soften around the edges, he pushed a thick wad of something into my guts – actually into my guts.

Shadows moved through the trees. They had us and they knew it. They weren't going to waste bullets.

"Run, Gabe. Run."

I saw his reluctance, but he also knew I was right, if Maddox caught him it would be game over. Without Gabriel we had no eye witness and Maddox could take her time hunting the others down to retrieve the information. Or she could simply blow the mountain up for all I knew. Either way, if Gabriel died the chances of Brant taking down Jupiter Section slimmed to almost nothing.

He rose, released a volley of fire and raced through the remaining trees towards the meadow. My job now was just to keep them from reaching the tree line so they couldn't go after him and pick him off as he crossed the open ground. My vision blurred. For some reason my jaw hurt and the pain on my right side made my left weak. I'd never manage to get to my feet but at least my ankle had shut the fuck up.

I didn't bother trying to use the sight on my weapon. I'd never curl up enough in my body armour to see through it and I wasn't a good shot from my left side.

The inevitability of my death struck me for the first time. This was it. This was my Butch Cassidy and Sundance moment. The final moments of my life. With each round I managed to squeeze out of my weapon I had flashes of memories.

The farm, my family. They made tears form and fall, further blurring my vision. I wished I'd taken the time to phone them on the journey to Alaska, but I hadn't wanted to worry them, and they knew that when I went dark, I was on a mission. I missed the farm. The rolling hills, the narrow and wooded combes, the tall oaks spreading their branches and the ash trees that had yet to catch the deadly disease wiping them out of England for the first time in history.

I could smell my mum's Easter biscuits over the stench of blood, burned gunpowder and sharp pine. The cinnamon made my mouth water and I could almost feel the biscuit crumble in my mouth covered in grains of sugar.

The thought crossed my mind that my sister would fancy Gabriel something fierce and I wondered if the man I loved would ever go to my home to talk to my family of my last moments in a forest in Alaska. I believed in what we were fighting to overcome but it seemed a terrible waste. I'd just fallen in love for the first time.

My finger clicked on the trigger, but nothing happened. I'd gone through thirty rounds and unless I could change magazines with only my left hand, I was fucked.

The chuckle burbling in my chest made that the funniest thought ever. As if changing magazines could save my life now.

A dark shape and terrific noise accompanied by a wind so fierce the trees bent swept overhead. "Shit, Maddox has cavalry." Men rushed towards me, but it was too late. They didn't have to waste their bullets on me.

I closed my eyes and walked into the image of Gabriel's beautiful body ready to welcome me home.

23

SOUND RETURNED FIRST. VOICES IN hushed whispers. All unfamiliar. Beeping, relentless beeping. A steady sound but irritating in its repetitiveness. I listened to the sound, blurring, sharpening, becoming loud, then fading.

With time. A lot of beeps later. Light caressed my eyelids. I became aware of more than just the light. Something held my jaws open and I couldn't swallow. My chest rose and fell but I didn't seem to be the one making it happen. As far as I could tell, my toes were all there, but I seemed to be missing control of some fingers. The light vanished again and so did the beeping.

Voices again drew me forwards and this time I managed to advance over the line, my eyes opened, and I swallowed. *Damn me, I'm alive.*

A slim shape moved around a small room in dim light and the smell of antiseptic and something unpleasant filtered through the oxygen being pumped up my nose.

"Well, hello, Nick. It's lovely to see you."

I blinked, the world a dizzying swaying place like a storm-tossed boat. A cool hand touched my forehead.

"You're safe, soldier. You just relax. The morphine will wear off and things will start to make a bit more sense. We've been waiting for you to come back. Almost made it last week but not quite. You needed a bit more time apparently."

Last week?

I struggled to push myself up the bed, so I could start asking questions, assert control over the situation, but I tilted to the right and the bed seemed to slip under me.

"Whoa, there. It'll take a while to get used to things. Just lie still and I'll find your mum. She's here most of the time, so I'm sure she's outside somewhere."

Mum? What the fuck was my mum doing here? What the fuck was I doing here? Where was here?

Panic flashed through me – Gabriel. Where was Gabriel? Colonel Brant? Lancing?

The machines changed their tempo but even as I tried to organise my limbs they wouldn't listen, and I slumped back into sleep.

I woke with a start. "Mum?"

"I'm here, love," came her soft West Country accent. Then her rough fingers on my head and holding my left hand.

I turned my head. "Mum."

She had tears in her hazel eyes. "Hello, son. It's good to see you. It's been a while." The soft light, some coming in from outside through the closed blinds, made her white hair a halo.

"Mum, what happened?" I realised my accent had thickened just by having her close.

"Oh, my poor boy. I have some news that the doctors thought should come from me. Your father had to stay on the farm, but your sister is here with me. Though she's proving difficult in London –"

"Mum, focus," I managed to cut her off. "I need water." I tried to lift my right arm.

"Here, son. I have a paper straw so we don't spill any. Best thing they did getting rid of those silly plastic jobbies –"

"Mum."

She pushed the straw into my mouth, and I took some sips then pushed the straw out and glared at her. For the first time in my life she looked small. Technically she was small. She just never gave me that impression, even when I hugged her with both arms wrapped tight around her slight shoulders.

"Nicky, son… You were shot."

"I know."

"Twice."

"No."

"Yes, son. One bullet went between the plates in your body armour – or that's what your colonel told me – lovely lady that one – then the other took your arm."

"I took a bullet in my arm?"

A tear rolled down her cheek and she squeezed my left hand so tight it hurt. "No, son. The bullet took your arm. By the time your friend, Gabriel, got back to you the damage was too great. He did what he could, he's well trained so they say, but it wasn't enough. He saved your life though. Before he had to run. He stopped the bleeding in your guts and your arm enough to keep you alive so they could air lift you out…"

She sniffed and fidgeted in her seat and I sensed her reluctance. It confused and upset me making anger bubble under the surface.

"I'm so sorry, son. They had to remove your right arm and you've had a lot of surgery on your liver, you lost a kidney – very careless, boy – and your colon is a bit of a mess, which of course your sister thinks is funny because they don't know if you'll be able to go normally again –"

"What?"

"A bag, son. But they say the coma has helped your body and mind heal so that's good. They think you'll be all back to normal in no time, you'll just have to watch what you eat and not drink too much in the future."

I stared at the light over my mum's shoulder and let the words float about my head held by fairies in the dust motes. I'd not 'lost' my arm. They'd taken it off because some fucker had shot me. Then other words made sense. Gabriel had saved my life.

"Gabriel?"

"Your colonel wanted to talk to you about him. I've called her, she's on her way. We're in St George's Hospital. She pulled some strings – well ropes really, I think – to get you here so we could be close. Friends on the board or something. Canny woman –"

"Mum, please."

She looked as if I'd pulled all the stuffing out of her. "Your friend, he's not here. He had to stay in the US, though she seems to think he'll be okay. He wasn't hurt. You were though. You were hurt. Your bloody heart stopped. You died on me, son."

Her tears were such a rare creature to see that I had no idea how to help or how to stop them. My mum was a farmer's wife, from farming stock, women don't come much tougher. I remembered her crying when the doctors told her about my scars as a boy, first time I saw her cry. Then the second, my passing out parade in the Marines. The third, my first deployment to a war zone. But none of those events had made this many tears.

"Mum, it's okay. I'm alive." I tried to reach over with my right arm and for the first time saw its termination point, swaddled in thick white bandages. "Fuck me."

It didn't look like it should be there, the shoulder joint huge, the biceps big as always, then nothing. I wanted to slide away, leaving it behind, and tried to move but the damn thing came with me.

"No, this isn't right, this isn't right." The panic spread. My heart rate doubled, the machines screaming in alarm. I had to run, had to escape the strange vision before me. The remains of my right arm wafted about in space. An alien creature sucking the life out of me. I twisted and turned but there was no way out, no escape, no options. This terrible new reality smacked me.

I heard Mum's voice but couldn't track the words, they made sense, no sense and no meaning. I couldn't hear the words.

People surrounded the bed and more words. Lots of hands, none of them my right one as I tried to push back with the stump I couldn't use or evade. Then darkness. Lovely, warm, safe, nothing.

The next time I woke up, which I had to do because the pain in my arm burned white hot, Brant sat next to my bedside looking tired.

"Good morning, Wilde."

"What happened?" The words were croaked, and Brant rose to give me water. After a few moments I managed the question again.

When she spoke, while I sipped, she delivered a well-rehearsed report. "We retrieved the data, the US cavalry arrived thanks to Sergeant Greenbrook, who despite being on desk duty in London still managed to pull our arses out of the fire, and Jupiter Section is being dismantled. Both here and in the US. There will be trials, most behind closed doors sadly, and we have had any number of resignations both in business, government and the military. You're a hero, Nick."

I didn't feel like one.

"Where's Gabe?"

"Sergeant Cabrera offered to remain with the US State Department to act as a witness. He'll then go into the Witness Protection Programme run by the US Marshals. He is key to many facets of the investigation so felt it expedient to remain under their custody."

Of course he would. Why would he be here? With me? He had a new life to look forwards to in the US with a clear name I should imagine. I ought to check that bit before allowing myself to wallow. My heart ached though, ached with a longing that twisted around the blank space of my right arm and squeezed hard.

"He's not being charged with anything?" I asked.

Brant shook her head. "Full immunity in exchange for his full co-operation. Your actions in Myanmar not only saved his life, it's saved the lives of countless people by ripping the heart out of a massive conspiracy that's been going on for years. They make the East India Company look like chicken feed."

I didn't want a history lesson, I wanted current affairs.

"What happened to me?" I lifted the inescapable lump on my right side.

Brant glanced at my arm and grew a little pale. "We reached the cabin with Gabriel. He was almost out of his mind in his desperation to return to you. Once Gabriel convinced Vulture we were friendlies, he handed over the intel, though I did offer to shoot the old turkey, and then the FBI turned up in a Black Hawk." Her expression turned speculative. "To be fair, I didn't know they could do that. After a lot of explaining, some violence on Gabriel's side, we managed to convince them to find you..."

She studied her hands. They were deeply freckled, and her short nails were clean where her fingers were clasped together. I realised I'd never do that again. Never clasp my fingers. Never scratch my balls with my right hand. Never hold a pen. How the hell was I going to learn to write? Or wipe my arse, presuming I wasn't going to have a bag forever? Can you blow your nose with one hand?

Panic squeezed my heart. My thoughts spun in a vortex of blood, trees, the *crack* and flash of firearms, Gabriel's screams and pain, so much pain. The scent of pine needles washed over me. A vision of lying in them, feeling their prickle on my neck as boots raced past my position and the heli overhead making the trees shower me in more needles. They filled my mouth and eyes as I fought to stay in the world with Gabriel. Despite the morphine he'd hit me with the pain circled me, its sharp teeth tearing at my broken flesh.

A firm hand gripped my wrist. "Breathe, Nick. Just breathe."

I stared into her kind and knowing brown eyes and did just that, in slow measured breaths. Lots of soldiers came home in several pieces. I'd live. I'd manage. Babies learned to write, to pee, to poo favouring one hand, how hard could it be if babies could do it?

Brant recognised my return to the room and gave me a soft smile before continuing with her story. "When you were found it was clear you were in a bad way, very bad. Gabriel and the FBI medic managed to stabilise you until the heli reached Anchorage, Juneau was just too far away, and we didn't have time to reach the capital. The specialists in Ottawa were the ones to take your arm. Sepsis was threatening by then and your organs were a mess. You've been in an induced coma for four weeks. The good news, and what we've all been worried about, is that you came round the minute you were taken off the heavy medication. It's a bit more complicated than that, but that's what I do know."

"Can I talk to Gabriel?" I asked.

Time for Brant to study her hands again. "No. They have him squirreled away. He's safe, we know that, but there's no outside contact until the trials have been settled. Then he'll go into Witness Protection…"

"And vanish off the face of the earth."

"Sadly, yes. I'm sorry, Nick. I never meant for this to happen."

"It's alright, Colonel. It's the job isn't it?"

"I'm afraid it is. The good news is that Gabriel gave me an overview of what's been happening to you in your regiment. Once we have your go ahead, Sergeant Stanton will be facing charges of bullying and harassment."

Christ, that seemed the least of my worries now. It wasn't like I could return to my job.

"Son," Brant said, drawing my attention back to her. "You need to go after Stanton. I'll be there, every step. You are working for Unit Twelve until you say otherwise, so I'm your CO now. We'll go after him together. I won't have people bullied or endangered because of prejudice in my army.

I'm far too proud of my country to let that happen. I just need you to help. Your behaviour in the field was exemplary, your bravery and sacrifice should be honoured by your Regiment brothers. I want to make sure that happens. The SAS and Paratroopers are our elite but that doesn't mean they get to step outside the law."

I nodded, which made the room roll in unpleasant ways. "Thank you, ma'am. I will take it under advisement."

"As for your arm. Get used to it, soldier, the faster the better, learn to use the prosthetic they'll give you. Work it like you did your training in firearms. You'll soon find recovering is worth the effort it'll cost."

I knew she wanted to inject some of the martial energy into me that we all use to help us survive life in the field or our first enemy contact. Sadly, I didn't feel it, not lying in a hospital bed missing my dominant hand. "Not like I can use a gun again."

"No, but you can fight just the same. You'll just need to find a new way to do it. You're a warrior, Nick, that spirit never dies unless you allow it."

"Any advice on a broken heart while you're here?" I couldn't control the tears any more. Everything seemed too raw, too new, too shattered. God, I missed Gabriel. I missed him so much I felt my heart wail at the loss.

"Time, son. Time and the love of those around you. I have to say, your family are amazing people."

I smiled. "I think my mum might have a small crush on you."

Brant laughed and I thought I saw colour stain her cheeks. "She's a good friend already. I hope to come and visit the farm one day."

Colonel Brant left soon after, tiredness seeping into me all too quickly. After everything I'd been through with Gabriel, our short time together seemed to stretch into eternity, but it had been barely two weeks. How could losing him hurt so much? I lay in my hospital bed and stared at the remains of my right arm. Brant was right of course, I had to fight to get my life back. Everything had changed in the flash of a single bullet.

I guessed I should be grateful it didn't hit my head.

ONE YEAR LATER

24

"DAMN IT." I DROPPED THE piece of bailing twine for the hundredth time and flexed my left hand in frustration.

"Nick?" Dad's voice came from outside the barn and I turned.

"In here, Dad. I'm at the lambing pen." I bent to pick up the errant twine.

"What are you doing?" His large bulk covered the light coming in from the half-closed barn door.

"I'm just trying to get this pen ready for Meg's puppies when they come." Meg was my sister's latest rescue and far too pregnant to go to the vet for sterilisation according to my mum and my sister, which meant more puppies at some point in the next week. Like the world needed more puppies. Trouble was, I might be able to blow up or shoot enemy combatants, but I couldn't drown puppies. Fearsome soldier that I am... was...

Forcing my thoughts to calm I focused on other things. Mental discipline had become my saviour over the months since I'd been returned to the farm. The summer had come in full and strong this year. The sheep were doing well on the grass and the cows were providing a lot of milk. The farm might break-even if we were careful, which meant minimising the stray animal intake – or at least trying to prevent it spreading to the rescue of horses at least.

"Here, let me get that. Knots were never your strong point." Dad took the twine and tied the metal fence to the wooden one in seconds. A job I'd probably been trying to do for at least fifteen minutes. I tried to stem the flow of anger at his help but without much success and it cost me dearly in patience and acceptance of my limitations.

The year had proved harder than any I'd endured before. The four-week coma had taken its toll and I'd struggled to come to terms with re-learning simple things and remembering current events – like when I'd last eaten a meal. Comas did funny things to the brain. Far harder, and not really a surprise, was my new disability. I had prosthetics fitted but none felt right or comfortable and having one that could work with my nerves was way outside our financial capabilities. The army could only give me so much, the rest I'd have to find myself. My specialist in Bristol told me that due to the nerve damage remaining in the limb they would need to take more off the stump to find enough nerves to join to the hardware.

I couldn't face it.

I couldn't face any of it.

I couldn't look in the mirror. I couldn't buy clothes. I couldn't talk about my feelings in the therapy sessions I attended so I didn't worry my parents. Simon, the therapist, said it meant I was wasting money but just getting off the farm to go for a walk and talking to him helped ease some of my nightmares, because apparently that was a thing for me now as well. Nightmares, daymares, absences, panic attacks, shock at loud noises – the whole nine yards.

"Your mum rang by the way. She and Jessie are on their way back from the station." Dad moved around the barn, trying to engage me. I could feel his anxiety and I hated myself just a little more.

"Good," I offered as a sacrifice to his needs. "They'll be back before dark. That's good. Did they enjoy their shopping trip in Bristol?" They'd been acting like a couple of schoolgirls for days so they were up to something. I just hoped I wouldn't have to be attending my sister's wedding to her latest walking disaster. I also had to hope they didn't spend too much.

"Seemed happy enough. Listen, son, I need to talk to you about something and it's a good idea to do it before they get back." He leaned against the old horsebox and folded his arms over his large chest. We were both big men but somewhere along the line I'd become taller, broader, far more dangerous, though I wished I could cross my arms as well. Instead I shoved my left hand into the pocket of my faded fatigues. It made me feel about sixteen again, so I shifted and stood straight as if speaking to my superior officer.

"Okay."

He eyed my stance, but I refused to move so he sighed and tried to relax. "I'm worried, Nick."

"I'm fine. Well, I'm as fine as I can be."

"It's not about your arm, son. We know how that's working out... and it is working out. You can drive the tractor, you've the automatic car, we're finding ways of making the gates work more easily. It's coming together, it's just..."

"What, Dad?"

He shuffled his feet and muttered, "I don't know why your mother won't talk to you about this stuff – it shouldn't be me."

Colour me a rainbow was Dad trying to discuss romance with me? The blush on his rough cheeks made it a possibility.

"Dad, I'm fine. I like being single. It suits me while I'm adjusting and finding gay men interested in someone like me is a bit on the impossible side right now."

"We know you miss your American –"

"Don't bring Gabriel into this, I don't want to talk about him."

"Son –"

"No, Dad. I mean it. I'm okay as I am."

I watched my father struggle with the instructions he had given himself about how to parent his adult, but broken, boy. "It's been a year and no word, Nick. It's time to move on and you need more than this place after what you've been through, what you're going through still. I don't believe all gay men want some picture-perfect man. You have such a good heart, Nicky, any guy would be lucky to have you."

I felt my teeth crack. "Finished, Dad?"

He looked flustered. "Well..."

"Good. You've said your piece. I've listened like a good boy, now you can tell Mum and Jessie that I'm fine."

Dad huffed at my sharp tone and picked at the rust on the old plough. "It wasn't their idea. They've got a bee in their bonnets about something else." He nodded though, making it clear he'd done his duty. I seemed to remember our conversation about safe sex had gone much the same. The light from the barn door coloured his short grey hair with flashes of gold making it look like it did twenty years before. "Alright. I've done my part.

When you're ready, come in for supper. We have a good ham salad and some nice fresh bread your mum made."

"Sure, I'll be in, in a minute." I watched him leave the barn and felt angry with myself for not appreciating him more. He just wanted to help his son find a bit of the happiness he had, a lifelong partnership of equals, but I couldn't quite let him or anyone else fix my broken heart.

How the hell could I convince them to drop this? I couldn't stop thinking about Gabriel. Every moment of every fucking day he stood beside me. How many imaginary conversations had I had with the memory of him over the last year? We'd even had full scale arguments as I'd trudged up the hills and down into the combes looking for sheep in the snow. Wrestling them out of drifts in November when a surprise storm hit the South West hadn't been fun but that's when I'd begun to understand I didn't have to use two hands to be of use on the farm. He'd been with me then and each step I took in the world, both metaphorically and literally, the memory of him kept me company.

We'd never had a goodbye. Well, he had according to Colonel Brant, but I hadn't. He'd wept over my broken body even as the FBI took him into custody. It felt like an untold story. A void inside me that couldn't heal. He was out there, somewhere in the world, and I'd never see him, but I felt him, all the fucking time – reaching out to me.

The physical therapy, the farm, the family, it just distracted me from my time with him. Time I valued more and more. I knew it couldn't be healthy, but I loved him, and we had no ending. I couldn't let go.

Then the self-doubt took control some days and I fought to push him away. I'd go into town, a small place on the edge of Somerset that hadn't changed much in centuries, or that's how it felt to me, and have a drink with 'friends'. People I'd gone to school with who had never moved away or moved and returned with children and partners. People who had some success in the world and others who had failed – like me. Those nights I'd drink too much and tell war stories from my time in the Marines. I never spoke about the SAS, I didn't want to share that part of my life, but some of them knew because of Jessie.

My little sister. The bolt of lightning in my life that I often needed to shock me from the depths of my self-created slurry pit of misery and loneliness. She even tried to set me up with a Grinder profile. A pitiful disappointment on all counts. I'd almost killed her when I found out, then wept in my room when no one responded to me.

The Regiment had forgotten me almost as soon as I touched base with the Head Shed at Credenhill. I'd been pensioned off, but things became more complicated when Brant insisted I make a formal complaint against Sergeant Stanton for harassment and bullying. They'd closed ranks. Right up until Luke Sinclair, Jacob Hayes, Sam Locke and Macalister joined ranks behind me and forced the matter. They were good men and I'd met up with them more than once over the months.

Stanton ended up facing charges on all counts and was looking at a full court-martial. Until he shot himself.

Brant rang me in the middle of the night to tell me. His son had come out as gay and Stanton hospitalised the fourteen-year-old the beating was so bad. Fourteen years old against a man with twenty years in the Regiment. Stanton could have killed him.

I attended the man's funeral.

It was a horrible affair.

The one blessing to come out of the entire sordid mess turned out to be my friendship with Stanton's son, Rex. With his mother's blessing we talked once a week, shooting the shit and being 'gay'. Jessie or Rex's mum often sat in on the conversations so nothing could be misconstrued but it felt good giving the lad a bit of support as he came out to the world. I just wanted to keep him safe and it was clear he was not going to become a soldier. More likely a drag queen by the looks of his latest attempts at finding his Gay Pride home.

Each day though moved me further away from Gabriel. Further away from my life as a soldier. Further away from the future I wished for on every rainbow and shooting star to cross my path as I wandered the farm.

The past year had taken its toll, I couldn't deny that, but perhaps Dad had a point. Maybe I did need to move on, not romantically, there wasn't a man in the world who'd want an ugly one armed ex-soldier who lived on a farm in the middle of nowhere, but I needed to lay Gabriel's ghost to rest. My sister could come up with a way I could say goodbye to him. Goodbye to the dreams I'd indulged in over the few days we'd been together, wrapped up in each other trying to survive. Some kind of ceremony to rid a foolish romantic of his wishes... his hope.

I heard Mum's car pull up in the yard and sighed. It had grown late in the afternoon and I'd been in the barn for hours, leaving Dad with the jobs on the farm. The time hadn't been wasted, I looked around and realised I'd been tidying and cleaning without thinking about it – we now had a very well organised barn, almost military style organised. I knocked the dust off my hand by rubbing it against my thigh.

Voices came from Mum and Dad before the barn door opened. "Alright, I'm sorry I forgot lunch, I'll come in now," I yelled. I'd been sat on a small hay bale wool gathering my memories, so I stood and picked it up in one hand, the twine stretching and the bale threatening to collapse. I started to turn, daring the stupid thing to fall apart before I moved it to the whelping pen for the dog.

25

"HELLO, ENGLISH."

I put the bale down and stopped turning.

"Hello."

"You're not going to let me look at you?"

Tears pricked my eyes. "If I do you might vanish. Not sure I can deal with that. You have an annoying habit of vanishing on me."

"Sorry. I never wanted to leave you. It wasn't my choice."

"I know."

Footsteps. Heat at my back. Breathing filling the barn which now seemed so small. "Look at me."

"I've heard your voice before, and you've not been there." Was I mad? Had I finally cracked? I sounded petulant and angry. Could you be petulant and angry with a hallucination? My entire body vibrated with the need to turn but my soul couldn't allow my legs that privilege because what if they were wrong? What if they led us to our downfall?

"I'm here now, Nick."

My breathing hitched as I caught a scent in my nose and my heart raced to keep up with my thoughts.

"How are you here?"

"Technically your mum and sister picked me up from Bristol."

That American accent sounded so strange on the farm. It never sounded strange out in the world we'd once shared. Here it sounded so dangerously like the future.

"Turn around, Nick."

I bowed my head. "I'm not the same man." My stump moved. The shirt I wore filthy with dust and sweat, the knot on the sleeve flapping.

Breath whispered over my neck. "To me you are. I'm not going anywhere, Nick." Strong arms wrapped around my waist and chest, under my stump. I heard my mum and sister in the doorway, Mum trying to get Jessie to leave.

"Gabriel?"

"Unless you know any other stray Americans who can find this farm," he murmured, and a soft kiss landed on that magic spot on my neck.

I turned at last.

I looked into the darkest eyes I'd ever seen. I cupped his jaw, the reality of his presence beginning to be real, dark stubble with white flecks rubbed my palm. His black hair had grown out even more and tumbled in dark curls around his beautiful face. Silver coloured his temples and just added to the effect.

"I want to wrap both arms around you," I whispered.

Tears filled his eyes. "You are. I can feel them both, Nick. Hold me tight. Never let go." He pulled me with some aggression tight to his body and buried his face in my neck.

This has to be a dream. A cruel dream. One born of temptation and desperation.

His scent filled my lungs on every inhale and mixed with the fresh summer hay stored in the barn. "Gabriel…"

He moved enough to press a kiss against my lips, a starving man reaching for salvation, and I allowed him to slip inside my body. The tentative lick of pleasure acted like petrol, the fire inside me ignited in such a rush I twisted him around and pushed him into the side of the horse box. He grunted at the pressure and slid his strong thigh between mine. Within seconds we were rutting, animalistic noises filling the large space, too drunk on each other in that moment to consider anything other than reclaiming what had been denied for so long.

Gabriel pushed my shirt up and I reached for his buttons without thinking, my right arm moving to remove his clothing…

The action brought me back to awareness with a jolt so hard and terrible I ripped from his grasp.

"Nick, don't…" He grabbed at my shoulder.

"Stop." The barked command stilled us both. Heavy breaths and pounding hearts slowed. I rubbed my hand through my sweaty short hair, the buzz cut making my hard features worse.

"Stop." Now a whisper and full of agony. It welled up inside me, drowning the flames of desire.

A gentle hand on my back. "Sorry. I've been waiting so long to see you. I didn't think through how this might feel for you. I'll give you some space."

"Take one step away from me, Gabriel Cabrera and I might be forced to nail your feet to the floor. Just give me a minute to catch up."

He laughed. "You can have all the minutes you need, Nick."

I squared my shoulders and turned to look into the face of my angel. How could this really be happening to me? I needed to think. "Want to go for a walk? I need a walk. Walk and talk."

"I can walk. I've been travelling for hours, it's a long way from Arizona." He held out his hand and I reached for him.

When we left the barn, my family stood around the car, my mum trying vainly not to cry happy tears and my sister grinning like a wolf with a chew toy.

"We're going for a walk. We'll be back for supper. You can all stop being weird," I told them. My dad, who obviously hadn't been in on the conspiracy, grabbed both women and dragged them back to the farmhouse among their protests.

"That's a beautiful home," Gabriel said, casting an eye over the family farmhouse.

I looked at our nest and smiled. "It is. Built in 1650 by the local landowner. A minor baron or something." Oh, this I could do, I could talk about the farm, it made all this seem more normal. The late afternoon sun warmed the golden stones and the wisteria tangled with my mother's roses. The windows were leaded and there were thick honey coloured lintels. It might be cold in the winter with endless draughts, but it did look stunning in the sunlight.

We strolled through the farmyard, hands clasped and in silence, while I tried to make sense of all the words tumbling through me. I settled for keeping it simple for a bit. "How are you?"

He pulled my hand to his chest and kissed my knuckles. "It's been a long and lonely year if that's what you're asking. My only solace all year has been the knowledge I'd reach you eventually. Some way, somehow, we'd find each other again."

Okay, simple questions weren't going to work. Gabriel had too much to say, I could see it ready to spill out of him.

"Talk."

He nodded. "I'm sorry I left you. They didn't give me much of a choice. I wanted to explain why we had to separate when you woke but time was running out because they couldn't hold Maddox forever without a sworn statement. I had to vanish into the system. I've been giving testimony for the best part of a year. Everything – all of it – has come out behind closed doors. It can't be made public for obvious reasons. If the public knew how close the US Government came to losing control it would cause an economic and social collapse."

"Where is Maddox?"

"On death row along with several other high-ranking officials."

"Fuck, you lot don't mess about."

"It was treason. Colonel Brant and her team are rounding up others. Cleaning house in SIS and the UK Government."

"Okay, so you had to leave."

"I promised I'd come back. I swear to you. I promised I'd find you." Gabriel hugged my hand again which made opening the gate impossible. I tugged my hand free, snagged the gate open and we walked through but he wasn't going to let me go easily and reclaimed his prize. The summer grass and flowers were still damp from the rain the night before but the glow of nature at her best made everything around me seem cinematic.

"But how are you here?" I asked. We strode up the hill, through another gate and into the top field so we could walk towards the largest woodland on the land. I'd kept my promise to the trees I'd blown up in Myanmar – I'd planted an orchard of rare and ancient breeds of apple trees.

"I couldn't have any contact with the outside world. They had to keep me in lockdown, mostly so no one from Jupiter Section could find me and kill me, it meant I couldn't reach out. I didn't want to endanger you, or your family and it seemed the best course of action. It's the only reason I agreed to go with them – if they, being the CIA, Homeland Security and the FBI, promised to leave you out of all of it. Once I gave them everything they wanted, they continued to keep me locked up safe, but I managed to reach out to Colonel Brant through her Sergeant Lydia Greenbrook. Apparently, she'd been keeping an eye on things in case I needed the British contingent to dig us out of the shit again."

"Sounds about right."

He grunted. "More than you know. Lydia managed to hack into your sister's email account, and I reached out. I've been emailing her and your mom for a few weeks."

"Bastards, they never said."

"We weren't sure when I could get here. Or if I could escape WITSEC. Your mom said it wouldn't be wise to build your hopes up just in case I didn't manage to reach the UK unimpeded."

Sharp woman my mother. I would have been on a plane in an instant and made the world a more complicated place for Gabriel. We walked into the cool woodland, the old trees reaching out to shelter us from the summer sun. It smelt safe and familiar. We avoided the puddles and followed the path to a clearing I loved.

"Now you're here." I liked to state the blindingly obvious sometimes, just for kicks.

"Now I'm here and if you'll have me, it can be for as long as you want." He glanced at me. The uncertainty in his dark eyes was at odds with his natural confidence now he'd recovered physically from his time in prison.

I pulled him down to the shorter grass and we sat.

"Wow, where are we?" he asked taking in his surroundings for the first time.

"My favourite place on the farm," I said. "Over there," I pointed to our right with my left hand, "is the slag heap of the old quarry. They say it was Roman originally. Then medieval. Lastly, the Victorians used it. There are still the remains of houses down there at the bottom of the quarry. Down here," I pointed into the deep hole we sat near, "is the quarry itself. It's said to be bottomless. I've certainly never found the bottom."

"Look at the colour." He stared over the edge of the very sharp cliff face into the small pond or lake. Trees, shrubs and flowers clung to the sides surrounding the pool and the only way into and out of the deep hole was a path fraught with dangers. The pool itself reflected back a deep blue, which made it appear inviting – it wasn't. Cold didn't begin to describe it because it never received much light, the 30 metre cliffs surrounding its 10-metre diameter wet centre, shielded the water from the warmth of the sun all year round.

I breathed in the fresh air and looked out over the rolling hills, the trees, the farmland and smattering of houses. The scene so familiar but now blessed by company I'd never thought would be here, beside me. I could see the effect on Gabriel. Shoulders dropping, face relaxing, breathing deeper than before and the sunlight creating a halo around his dark hair revealing shades of red I'd never seen before. He wore it longer even than when I'd found him in Myanmar. I knew those soft curls would tangle in my fingers if I reached up to caress them, but the intimate gesture felt like a step too far right now.

"I can see why you wanted to come home," he murmured. "It's beautiful here."

I laughed at his wonder. "Not so lovely when we get a wet summer or endless rain for weeks during the winter."

He closed his eyes and it gave me the opportunity to see all the small changes in him since we'd been apart. In Myanmar and the madness that followed, Gabriel, though still far out of my league, looked like a hollowed-out version of the man before me. From hunger, dehydration, extreme fatigue and stress for three months, I'd not known him at his best. Now however, after US Army medical care, a year of good food and from what I could see under the long-sleeved shirt, the workouts he'd been doing, he looked magnificent.

"Why are you here?" I hadn't meant for the question to escape.

He opened his dark eyes and fixed them on me. "Still doubting me? I travelled halfway around the world just to sit in this magical place with you and yet you still doubt me." He didn't sound pissed off, he sounded amused.

My heart ached but I had to admit – I did doubt him. I didn't bother to say anything, he could read me well enough already. "I'm sorry."

With some reluctance, as if the scenery would vanish if he didn't watch it, he turned back to face me by crossing his legs. He must be doing yoga; I couldn't match that movement.

"Nick, I am here *for* you. I am here *because* of you. I am here because I have thought about you every day for the past," he did some maths in his head, "384 days." He took hold of my hand. "I knew you were going to lose your arm when I left. I know you must have terrible scarring over your belly and back from the gunshot in your guts. I know you don't think you are beautiful enough, clever enough, funny enough or whatever other shit is going on in your head, but I'm telling you right now – I don't want to be anywhere else in the world. I don't want to be with anyone else and I haven't been with anyone else."

I struggled to meet his gaze.

"Hey, look at me, soldier."

I managed to lift my eyes to his and tried a smile.

He frowned. "I'm serious, English. I'm in love with you. I've done all this so I could come home to you." Now he sounded pissed off with me.

The words struck deep and true, but I didn't know what to do with them.

His frown turned into a scowl. "Unless you've met someone else? I mean, I asked your mum and she said no but I guess she could have been wrong." He dropped my hand. "I wouldn't blame you; I'd just ask you to give me a chance to prove I'm the one, not whoever you have met since moving back here…"

I chuckled.

A flash of total indignation marred his handsome face. "Are you laughing at my declaration of love?"

To be honest it was funny. I nodded. "Kind of, yes."

He twisted to move away from me.

"Don't, Gabe, I'm sorry. I'm not laughing at you – I'm laughing at how fucking weird this is. I feel like I'm in some film of my life, not my actual life. I've yearned for you every fucking day. I've poured so many tears onto this land I'm sure I'm the one irrigating it not the rain. I've imagined this moment a thousand ways and cursed myself for being such a fool. I'm struggling to believe this is real. I wanted you the moment I wrapped my arm around your waist to lift you from that hook in the ceiling. I loved you the moment I watched you dance in the monsoon rain, trying to wash the filth off your beautiful body. I want to worship every inch of you and there are many more inches now than before. What did you do? Spend every day in a gym with a big sweaty trainer?"

The scowl had softened while I'd been talking and he finished up with a soft and goofy smile, looking up at me through dark lashes.

"So, you're happy I'm here? You aren't sleeping with anyone else?" he asked.

I laughed. "How could I? Trust me the pickings in Somerset aren't great and being a one-armed bandit don't help any. Even if I could look at another man why would they want me? It's why I'm surprised you're here."

He picked a daisy from the stubby rabbit shorn grass and tucked it behind my ear. "So, no other men have been on my territory?"

"No other men have been anywhere near your territory."

"And you've been thinking about what you'd like to do to me?" The flash of mischief in his eyes made me wary.

"Yes, though jacking off with my left hand is still weird." Truth be told I'd struggled to masturbate at all because it left me feeling more depressed than relieved.

He moved onto his knees and pushed me back on the grass. I went without protest.

"Are we going to be disturbed up here?" he asked.

"Possibly by walkers but it's a Tuesday afternoon not the weekend so it's unlikely I guess."

He moved over me and began unpopping my shirt. I didn't like small buttons these days. My breath hissed through my teeth when his fingers grazed the skin now showing. He traced delicate lines along the scars through the tangle of hair and I fought the need to drag him down and smother him in my weight, scent, kisses and more.

Those dark eyes were serious now and I reached up to push back the tangle of curls. "You alright?"

He looked into me and I gasped. No barriers were in that gaze. I peered into the black depths of his eyes and touched parts of Gabriel I doubted he'd ever shown anyone. "I had a lot of therapy in the States," he whispered. "I'll share some of it with you over time, Nick, but I needed to square away the pain of the torture and what it did to me."

"I know, babe. Whatever you need from me, however long it takes."

"I want to be inside you. I want to make love to you."

I could see the truth of his statement.

"I want that to."

"I need more time, but I want you to make love to me as well. I want to give you everything, Nick."

My expression softened in a way I hadn't felt in a year and I continued to play with a stray curl. "One step at a time, beautiful."

He smiled and I brushed my thumb over his soft lips and the prickle of hair. The rest of the buttons on my shirt came free and he ran his hand over my chest and down my belly, not looking, just feeling as we swam deeper, ever deeper, into each other. The intensity grew and I found it hard to breathe until I relaxed the bonds holding my broken heart together and let go. He watched it happen and the smile he gave in return to my surrender warmed the loneliest parts of my soul.

In return for my surrender he dipped and took possession of my lips. I dragged his weight over my hips and as the kiss grew, we rocked together, not wanting to release our trapped cocks, just needing to explore mouths, jaws, throats. I pulled his shirt off at last and marvelled at the scarred but sculpted body. Rolling him onto his back I kissed down his chest, over his collarbones, licked and sucked his nipples, the inside of his elbow and growled at his heavy musky scent smothering me.

The sun warmed my back. The light softened our surroundings into a hazy summer late afternoon. The birds filled the air with twitters and song, the crows called overhead and a buzzard screamed his joy from the sky. We were desperate in our need and locked together. My balls ached with the desire to fulfil our union.

"We should go home."

"I've booked a hotel room in town," he said under me as dazed as I was. "I didn't know if you wanted me to stay at the farm."

"You'll be lucky if I ever let you leave it again. You're staying at the farm." I found without an elbow on my right side I couldn't lean over him and touch him easily. I didn't want to drag my stump down that perfect torso. He'd not pushed my shirt off my arms, just opened it so our skin to skin contact would send endless shivers over our flesh.

He brushed a hand over my right shoulder and gripped it. "Can I see the arm while we are here? I need to see how I failed you before we go any further with this."

I drew back, shaking off the lustful haze. "Failed me?"

Gabriel nodded. "I hope this is the last confession I need to make to you. I didn't check our surroundings properly when we stopped moving and agreed to take up the rearguard position. I didn't do a full sweep. I didn't see the shooter coming on our flank. I killed him but not until after he'd done this." He squeezed my shoulder.

"Neither did I."

"But –"

I gripped his hair in my left fist and tightened it until he met my eyes. "Listen to me. This was not your fault. Shit happens. We were exhausted. You were – amazing. There is no other way to describe what you did to survive prison, our escape, our rescue, then a run through Alaska. What you did is worthy of a legend being told. You saved my life. No other soldier could have helped me make it alive to a hospital. Gabe, I have never blamed you. Not once."

"I have."

"Don't. And if you need to look at my arm here, then do it."

That soulful gaze didn't waver for a moment as he pushed the shirt off my shoulder and down the stump. The breeze tickled over the bits of me that weren't numb and other bits of me that were hypersensitive. Those black eyes finally saw my shoulder and down to the empty space. They took in the mess and they didn't flinch.

"Can I touch?"

I nodded, captivated by his gentle exploration. He lifted his head off the ground and lay a tender kiss just above the horror story of scars that ended in the absence of my arm.

"Tell me if I hurt you." The words were as quiet and as full of meaning as a flower opening its petals to the sun.

I nodded. My only option. His care struck me dumb. I didn't let the doctors and nurses near it these days. I'd never allowed my mother to touch it but as he rolled me onto my back and lay over my chest, he stole my stalwart courage with his gentle strokes and tender kisses. They weren't lustful. They were healing. Like a parent kissing a sore knee or scuffed palms. He nosed and rubbed his beard over the pink and puckered scars making me laugh, which made him chuckle, the rumble setting off another round of giggles from me. The damn thing was ticklish, and I'd never known.

Gabriel laughed as I squirmed under him, none too anxious to escape his attentions. It didn't make me horny in the least, but it did feel… well, *nice*, to have someone else touch it. Somehow it made it less *it* and more *me* for the first time since I'd woken up in that hospital bed.

The sun began to slide towards the hilly horizon and Gabriel yawned. "Fuck, sorry, jetlag. I'm all over the place."

"Come on, the quarry isn't going anywhere, we'll explore the farm tomorrow and every day after that."

We rose from the warm ground and made our way back to the farmhouse, fingers entwined, sharing bits of the last year with each other. When we reached home the family were waiting in the kitchen with a wonderful summer salad laid out everywhere. We all sat and began to tuck into the food. Gabriel took my family's teasing in good stead until my sister said, "How could you fall for an ugly mug like that?"

He grew still and I watched his eyes flash with sudden rage. "Your brother is the most beautiful man I've ever met. I love him. Please, understand this, Jessie, there will be no more teasing like that in my presence."

"Oh," mum gasped from the end of the table. "That's the loveliest thing anyone has ever said about my boy, except me."

"Mum…" I protested.

My sister's eyes had widened, and she nodded her approval. "Fair enough. Does this mean I can't call him stumpy anymore?"

"Jessica." A sharp retort from my father.

I laughed.

"It very much means you can't call him that anymore," Gabriel said, removing the righteous anger from his voice and unable to help a small chuckle.

Jessica didn't seem fazed at all. I had no doubt she'd find other ways to wind me up, it's what little sisters are for, after all.

With dinner finished I showed Gabriel up to the bedroom and bathroom. He looked around my room in silence for a bit, so I left him to explore while I returned to washing up duties. Jessie and Dad were on milking tonight which meant I'd be doing the morning run, but the army had instilled a love of the quiet in the world for early mornings, so I didn't mind.

Mum stood at the sink while I cleared the table and started wiping down surfaces before drying up. We worked in silence for a bit before she said, "Sorry I didn't tell you he was coming."

"Bad mother of the year award." I poked her.

She narrowed her eyes at me, and I hugged her to me, kissing her crown. "You did amazing. Thank you."

"You know your room isn't soundproofed, right?"

I laughed. "Yeah, I know, Mum, thanks for that."

"Just saying. Not sure how much I want to know about my son's love life."

"I'm fairly sure Gabriel doesn't want you to know anything about our sex life."

"He really does love you, though, Nicky. And he's *so* pretty."

"I did tell you and yes, he really does seem to love me."

She bumped against me. "Don't sound surprised, Nicky, you deserve it."

"Hope so."

We finished up and I showered in the cloakroom downstairs. I'd had two men stay at the farmhouse over the years but never had sex in the house. It felt odd, walking up those old stairs, to go to my lover in my old room, to find him on my bed. At least I hoped that's where he was waiting for me.

I reached for the top of the steps, my hand polishing the newel post for a moment as countless people had over the centuries, so it shone deep and smooth, before I walked to my room. I knocked lightly on the door, didn't hear anything but stepped inside. Gabriel lay on his back, naked, on my large bed and deep in sleep. I leaned against the doorway for a moment, hand tucked into my pocket and stared at him in wonder.

The scarring had faded to almost nothing in most places over his ample genitals and thighs, the hair grown back where it had been burned away. As thick and dark as the hair on his head, but coarser. I wanted to bury my nose in his scent. Instead, I pulled off my clothes in silence and found a blanket to drape over him to keep the chill off before I lay down next to him.

Within moments he mumbled, rolled and reached over the space between us. Gabriel tucked himself into my side and I found his deep breathing the best of narcotics. I fell deeply asleep.

26

MOONLIGHT, THE SOFTEST OF SILVER, filtered through the leaves of the wisteria outside my bedroom window and cast mercurial shadows over Gabriel's angelic features. I woke up because he drifted on a raft in dreams made of sound and movement. I needed to calm him, bring him safely back to shore.

He sighed and I nuzzled his neck.

"Jetlag sucks," he mumbled.

"It's zero-one-hundred-hours."

"Not getting up time then?"

"Not even for a farmer," I told him, stroking down his ribs.

"I've a hard-on suitable for knocking in nails down here." He sounded like he was complaining.

"Need some help with it?" Rather than nuzzle, I bit. We were both biters, I remembered the ship as we learned each other's bodies, floating away from danger – only to find more. My stump ached for a moment, but I pushed back against the phantom pain.

Gabriel shuddered and stretched his long lean body, pressing his hips back. I wore a loose-fitting pair of summer weight pyjamas that didn't control my cock at all. When I thrust against his hard backside I groaned, and he arched his spine wanting more.

"Feels so good to be in your arms."

"Arm," I qualified.

"I still feel both, Nick. I swear I do." He rolled over and we were nose to nose. His eyes were as dark and bottomless as the quarry lake. Stray shafts of silver light made the silver in his black curls glint.

I reached up and traced his jaw and brow with my fingertips, exploring the landscape of this dream creature in my bed. "The doctors don't like it when I tell them the arm is still there."

"Then they don't understand, I feel it because I feel safe with you. It's like you, your energy, have kept me safe all these long months I've been alone. Every step I've taken, Nick, you've been there making me fight so I could come home to you."

"Oof, don't say things like that or I'll be crying like a baby." I tried to chuckle, but my voice betrayed me, the rumbling bass even thicker than usual.

"I'm going to tell you how beautiful you are every day we are together, just so you learn to love yourself a little more," he said, pulling the end of my nose. I kissed his fingertips.

He leaned in and we kissed. Warmth, soft lips, exploring tongues and teeth. Nips and licks, sighs and needy moans. We were tangled together, Gabriel's strong thigh between my legs so I could rub against him, the heads of our eager cocks touching, bouncing, almost jousting together making us whimper and hiss. Maybe we needed more, maybe we didn't, in that moment we just wanted to be with each other and know we wouldn't be parting. We rubbed noses, bumped foreheads and whispered words of love.

His fingers tangled with mine and the strength in them filled me with comfort. The few times in my life I'd held a woman's hand, mostly those belonging to my relatives, they were small, soft and even my sister's hands were weak in comparison. This strong grip held me firm in a world I'd felt shifting around me too much over the last year. Losing the army. Losing my arm. The external threat of debt to the farm hanging over me... It all rocked me, buffeted me in a storm I would never be able to change or control. Having this strong grip on my good arm – there weren't words beautiful enough to describe the simple joy of it.

I tended to appreciate things like hands and arms now I was missing one.

Gabriel's grip tightened further for a moment as he closed his eyes and rubbed hard into my taut belly, gaining pleasure from the friction. I took the opportunity to bite his throat, grabbing the Adam's apple between my teeth. The strangled whimper and stillness it induced in his body reminded me of a kitten being held by its mother. His breath came in short bursts and it made me growl.

"Nick..."

I liked that; my name tinged with a begging need for more, but he didn't quite understand what the 'more' was he wanted. I licked the area I'd bitten, my tongue rasping on the stubble. He drew his hand away from mine and his fingers danced over my flank and back, petal light and tender as he tried to focus on me again.

"What's happening to me?" he whispered.

"We're making love, baby," I murmured. "We're safe, so safe. No bad guys here, no monsters under the bed and it's not a dream."

He kissed me again, this time with more urgency. Hungry and desperate he wanted more and rolled me onto my back to get it. I lay under him, happy to feel his weight press me into my bed. My left hand slid down his back, under the sleep pants he wore and clutched his backside.

"You are too dressed," he decided. In seconds he'd wriggled out of the bedding and removed my clothing in one swift yank.

He knelt between my ankles and looked at me. "I want to fuck you. I want to be inside you." The moonlight shone on his warm skin. The dips and planes of his muscled body kissed by light and shadow. I half expected wings to burst from his back, as they would for his namesake. He looked so perfect in his masculinity. The scars littering his face and body were invisible in the subtle shades of silvered colour dancing through my bedroom window. Ageless, timeless, unbowed by life and its bitter experiences, he looked – no, he was – divine.

I felt breathless and more than a little scared by the immense weight of emotion rising ever higher through my belly and into my chest. My immediate sexual desire waned under the onslaught of deeper passions. "God, I love you so much, Gabriel."

No other words were uttered with such devotion, such reverence. I wanted to weep. I wanted to kiss every part of his body and murmur benedictions over them. I wanted to rip open my chest and keep him inside me, safe, and forever.

As if hearing my thoughts, he bowed his head, lifted my right foot and brought it to his lips. He kissed the soft arch, then the top. He moved to kiss the inside of my ankle before doing it again on the other side. He rubbed his prickly jaw up the hairy, large calf muscle and kissed the inside of my knee, drawing a hiss from me. A lick at the back of my knee had me stifling a bark of laughter. He grinned, devilment making his eyes moon bright.

Hooking both legs over his shoulders he preceded to torture me by attacking my knees. We were more than capable of hurting each other if we used any strength to stop the game but neither of us did; we just started to fight like schoolboys. More laughter ensued as I tried to tickle him in return, but I couldn't stay upright long enough with just one arm.

"Enough!" I half whispered, knowing my sister was asleep next door. He gave up and I flopped back on the bed in a state of exhaustion, cock at half-mast, very confused by this state of affairs.

Gabriel sat back on his heels, grinning from ear to ear, a Cheshire cat. He still had one of my legs over his shoulder and he rubbed his rough palm up and down my thigh. "I love you too, English. I didn't know it was possible to feel like this with another person, never mind another man." He rested his head on my shin for a moment, studying me. "I really want to be a part of all this, Nick. I want to be a part of your life."

"You already are, you have been since the moment I found you. That's never going to change, Gabe. I don't want you to be a *part* of my life. I want you to be *central* to my life."

He nodded, his smile softening and become almost secret, like he had plans I didn't know about. "We'll talk more in the morning when I'm properly awake. Right now, I want to make love to you." Another kiss and a small nip on the big muscle of my thigh. I sucked in a sharp breath. He watched my reactions as he kissed and nipped all the way up my leg and each time he inched closer to my balls the urge to buck up against something increased. I reached for my cock, needing something more but he knocked my hand away. The torture continued.

"I confess..." I bleated.

That low, husky chuckle made me think of sexy dark things in hidden dark places. "Confess to what?"

"Whatever you want." A breathless and agonised moan leaked out of me as he took one ball in his mouth and rolled it over his tongue.

"Tell me what you want me to do to you, Nick." The order came, then he drew my ball back into the hot, wet cavern of his mouth.

Words? I needed to find actual words? Fuck, that was hard work when all

I could think about was how amazing his mouth felt sucking on my bollocks. "I want you to drive me crazy with a blow job, Gabe. I want to fuck into your mouth for as long as I can stand it – which won't be long."

"We can do that, baby," he murmured, before turning his attention to the other side.

I put my arm over my face hardly able to breathe for the sensations radiating out from my balls. "I want to feel your fingers stretch me open. I want to feel your cock inside me. I want to feel you come hard. I want you to fuck me hard."

"I think you might have the list in the wrong order, there."

"I think you're lucky I can speak at all."

"Where is the lube, Nick?"

"Condoms? I don't..." Panic gripped my heart at the thought of not getting him inside me.

"Do we need them? I haven't been with anyone else, you said you haven't, we've both had more blood tests than the average soldier –"

"Good enough for me," I decided. It wasn't like I ever wanted to share with anyone else – ever. I reached over to my bedside and found the bottle of lube I'd bought in a vain attempt to make masturbation with my left hand a little less depressing.

Gabriel took the bottle from me and I watched him suck his top lip between his teeth. "Um, Nick, I've never... I mean I watched some porn – which disturbed me to be honest – but I've never..."

A part of me wanted to take the piss, because being a British soldier it's what I did best, but this time between us – this night we shared – it was too special for such things. "I doubt you'll do anything wrong, Gabe, but if I need to, I'll make sure you know what's right and what's wrong. Just follow your instincts, they've never led you astray before." Personally, I was never sure porn had much to do with normal sex between a couple regardless of the genders involved.

He squirted some lubrication onto his fingers and frowned a bit at the slick slide as he rubbed it around, then he seemed to make up his mind, gave a half shrug to himself at whatever had been going through his head, and decided to go into battle.

Before he did anything else, he licked up the shaft of my cock, pressing down on the vein and popped me into his mouth. I may have yelped and whimpered, but the sound was so unmanly I refused to acknowledge its presence.

I hardly noticed his fingers begin their exploration because all I could think about was the intense heat of his mouth as he worked up and down my shaft. His tongue licked and pressed, experimenting, remembering, enjoying. My balls were so tight I feared I'd lose all control. It felt like we'd been doing this to each other since the moment he arrived. The slow torture of the day finally reaching a peak.

"Christ, Nick, don't think about peaks," I murmured making Gabriel chuckle which did really bad things to my self-control. "Fuck, baby, I can't..."

He gazed up at me and nodded, which just drove me further into his mouth. Fingertips brushed my tight entrance and the thick blunt finger pushed just a little. The heat inside me burned flash bright and I lost control, cursing myself as I thrust up into his mouth, while Gabriel tried to control me and not choke.

"Fuck, I'm sorry..."

"Don't stop," he said. "Fuck don't stop, Nick, you look amazing. You taste even better. I want to make you come again. This time I'll be inside you." He pushed up with his finger, licked my cock and I almost leapt off the bed.

"Yes," I moaned. The orgasm may have taken the edge off, but it wasn't enough to stop me – or even slow me down apparently. I opened my legs, used my left hand to brace on the bed and used my considerable stomach muscles to hold me off the mattress while I worked him deeper inside my arse. "It's been so fucking long."

"How long?" Gabriel said, watching and playing with the lube on his cock.

"Years. Lots of years since anyone has been inside me."

"You want me?"

"Fuck yes. I want you deep and hard, baby. I want it all. I want to feel the burn, the stretch." The moment he added two fingers I became inarticulate. The burn and stretch with just his fingers blew my tiny mind.

He kissed the inside of my knee and thigh as he worked deeper, watching me fuck his fingers with wanton abandon, whispering words of desire and encouragement. Sweat formed and gathered over my chest and belly. He bent over me the moment two fingers were in deep and sucked my balls again. My cock grew hard almost too fast, blood fleeing my brain now it had something more fun to do than fuel my miserable thoughts.

"Now, Gabriel."

"I haven't opened you all the way up yet," he said.

"Fuck me, now." The order came from the depths of my desire.

"I'm not going to last long, Nick. I need to make sure –" He grunted as I pulled off his fingers, flipped over and lifted myself up onto one arm and my knees.

I looked over my shoulder at him. "More lube, no more words."

He grinned and followed my instructions. I made a mental note to make sure I did my own washing tomorrow; I did not want my mother doing my bedsheets. Fingers found their way back inside me and he guided my hips towards his cock so I didn't have to keep my weight on one arm. I made some noises that might once have been words before he removed his fingers and held his cock still while I lowered my hips over his groin. The pressure, the pain, the beginnings of the intense feeling of being too full to think, began to creep over me as I worked myself downwards, up and downwards, up…

"Oh, fuck, that feels good," I groaned, as I pushed out and down all at once.

Gabriel trembled and his forehead hit my shoulder. "Oh, Nick, baby, I can't. Oh, fuck, you're so tight, so hot. I can't…" He wrapped his arms around my belly and my torso, holding my sweating back to his chest as I took him all the way inside.

We both paused, panting, hot breaths combining with the moonlight spilling through the window. The air smelt of man, of sex, and the wild fields of the world outside our cave. He nipped my shoulder, tightened his arms and pushed up, deeper, just a little more. I cried out.

"I'm going to need to go hard and fast, baby," he said into my ear then he licked it.

"Yes."

"Can you take it like this?" he asked.

"I can take our weight on one arm, if that's what you're asking?" I said. I rose up and pressed down again, making him whine. I did it again and again, not moving very far but making sure we experienced all my body could give in this position. More, ever more but never enough.

Gabriel suddenly took over. No more words now. All dominance and desperation. He pushed me forwards, forced my head to the mattress, holding the back of my neck, widening my knees by nudging them apart to the point of pain and he thrust deep.

Hard and fast. Fingers gripping my neck and my hip so hard I'd feel it for days.

I reached for my cock, left hand free to add to my pleasure and it did. My balls tightened, the fire in my spine and belly built.

"Fuck, yes, harder," I groaned into the sheets.

"Nick…" Gabriel grew impossibly larger inside me. I thought I'd split into two before he finished. He filled me, thrusts becoming erratic and uncontrolled. He cried out and I felt him pulse, spill, hot and heavy deep inside.

His fingers lost their control of my neck, reached for my cock and with our fingers meshed together I came again, drawing more cries of pleasure from him and me as he stroked over my prostate. The orgasm rolled on and on.

All things end though.

He pulled out, a breathless mess of a man, making us both feel a little lost the moment we disconnected. He rolled me over onto my back and lay on me, tucking his head into my neck, almost all his weight covering my entire body, legs tangled. He smeared come over my belly and I held him close, kissing his sweaty hair, thinking about what this must mean to him after what happened in Myanmar.

"You alright?" I asked.

"Just don't let go yet."

"Never, baby."

"I need to clean you."

"It can wait for now."

He snuggled deeper and despite our best intentions we were asleep in moments, our pact sealed. We created real love that night in the moonlight.

27

MY PHONE WOKE ME JUST as dawn made itself known through the open curtains. Milking time. Gabriel grumbled as I untangled him from my body. I shoved my pillow under his searching arm, and it seemed to settle him. I went into my small bathroom and cleaned up.

I dressed in overalls and yawned as I wandered down the stairs. I'd been milking cows all my life so making it out the door with the dogs and walking up the Bracken field whistling the cows in didn't take any thought. Leaving all of me to concentrate on the long, lean, miracle lying in my bed and the feeling of being well and truly fucked. I had never experienced sex like last night, but maybe that's because no one had ever made love to me before. Every part of my body vibrated.

The cows came in, followed me down to the yard with the dogs helping to remind them of the routine, and on into the parlour. We didn't have many cows now, only twenty-five head, but it kept us in milk and the local dairy which supplied a few farm shops and milk rounds in the area.

With dawn well on the way Dad came out to help me with the clean-up and we let the cows back into the pasture. I saw Gabriel sitting on my mum's bench outside the kitchen door, enjoying the morning sun with a big cup of coffee in his hands and my heart smiled. I didn't know a heart could smile but it's entirely possible, right now mine beamed like a mid-summer dawn.

He grinned as I stomped over the lawn in my wellies. "I'm lovin' the farmer look. Much hotter than soldier as far as I'm concerned. Do you wear dungarees as well, with no shirt on? Or the lumberjack look in the winter? Maybe grow the beard out a bit more?" He reached up and tugged on it.

I bent down and kissed the offered lips. "I didn't think you liked beards? You taste of coffee. Yes, I do wear dungarees, though with a t-shirt."

"A white one? That then gets wet in a mysterious industrial accident? The beard is growing on me, it's nice on the inside of my thighs."

I laughed while feeling the heat flush my face and he grinned at me over the rim of his coffee cup.

"Your mom is making breakfast, though I'm not sure anyone should eat that much meat this time of the day – or ever."

Stealing his coffee cup from his unresisting hands I took a slurp. "I agree but don't tell her that. She doesn't normally make breakfast for us. I think it's for your benefit. She's normally out the door on the day job before I've done milking."

"She doesn't work on the farm?" he asked.

I shook my head. "No, she works in the local care home. The farm can't support three incomes. When I came out of hospital, she already had the job so I could help Dad on the farm. With my disability from the army we manage but things are tight."

The farm's perilous financial situation kept me up at night on a regular basis, but my parents were determined I have a job that made me feel safe and capable. It did make me feel safe, but not always capable, still, I was learning to cope and that made today a good day.

"Is the farm profitable?" Gabriel asked. He saw my eyes and mouth tighten. "Sorry, love. I don't mean anything by it, I just want to help if I can." Those long clever fingers rubbed my thigh in reassurance.

I considered my options. We were going bankrupt. Slowly to be sure, but it was happening and without significant investment in the farm buildings and a new business model we weren't going to make it another two years. At least that would get my parents to retirement and we could sell the land and maybe the house to buy them something small somewhere nice. Maybe in the village, though the prices around here were too high for most locals. It would break my heart to lose the farm, but we were mortgaged to the point of being in negative equity if another housing crisis hit the market.

Which meant I could lie to Gabriel about our financial situation so I could pretend I was the successful and bountiful landowner. I could give him a half-truth and still be able to hold my head up in prideful defiance of the coming disaster. Or I could be honest. I could tell him we were in deep shit and if he wanted to remain a part of my family he needed to know I was an emotional, physical and financial mess without the means to support him in the UK.

Pride – the one thing I'd been denied for so long I didn't remember what it felt like to have any. I'd come to terms with the future months ago. I didn't like it and I'd work hard to prevent my predictions from coming true, but I had to face reality.

Lying to Gabriel had never really been an option. He'd see through it in no time and I had never lied to him before.

"Honestly, and I know this is yet another nail in my coffin, we are deep in the shit – really deep, Gabe. We can't afford to get the tractor MOTed at the end of next month the way things are at the moment. When I thought Mum and Jessie were going clothes shopping in Bristol, I almost had a heart attack because I'd need to find the money to pay the credit card statement. Mum's been keeping the accounts in good order, but she can't do the projections I can, so I see the future in the spreadsheets." I studied the sparrows picking at the gravel to find yummies. "Guess you need to know how much of a liability I really am. A one-armed farmer going bankrupt."

He leaned against my right shoulder, propping his chin on the edge, my arm not in his way as he snuggled closer. "You're making assumptions about what I want from life again, Nick."

I twisted and looked down, unable to resist giving his nose a quick kiss. "Yep. I am."

Those dark eyes blinked, the black lashes thick, and when they opened, I could read the depth of his love. It reached so far into his soul it made tears spring into my eyes, blurring the perfect vision before me. He shifted, wrapping his arms around my waist.

"I have nothing in the States, Nick. No family, no home, no job, no friends. I am alone. I understand more about how lonely that is after this last year. Every day I wanted to turn to you to ask a question, seek an opinion, hug someone I trusted with my life. Meeting you has made me realise how alone I've been for years. Since leaving the Rangers I hardly went home. My father died of cancer and I wasn't there – his sister held his hand as the end came. I've told myself for years that what I did for the US flag was more important than family. More important than my happiness, safety, welfare and more important than those I love. I was wrong."

Mum yelled about breakfast being ready. I twisted in his arms and he straightened.

"What are you telling me, Gabe?"

He ran his fingers through my buzz cut and removed a stray piece of grass. "I know that technically we haven't been together long enough to say this, but I know what I want for my future." His focus returned to mine.

"Okay, what is it?" Squirrels were chasing each other around in my guts, which had to be the reason for the sudden excited jiggle.

"When I sold the ranch, received my back pay and organised some substantial compensation from the US Government for being left in Myanmar, as well as what I've saved by always working, I've come out of things financially secure for more than one lifetime." He watched my face, reading every twitch.

"Good, I'm glad you'll be okay." A wave of relief took me, I wouldn't have to provide for Gabriel.

He frowned as if I were being very dumb. "I'm looking to buy a new home, start a new life, invest in my future before I'm too old and broken to enjoy it. I want to invest in your farm. I've more than enough to become a full partner. We could buy it off your folks. They could live in the farmhouse and we'll build something new – maybe near the quarry. There's an old barn I could see on the other side."

"It's an 18th century tithe barn, it's falling to pieces," I whispered by rote.

"Then we should be able to get planning permission, right?" he asked.

"Um…"

He took my left hand in his and kissed the scarred, thick knuckles. "I love you, English. I want to live with you. One day I'm going to want to marry you. I know that, I just have to convince you and I will. I know you struggle with trust. I know you struggle with self-confidence and how that affects your relationship with the world. But, and it's important you really listen to this bit, Nick, I want forever, and I want it here. I've done the research. I know how much real estate you have; how much land is worth in Somerset. I know how much the farm is worth if it wasn't carrying debt. I can give you a fair price to buy in and we can invest in the business. I've had my accountant –"

"You have an accountant?"

He laughed. "Yep, and a UK lawyer. Let me sweep in like a fucking handsome prince and rescue you from the future you don't want. Just like you rescued me from that prison cell. Let's build a future."

I laughed. A scary, hysterical sound. "You can't do that."

"Why not? With the right kind of investment, we could have a great business here. I've some initial plans but I didn't want to bulldoze you with too much and I'm sure you have your own ideas." He looked scared like I'd say no on the spot and throw him out.

"We've only spent a handful of days together, Gabriel. We have no idea if we could make this work. I've never lived with someone romantically. You've never been with another guy –"

Now he looked offended and I snapped my mouth shut. "Why on earth does any of that matter? Do you want to live with anyone else?"

"Never."

"Do you want to keep the farm?"

"Yes."

"Do you want me to stay here?"

I reached for his jaw and swept my thumb over the prickly surface. "Always."

"Then that's what we'll do. My parents fell in love the moment they met. They were married within six weeks. They were both eighteen. They just knew. I know. I had no idea what love was until I met you, but when I left you in that hospital bed, I understood why my father died the day my mother did. He may have walked and talked but his heart went into the ground with her."

I realised my head nodded without conscious thought, my mind agreeing with his plans before I could fully comprehend the implications. "You know we can't tell my parents until we have a full business plan?"

"I know." He grinned, the corners of his eyes crinkling. "So, you agree?"

I couldn't stop the smile. "I agree. We'll be business partners."

"And one day we'll get married?"

Barely able to hold the sunshine and rainbows that were my heart and soul inside my body I nodded, lacking the words necessary to tell this beautiful creature of my dreams how much I loved him. How fucking grateful I was for every miserable moment I'd spent in the SAS and in the past year, just to sit in this place, with him, right now and feel this perfect clarity of love.

He rubbed my back, just as overwhelmed. "Come on, let's go eat our own body weight in breakfast. Then you can show me what I'm really buying into, Nick Wilde."

Before he left the bench, I leaned in and pressed my lips to his, then I looked into his eyes. "Gabriel Cabrera, from the very bottom of my soul, I love you and thank you for saving my life."

His dark eyes were bright with unshed tears. "I love you and I will always be thankful it was you who lifted me off that hook, despite all it cost you."

"No regrets, Gabe. I have no regrets. I have never regretted that moment, no matter how hard this last year has been for me. Knowing you were out there in the world has meant more to me than any grief over losing an arm."

Mum chose that moment to pop her head out of the door. "Come on, boys, breakfast is spoiling. You have a long day ahead of you, I'm sure."

She looked at the pair of us as if using her psychic mother ninja skills to work out what the hell was going on before giving us the sweetest, softest smile I'd ever seen on her face.

"I'm glad for you both, you know that? I always wanted another boy in the family." She vanished back into the house before Gabriel could answer.

He took my hand in his; we rose off the bench and walked together in the cool interior of the old farmhouse.

The End

Find Sarah Luddington at sarah@fictionwriter.co.uk

I don't have a newsletter to join or a Facebook group.
However, if you enjoyed this story, or even if you didn't, could I
trouble you for a review? They are the life blood of authors and they
matter, they really matter.
Many thanks.

Also available through Mirador Publishing:

The Prophecy
Vampire
All the following are M/M stand alone or series
Seelie
Unforbidden: A Queer Collection
Chords for the Dead
Men of Sherwood: A Rogue's Tale

The Knights of Camelot Series:
Lancelot and the King
Lancelot and the Sword
Lancelot and the Grail
Lancelot's Challenge
Lancelot's Burden
Lancelot's Curse
Betrayal of Lancelot
Passion of Lancelot
Revenge of Lancelot

Lancelot the Lost Years: The Spear

Sons of Camelot Series:
The Pendragon Legacy
The Du Lac Legacy
Albion's Legacy

Shadow Ops
Fortune's Solider: Alpha
Ultimate Sanction: Bravo
Final Play: Charlie

About the author

A LITTLE ABOUT ME, I live in a tumble down house in the Southern mountains of Spain with my husband who writes comedy. We have far too many dogs. I'm crap at social media but I try and I'm not good at sharing my life, mostly because I can't believe anyone would be interested.

I love writing, it's my grand passion and the only reason to get out of bed, well, that and the Belgium shepherd that lands on my head every morning. I love reading as well and if you follow my newsletter I'll be posting about other authors I've fallen in love with. I crave stories, so films and TV are a huge part of my life.

I do all I can to support the LGBTQ community. It's important to remember there are many people out there who are victimised for being gay or trans. Just because the law says it's okay to be gay, doesn't mean people don't suffer – we must keep fighting! I'd bang on about all the countries where it's still illegal or you face death for being gay but you guys know about this stuff.

On a lighter note, I also love walking the hounds and trying to keep them out of trouble. I love my swords, bows and pretending to be what I secretly *("Yeah right, it's such a secret." Husband rolls his eyes at me)*, want to be – a knight. I'm a hopeless romantic who would love to rescue the princess or the prince and doesn't really care what gender she is as she's doing the rescuing just so long as the bad guys put up a good fight.

So, that's me. Not complicated, just a human trying to figure out the best way to live. I hope you are to and if you want to share, come and chatter to a fellow traveller through the world and collector of stories.